#HATER

The Hashtag Series #2

by Cambria Hebert

#1HATER

Chapter One

> #TravelTrivia
> More people are killed yearly by donkeys than by airplane crashes.
> #YouAreSafe
> #UnlessYouHaveADonkey
> ... Alpha BuzzFeed

RIMMEL

The white-knuckled grip I punished the armrests with did not loosen until the plane came to an absolute stop.

Even then, my fingers only loosened as the loud sounds of the tunnel thing passengers walked through to enter into the airport terminal was rolled over and attached to the plane. The air was stuffy in here. Not really stale, but not fresh either. Everyone around me was restless. The flight had been full of turbulence, and the crying baby in the back did nothing to soothe everyone's frazzled nerves.

I hated flying.

But God, I was so glad to be back. I never thought I'd miss Maryland and its cold seasons this much.

'Course, it wasn't really the place I missed.

It was a person.

Everyone started to file toward the door, crowding each other in their attempt to get the hell out of this flying deathtrap. I stood and waited for my turn, hefting my purse over my shoulder, and turned my cell phone back on.

The second it lit up and I was able, I shot out a text.

LANDED. GETTING OFF NOW.

Romeo's response was instant, and I smiled.

I'M WAITING.

I glanced out the tiny window behind me as if I would see him standing out there on the tarmac. I knew he wasn't, but I couldn't stop my eyes from scanning the open space. Butterflies somersaulted beneath my ribcage as a man passing by my row stopped and motioned for me to go ahead.

I shot him a grateful smile and slid past him into the aisle. The flight attendant smiled and wished everyone well as we all stepped off the plane and onto the walkway that led to the terminal. I moved quickly, beyond anxious for my first glimpse of Romeo.

I'd been in Florida almost two weeks, but it felt like a freaking eternity. As I went, I bumped into someone laden with a bulky piece of carry-on luggage and another bag, but I didn't stop. I muttered an apology and kept right on going.

When I burst into the terminal, my eyes swept around, bouncing from person to person in the crowded, bustling space. My stomach fell a little when I didn't see him, but I knew he probably couldn't come this far. He was probably at baggage claim.

I looked around for a sign to point me in the right direction and finally saw one labeled *Baggage Claim* with an arrow pointing off to the left.

But I didn't follow the arrow.

My eyes fixed on someone standing beneath the sign.

His hands were jammed into the pockets of his well-worn slouchy jeans. The relaxed action pulled the waistband low, highlighting his flat, narrow waist his Henley tee molded to. As usual, he was wearing his varsity jacket and his blond hair was a mess.

My gaze locked on his sapphire-blue eyes and didn't let go. His eyes, *ohmigod*, his eyes. The blue was so intense it served as an emergency brake on everything in my life. The second I looked at him, everything else came to a screeching halt. I no longer noticed the huge crowd rushing around.

The anxiety-causing flight was just a distant memory, and the two weeks I spent longing for his touch became something I would live through ten times over just to be in this moment with him again.

His lips pulled into a smile and the charm that oozed from every pore in his body made me almost lightheaded. Romeo pulled his hands out of his pockets and straightened, motioning for me.

I rushed across the space separating us, my bag slapping against my side as I, for once, gracefully maneuvered around the people in my path.

His chuckle brushed over me when I was just steps away, and I threw myself at him with a little sigh of relief. My legs wrapped around his waist and his arms locked around my back. I burrowed my head into his shoulder and inhaled deep, taking in his distinctive scent.

"Rim," he murmured, his voice low. I pulled back and his lips were on mine instantly.

The moment our lips touched, he stilled, his body and mouth pausing against mine. Before I could wonder why, he muttered a garbled curse against my mouth and then his lips began to move. He kissed me softly but fiercely. There was so much possession in the way he kissed me, in the way his arms locked around me that my heart stuttered.

I parted my lips so his tongue could sweep inside, and when my tongue met his, desire, hot and heavy, unfurled within me.

Someone chuckled as they walked by, and Romeo retreated slightly, still letting his mouth linger on mine before completely pulling away.

He rested his forehead against mine and he smiled. "I really fucking missed you."

"Me too," I whispered.

He dropped another quick kiss on my lips and then stood me back on my feet. I swayed a little, and he chuckled. "C'mon, let's get your suitcase so we can go. I want to be alone with you."

My stomach dipped and something inside me loosened.

We held hands through the large terminal. He didn't even let go when he snagged my stuff off the baggage claim belt.

Since I'd come from Florida, I was wearing only a short-sleeved T-shirt over a pair of loose sweatpants, so before we went outside into the cold Maryland air, I dug into my suitcase and pulled out the hoodie he gave me the night of our first kiss. I wore it all the time. After I pulled it on, I glanced over at him, smiling.

"What?" I asked.

"You took that to Florida?"

"Of course," I said. "The evenings can get chilly this time of year."

"And what did your dad have to say about you wearing some guy's sweatshirt around?"

"You aren't *some guy*. You're my boyfriend," I replied and reached for his hand.

"And you finally told your dad about us?" he pressed.

• • •

"Yes, I did." Even though we'd been dating a couple months now, I'd just told my dad over winter break. I wasn't sure what he would say when I told him I was dating. He took it better than I thought, even went as far as to say he was happy for me.

"And?"

"He took it a lot better than I thought he would."

The surprise in my voice was evident, and Romeo glanced at me. "You really thought he'd be upset?"

Yeah, I had. I mean, didn't all dads get upset when their little girls started dating? I shrugged, feeling silly. "I guess I wasn't sure how he'd take it."

When he asked me about the name on the back and I explained it was a nickname, a look of doubt crossed his face, and he said he wasn't sure how he felt about his daughter dating some guy who earned the name of a player.

I braced myself then for an argument, but none came. He seemed to cut off whatever lecture he was about to launch into and said as long as I was happy, that was all that mattered.

"He must know I'm good for you." Romeo kissed the side of my head as we walked outside. The wintry air took my breath, and I snuggled into the hoodie. "I parked as close as I could," he said, noticing the way I grimaced against the cold.

We hurried toward the lot where the Hellcat was parked in the short-term section. He opened the passenger door and ushered me inside, then tossed my stuff into the trunk. I leaned into the leather of the seat, marveling at how familiar this car was to me now.

It was a one-hour drive from the airport to campus. We didn't really talk much, despite having plenty to talk about. Every time I thought to say anything, his thumb would gently stroke the inside of my palm where our hands joined and my skin would break out in goose bumps.

The tension inside the car grew the longer we drove. I wanted him so badly I could barely think or see. For someone who'd gone almost her entire life without sex, the last two weeks shouldn't have been a problem, but *oh,* they were. I ached for him.

Just holding his hand made my skin tingle with anticipation.

When we finally got off the interstate, Romeo turned abruptly onto some empty back road with trees on each side. "Where are you going?" I asked as he pulled over onto the side of the road and let the car idle.

"I can't take it anymore, Rim."

He reached for me, practically lifting me out of the seat and pulling me across the center toward him. I was all too willing as I climbed into his lap to straddle him.

He reached up into the messy bun on my head and pulled out the hair tie. The heavy mess that was my hair tumbled down over my shoulders and back as he carefully removed my glasses before burying his hands in and pulling me close.

The kiss was all-consuming. It wasn't like at the airport where he kept his desire in check. Instead, it surged out around me, and I rocked into his already rigid length and moaned low in my throat.

My fingers slipped into his hair and massaged his scalp, and he worked his mouth over mine. I began to move atop him. I rocked back and forth, rotating my hips and pressing myself into the hardness beneath his jeans.

He murmured my name and his hands left my hair to grip my hips, urging me to move even faster.

So desperate for release, I sucked his bottom lip into my mouth and pulled at it with my tongue and teeth. A sound—more like a plea—burst from my throat, and he swallowed it.

I felt his smile against me and a strangled chuckle floated up. "Damn, Rimmel. I think you missed me as much as I missed you."

I was too far gone to talk. In response, I rocked against him again and shuddered at the urgency flooding my system. A frustrated sound bubbled up in my chest, and my hands slid down to either side of his neck.

"I know what you want, baby," he whispered as his hand slid into the waistband of my sweats.

My body stilled even as I yearned for him. His fingers delved into my pants, past the waistband of my panties, and brushed against the smooth center just above my slit.

"Romeo," I groaned and sagged forward, my forehead on his shoulder.

His free hand came up to grip the back of my neck as his fingers found the moist heat of my center and slid farther down.

I shuddered and he groaned. "You're already ready for me."

I couldn't say anything. All I could do was gasp as his finger flicked over my swollen clit and teased me with more. I reached for the waistband of his jeans, not caring at all that were weren't really in private. This car was private enough. I needed him so badly that I wasn't going to stop.

"Oh no you don't," he said, his voice strained. His words were a stark contrast to the way his hips tilted up, inviting my fingers. "There isn't enough space in here for me to have you the way I want."

A broken sound escaped me, and he chuckled. "But I'm gonna take care of you. Right here. Right now."

I shivered at his lusty promise as the pressure of his fingers increased and he pressed down on my sensitive button. The friction he created in my center with just his hand had my fingers curling into the front of his shirt, and I rocked into his touch.

My entire world blew apart as the orgasm quaked through my body. I shuddered and shook, coming apart in his lap as he continued to stroke me, using my own juices to further my pleasure. Even after his fingers slowed, I rocked against him. The aftereffects of the orgasm were almost as good as the real thing.

Long moments passed, and he removed his hand from my center and cupped my face. My eyes felt heavy; my brain was foggy as he kissed me softly before putting me back into the seat and pulling the seatbelt across my chest.

"What about you?" I murmured when the car started moving again.

"Don't you worry about me, baby. When we get to my place, I'll get mine."

Even though he'd just released some of the tension in my body, I already needed more.

"I hope you're ready." He glanced at me with a wicked grin.

My pulse jumped.

Oh, I was ready.

CHAPTER TWO

> #ChampionshipsAreComing
> While you were off eating turkey and
> pie the WOLVES were kicking ass on
> the field!
> #24WillTakeUsAllTheWay
>
> ... Alpha BuzzFeed

ROMEO

Rimmel burrowed beneath the comforter on my bed and pressed her naked body farther against mine. Even though we'd already had sex three times since we got here, my body responded to her touch. Just the feel of her silky bare skin rubbing against me was enough to make me want her all over again.

She groaned and tucked her fingers between my side and the mattress. "I don't think I'm ever going to get used to the cold air here."

I chuckled and kissed her forehead. "Just wait 'til it snows."

"Ugh," she moaned.

"I'll turn the heat up," I said and started to move from beneath her. She clutched me closer and made a sound of determination. I laughed. It thrilled the shit out of me that she liked having me so close. "I thought you were cold," I said affectionately.

"But you're warm."

"I'll come right back."

"Kiss me," she demanded. She was definitely a shy person, but the more time we spent together, the less shy she was with me when we were alone. I loved it. It was like getting a glimpse of the person no one else saw.

I rolled and pinned her beneath me, wrapping my arms under her back and pressing her naked torso against mine. Her mouth was willing and eager as her tongue stroked expertly against mine. It was a lazy kiss, and it wasn't short. I could explore the depths of her mouth for hours on end and still find new ways to make her groan.

When the urge to plunge into her center became almost too much, I eased back. Her eyes were unfocused and her lips were swollen as she smiled up at me.

I wanted her so fucking bad, just as badly as I had when I saw her searching through the airport crowd with anticipation in her eyes. Going through all the extra security just to be at the gate when she came through had been well worth the hassle. The way her face lit up when she saw me caused my chest to tighten.

I was used to attention from the opposite sex. Getting a girl to like me was never really a challenge.

But Rimmel was different.

She didn't bestow that look on just anyone. In fact, I'd never seen her look at anything or anyone the way she did me. Even the animals at the shelter, the ones she considered her friends.

It wasn't a small feat for someone to make me feel like I was special. It was almost something I'd grown used to. It wasn't really anything I didn't expect.

But with Rimmel, it was almost like she loved me in spite of all that.

"You're driving me crazy," I murmured, stroking her hair away from her face.

Her hand slid across the back of my shoulder and trailed down to my lower back.

I groaned. "You're gonna be hurting tomorrow, Rim."

"I don't care."

I smiled. "I know. But I do."

She made a face at me and I kissed her nose. Pulling back wasn't something I wanted to do, but her body needed a break. At least for an hour. "I got you a present."

Her eyes widened. "You did?"

"Did you really think I wouldn't get you a Christmas present?"

She shrugged beneath me. "I didn't expect you to. Besides, we spent Christmas apart."

"What kind of boyfriend doesn't get a present for his girl?" I asked and slipped out of bed.

She pulled the covers up over her, guarding against the air. I picked up my long-sleeved Henley from where I threw it on the floor and tossed it to her.

I went and turned up the heat and hit the switch for the gas fireplace on the wall opposite the bed.

Flames roared to life and filled the dim room with dancing orange.

"This sure beats my dorm room," she half sighed.

I laughed and turned. The breath I was taking in froze halfway to my lungs.

She was sitting in the center of my bed, the blankets rumpled and piled around her. My shirt was way too large and the neck slipped down low over one of her slim shoulders, exposing a wide patch of creamy skin. Her cheeks were pink and her lips were swollen. The long thick mass of her hair was tangled and messy, falling around her face and down her back.

I'd missed her.

I'd missed her even more than I'd let myself realize. But seeing her sitting there taking up so little space in my bed but so much room in my chest was sorta something I couldn't deny.

She tilted her head and looked at me, wrinkling her nose. "Do I look a mess?" she asked.

I shook my head, unable to speak. I never thought this would happen to me. I never thought I would love someone so much. So fast.

I turned and picked up the wrapped box near the door and brought it back to the bed. It was nothing fancy, since I'd wrapped it myself. It was covered in plain red paper and had a gold bow on top.

I held out the box and she took it, placing it in her lap on top of the blankets. Her eyes roamed my naked body, heat and appreciation in them. I grinned and reached for a pair of boxers and slid them on. If she kept looking at me like that, I wasn't going to last the next five minutes, let alone a couple hours.

I slipped into the bed beside her and lay on my side, propping myself up on my elbow. "You gonna open that?"

She bit her lip and glanced down at it. Murphy jumped up on the end of the bed and sat down, watching us with his tail swishing back and forth. Rimmel picked up the box and shook it.

When that gave away nothing, she smiled and ripped open the paper. I put the gift in a plain white box, so she set it in her lap and pulled the top off to look inside.

She glanced at me and grinned.

"Thought my Florida girl could use something to keep her warm when I'm not around."

"I love them," she said and pulled out a pair of white fur slipper boots. They had red ribbons at the top to tie them in place.

She slid her fingers over the soft white faux fur and sighed in appreciation. With one in each hand, she flung herself at me and wrapped her arms around my neck. "Thank you, Romeo," she said and kissed my cheek. "I love them."

"Try them on," I said.

Rimmel pushed the covers back and pulled her bare legs out to pull on the boots. She got one on and tied and then pushed her foot down in the other.

Her forehead wrinkled. "There's something in there," she said and quickly pulled it back off.

"What is it?"

"I'm not putting my hand in there!" she squealed. "It might be a bug."

"A bug?" I was amused. "How would a bug get in there?"

She screwed up her face and stuck out her tongue. "Who knows? Bugs are creepy like that."

I chuckled and shoved my hand down into the boot. She watched like she was expecting something to eat my hand off. I pulled out the square white box and held it out. "I think it might be for you," I said and winked.

Her eyes bounced between me and the box I held. "The slippers are more than enough."

"I know," I replied and held it out.

She took it and lifted the lid. I heard the rustling of tissue paper and then she stared down at it for a few seconds. "I need my glasses," she said, her voice whisper soft.

I reached behind me and pulled them off the table and handed them to her. She slid them on and glanced back down. "It's so beautiful."

Her voice was hushed like she somehow might disturb the contents of the box, and she stared down at it like it might disappear. It made me worry that maybe she didn't like it. Maybe she was trying to think of something to say.

"If you don't like it…" I started, and she gasped.

"Of course I like it." She glanced up. "I love it. I've never had anything like it."

Her eyes were sort of misty and it got to me. It was such a simple gift. I'd spent more money on my parents and, hell, even Braeden. But I knew Rimmel wouldn't like anything flashy. She wouldn't want anything that appeared like I was trying to impress her. I loved that about her. I loved the fact that she hadn't expected anything at all.

"Try it on," I said and reached into the box. There wasn't much to the bracelet. The saleslady called it a bangle. It was basically like a thick gold wire that would wrap around her wrist. In the center was a golden heart with two small loops on each side where the bracelet hooked together. I unclasped it and Rimmel slid her hand through. Once it was around her wrist, I rehooked it and adjusted it so the heart lay flat against the top of her wrist.

In the center of the heart, I had R&R engraved in the center. It looked like it had been carved by hand.

"It's so beautiful. It has our initials," she said, running her fingertip over the engraving.

"You know me," I half joked. "Any way I can get my name on you."

She looked up. I felt her hazel eyes on my face. "I love you."

She didn't say those three words very often. I think they scared her. I think they made her feel vulnerable, like putting out there just how much she cared about me would somehow jinx it, like I would somehow be taken away.

It didn't matter that I knew how she felt. Hearing her say it speared me deep down.

I grabbed her face and pulled it to mine. "I love you too, baby."

I kissed her slow and deep, penetrating her mouth the way her words penetrated my soul.

When she pulled back, she glanced down at the gold encircling her wrist and smiled.

"I got gold because it matches your mom's necklace."

"It's perfect."

Before I could pull her back, she bounded out of bed and into the other room.

"Hey!" I called after her.

She laughed and I heard a zipper being pulled. A second later, she reappeared, my shirt almost hanging to her knees, one furry boot on and the other missing.

I laughed and held out the other slipper. She came over and slid her foot in. When I was done tying the ribbon at the top, she pushed a small box under my nose. "I got you something too."

I snatched her around the waist and tossed her down on the bed, coming over her.

She laughed. "Open it!"

Still straddling her hips, I sat up and took the gift from her hand. It was a small rectangular box with a dark-green ribbon tied around the center. I undid the bow and lifted the lid.

Inside was a dog tag necklace on a silver chain. The dog tag itself wasn't silver, but a deep navy color.

I lifted it out of the box and held the tag in my palm. The front side had my name and jersey number on it.

ROMEO

#24

"Turn it over," she said, so I did.

The back was also engraved. It read: *Anything is possible.* And beneath the words was a four-leaf clover.

"Do you know how hard it is to shop for guys?" she said, partly amused.

I ran my finger over the clover.

"I know you gave up an easy path into the NFL when you told Omega to shove it. I know you wouldn't have done that if it weren't for me," Rimmel said, and I looked up from her gift. "I wanted you to know I believe in you. I know you're going to get there. I thought maybe the clover would bring you luck. Not that you need—"

I cut off her words with a kiss. A hot, searing kiss. She groaned as her fingers delved into my hair and her legs wrapped around my waist. Thoughts of giving her body a break were completely forgotten as I pushed my hand beneath the hem of my shirt and massaged her breast.

Her head fell to the side and I took advantage of the opportunity to kiss her bare shoulder. My cock was throbbing for her. I wanted in her so bad I could think of nothing else. The dog tag was still clutched in my hand as I shoved my boxers down, just enough so I was able to spring free.

Her entrance was already slick and hot. With one swift movement, I slid into her body in one long stroke.

Both of us gasped on contact. It was the first time I'd forgotten to put on a condom. Holy shit, she felt so tight and hot. Everything was magnified, the way her walls squeezed around my bare skin, the way her juices coated my throbbing manhood.

"Jesus," I groaned, fighting the urge to pound in her over and over again.

"Romeo," she whispered, her nails digging into my back.

"I know, baby. I forgot. I'm sorry. I'll fix it."

I started to pull out and she moaned, her fingers tightening against me. I swallowed thickly. This was the first time I'd been in a woman unwrapped. I had no idea it would feel like this. It was so, so much… *more.*

"Just one more," I murmured, pushing myself deep.

My entire body shuddered and Rimmel's knees began to shake.

In one fluid, fast motion, I pulled out. If I allowed myself just another second inside her like that, I wouldn't be able to pull out. Immediately, I missed her warmth. I reached for a condom as the need to bury myself bareback again roared within me.

I pulled on the condom as fast as I could and then surged back inside. I went at her hard, overcome with emotion and need. It didn't take long for both of us to strain against the other as release rocked through her and into me.

When it was over, I rolled to the side and blew out a shaky breath.

"Does that mean you like it?" she asked, rolling on her side to look at me.

I turned my head and grinned. "What do you think?"

"That felt really good," she whispered.

I groaned and scrubbed a hand over my face. It felt so good that I knew it was all I was going to be able to think about. I twisted to face her. "I've never been in anyone like that before."

Behind her glasses, her eyes widened. "Really?"

I nodded. "Do you trust me, Rimmel?" I asked.

• • •

"Of course," she replied without a second of hesitation.

"I want to get tested. Just to be sure of what I already know. I'm clean, but I want to prove it to you."

"I believe you," she said.

I knew she did. But I wanted to prove it. "Would you consider going on the pill?"

It was a lot to ask of her. We'd only been together a few months.

"Already taken care of," she said, taking me off guard.

"What? I thought you weren't on it."

"I wasn't. When I went home over the break, I made an appointment with my doctor and got some. I got tested while I was there. I'm clean."

I knew she would be. Hell, I wasn't even going to ask her to get tested. But she did it anyway; she did it for me.

"I don't want anything between us," I told her. "I want to be as close to you as I can get."

"I want that too," she whispered, cupping my jaw with her palm.

"You're sure?" I asked.

She nodded.

"As soon as I get tested and the results come back, I'm throwing out the condoms," I told her.

"I like that plan."

I groaned and pulled her against me. "Me too."

"Are you going to wear it?" she asked, her voice muffled against my chest.

I remembered the necklace clutched in my hand. I pulled back and held it between us. "Of course."

She looked shy as she pulled it out of my hand and held it out for me to slip my head through. The cool metal lay against my chest.

"I'm your biggest fan, you know," she whispered, and then her stomach growled loudly.

I laughed and kissed her swiftly. "My biggest fan is hungry."

She grimaced. "I didn't eat before my flight. I was afraid I'd get sick."

"Pizza. Movie. You in that shirt and nothing else," I said.

"Apple cider?" she asked.

. . .

She was obsessed with the stuff since she started coming to my games. "You know I have some in the kitchen," I told her.

"Deal," she said.

I ordered the pizza while she was in the kitchen making her cider.

When I came out, Murphy was sitting on the counter next to a cold can of soda she set out for me.

Most of the time waiting for the pizza was spent making out, and when the doorbell rang, I was partially irritated by the interruption. Rimmel padded along behind me in her slippers (which looked sexy as hell) and my shirt.

I kept my body angled in front of her so the delivery guy couldn't see how hot she looked.

When he walked away, I juggled the pizza boxes and moved to shut the door. But Rimmel didn't move back. She was standing stock still, staring past me out the door.

"What is it?" I asked and turned to see.

I saw nothing.

"Is that your mother in the window?" she asked, motioning with her chin.

I glanced up at the house, at one of the lit-up windows. My mom was looking out at us. When she noticed us looking, she disappeared back into the room.

Rimmel was quiet when she moved into the living room toward the couch and TV. I knew my mother made Rimmel uncomfortable. Judging from the one time they'd met, I couldn't say I blamed her.

"Hey," I said, setting down the boxes and rubbing my palm over her back.

She turned somber eyes on me. "She's never going to like me. Is she?"

The sadness in her tone caused anger to flare up inside me. "Of course she will," I murmured and pulled her into my side. "As soon as she gets to know you, she won't be able to help but love you."

I hadn't realized how much my mother's rebuff the night they met several weeks ago had bothered Rimmel. But I saw it now in the depths of her eyes. I wanted to take that away. I wanted to make it right.

But the truth was I wasn't sure what it was going to take to bring my mother around.

CHAPTER THREE

> #BoringBuzz
> Reminder: Classes require books.
> Get yours.
> #BookStoreIsOpen
> #HomeworkIsComing
>
> ... Alpha BuzzFeed

RIMMEL

Snowflakes swirled through the cold air. The gray sky hung low over everything outside, looking slightly ominous with the threat of more than just flurries.

I gazed out the window of Romeo's house, doing my best to avoid looking at the giant pool sitting right in my sight line. My hands were cupped around a white ceramic mug and the scent of cinnamon and cloves floated up to my nose, taking away some of my disgruntled feelings about the promise of snow.

I had to admit standing in here with the heat on full blast, hot cider in my hands and furry boots on my feet, the snow looked beautiful, even playful as is fell toward the ground. My freshman year was really my first experience with the stuff, having never traveled far beyond Florida until then.

I still remembered the wonder of my first snowfall. It was a short-lived feeling because the moment I had to step outside and trudge to classes, the magic melted like I wished the white stuff would.

I felt Romeo come up behind me, his large presence impossible to ignore. My body hummed in anticipation of his touch, and I reveled in that feeling because wanting him was something I would never tire of.

"Are you admiring the snow?" he murmured as both arms wrapped around my middle and he pulled me into the circle of his body. His chin rested on my shoulder and his breath flirted with the hair beside my ear.

"It's starting to stick to the ground," I replied, taking a deep breath and pushing closer against him. He smelled good, like his shampoo. It made me think of the hour we spent in the shower just a little while ago.

Romeo wrapped his hand around my mug and tugged gently. I released it and he straightened to take a sip of the liquid. I turned slightly to watch his throat work as he swallowed. His sapphire-blue eyes watched me over the rim and the chemistry that always seemed to be between us spiked the air.

He wasn't wearing a shirt, just a pair of jeans and the dog tag I gave him rested against his chest between his incredible muscles.

As he set aside the mug, I reached out to run my fingers across his chest, but he caught my hand and pressed a kiss to the tips of my fingers. "Don't tempt me," he half growled.

I batted my eyelashes innocently.

He chuckled. "As you pointed out, the snow is starting to stick. We should go before it starts coming down harder."

I didn't want to leave. Since arriving back from Florida, the only place I'd been was here. My dorm room was still there. I was still sharing with Ivy, but she wouldn't be back on campus until later today.

• • •

It was great seeing my dad and my grandparents, but these last two days here in this house with no one but Romeo had been the highlight of my winter break. I was sorry to see it end even though I knew it had to.

"I'll get dressed." I sighed and turned.

He laughed and pulled me back around. "We still have tonight." His eyes darkened with promise.

Classes didn't start until the day after tomorrow, and I didn't plan on staying at my dorm again tonight. But I needed to get my books. I'd never purchased them so late before. I just hoped they had some left.

My overfull suitcase was flung open on the floor of Romeo's room. Clothes spilled out the sides and threatened to fall on the floor. I'd had to sit on it to zip it up before flying back. When I left it, had only been half full.

When I was home, I mentioned to my grandmother that I was thinking about getting some clothes, ones that weren't so baggy. Considering she spent half my life trying to get me to wear the latest trends and I'd never once shown any interest, she acted like she'd won the lottery. She insisted on coming shopping (which I was glad because I had no idea what to pick) and she insisted on paying for it all. She also insisted on buying me three times what I actually needed.

Ivy was gonna flip when she saw all the new clothes.

The things I'd gotten were beautiful, but I had to admit I still preferred sweatpants, baggy tops, and messy hair. But I'd told myself this semester I'd lay off the pants that made me fall all over the place and try to wear things that were a little more flattering.

I pulled out a pair of skinny jeans in a washed-out color and ripped off the tags. Once I slid into those, I dug around for a warm top, my hand landing on a grey-and-white horizontally stripped sweater that was thick and warm. I pulled it on over my bra and white T-shirt and enjoyed the way the back hem fell over my butt.

The bangle Romeo gave me was still on my wrist. I planned to never take it off.

My hair was a disaster because all Romeo and I had done since arriving was alternate between the couch and the bed, so I ran my brush through the tangles and quickly piled it on top my head.

Romeo was by the door, lacing up a pair of brown leather boots. After he pulled his jeans over the laces, he straightened and smiled. He was dressed in a red long-sleeved T-shirt.

"New clothes?" he asked as he pulled on his varsity jacket.

"Yeah," I said a little self-consciously. I wasn't used to people looking at my clothes or noticing the way I dressed.

"You look hot," he said appreciatively.

I smiled.

"Where's your hoodie?" he asked.

I should have known he'd want me to wear his hoodie since we were going to campus. I glanced out the window. The snow was coming down a little heavier now.

I ran back into the bedroom and dug into the bottom of my suitcase and pulled out my new coat. I loved wearing Romeo's hoodie, but it was just too cold today. I needed a coat.

I pulled on the white puffer jacket and zipped it up as I walked. The interior was lined with fleece and was cozy warm. The oversized hood lay against my back and was wild with gray faux fur lining.

Romeo raised his eyebrow when I appeared, and I took his hand. "I don't need to wear your name today because you're going to be right next to me."

He grunted and we stepped out into the crisp winter air. I sucked in my breath at the chill and pressed into Romeo's side as we walked.

He chuckled and wrapped an arm around my shoulders.

My eyes couldn't help but stray toward the pool where wild snowflakes hit the water and dissolved instantly. There was also a slight cloud of steam rising off the top.

"Why don't your parents close the pool in the winter like everyone else?" I asked, my voice sounding grumpier than I intended.

I couldn't help it. My mother drowned in a pool. I found her body. Visions of the pink-tinted water and her lifeless form in the center made me shiver.

Romeo clutched me a little bit closer and angled his body so I couldn't see the pool anymore. Our steps quickened toward the Hellcat, the purr of its already running engine a familiar sound.

"Because my mother likes the way it looks lit up at night. She says it's pretty for parties and to watch the snowflakes melt in the heated water."

"Keeping it heated all winter has to be expensive," I murmured. The mention of his mother washed away the ugly memory of finding my own mother dead. Valerie didn't like me. She thought I wanted something from Romeo, a point she made very clear the night we met.

I tried not to show how much it bothered me, but it did. Maybe it was because I no longer had my mother here and a friendly relationship with Romeo's would have been nice. I know no one could ever replace my mother, but getting along with her was important to me.

"I'm sure it is," Romeo replied, drawing me out of my thoughts. He opened the passenger door of the Hellcat and motioned for me to climb in.

Once I was in, he reached around me and pulled the seatbelt across my chest. I didn't bother telling him I could buckle myself in. He never listened. "They don't keep it swimming temperature." He continued. "Just warm enough so it doesn't freeze."

Once he was in the driver's seat, he turned up the heat and it poured into the car. The remote start he had installed was the best thing ever. It meant never having to wait for the heat to warm up.

After the windshield wipers swiped all the snow off the glass, he pulled around toward the street. My eyes went back to the pool as he drove and they stayed fastened to it until it was out of site.

Campus wasn't as busy as usual, even though there were people milling around as students arrived back from winter break. Romeo's parking spot was vacant (as always) and he slid into it with ease. I braced myself against the cold once more as we rushed toward the building with the campus bookstore inside.

The scent of coffee and food greeted us at the door because the upstairs level of the building was the food court.

Downstairs, people milled about getting books and supplies, and the line at the register was longer than I would have liked. As usual, the second Romeo walked in, he was the center of attention. People called his name and gave him high-fives.

As he talked and joked with people who'd walked up to us, I focused on pulling out my list of books and supplies. I tried to slip through the crowd to start my shopping, but Romeo tightened his hand around mine. I glanced up and him and he smiled.

Even though he was preventing me from running away, I smiled back. I'd probably smile at him if I were dying. Just looking at him filled me up inside with joy. It was the reason I was learning to deal with his celebrity status. It came with him, and Romeo wasn't someone I was willing to give up.

"I love your coat," someone off to the side said.

Romeo nudged me because I hadn't realized she was speaking to me. I jumped a little and turned toward her. It was someone I'd never spoken to before. I'd seen her around. Part of me thought she might be a cheerleader.

"Thanks," I said, forcing myself not to shrink into his side. Romeo didn't need a girlfriend who ran from his life. He needed someone to embrace it just the way he'd embraced mine.

I gave the girl a rueful smile and said, "Trying to find a coat in Florida is next to impossible."

Her eyes widened a little when I gave more than a one-word response. But she recovered and smiled. "You're from Florida?"

I nodded.

She sighed. "So lucky. I'd love to live by the beach."

"Maybe someday," I said because I had no idea what else to say. This was the longest conversation I'd ever had with one of Romeo's friends. Besides Braeden of course.

As if I conjured him into being, Braeden materialized nearby and shouted, "Rome! Where you been hiding?"

The crowd parted slightly to make room for Romeo's best friend, and he grinned when he saw me standing there. "Ah," he said, "tutor girl is back."

I sighed dramatically. Was he ever going to stop calling me that?

Braeden pushed into the center of the small crowd and put his arm around me, and Romeo let go of my hand as Braden tugged me into his side. "He's been unbearable while you were gone," he said. I was aware of everyone watching the easy affection he showed me. It made me slightly uncomfortable, even if I did enjoy it.

"I doubt it," I said, poking him in the ribs. "You were probably just annoying."

People around us laughed, and Braeden hooted. "Rome, I need to borrow your girl. She knows all about books and I can't seem to find the one I need."

He shoved his wrinkled paper beneath my nose and steered me out of the crowd so I would help him.

I found the book in like three seconds and handed it to him with an *are you for real?* look on my face.

"Looked like it was getting a little crowded over there," he said, taking the book. His eyes held a knowing look.

He'd done that on purpose. He knew almost as well as Romeo how uncomfortable I could get.

"Thanks," I said, and I meant it.

"Anytime, tutor girl."

"I do have a name, you know?" I said.

"I know." He grinned. It was the only answer I got. He definitely didn't say he was going to start using it. "So is Missy back from break yet?"

I glanced at him. "You haven't talked to her?"

He shrugged. "Why would I?"

Because they were sleeping together… At least they had been before we all left. "Ummm," I said, suddenly feeling awkward. It seemed I probably shouldn't have to point out something like that to him.

Braeden chuckled and threw his arm across my shoulders and yanked me forward. His abrupt movements caused me to lose my balance and I fell against him. His chuckle turned into a laugh as he steadied me.

I straightened and then pushed at my glasses. "I think she comes back tomorrow."

"Cool."

I frowned. "You really haven't talked to her?"

"Nope." He shrugged like it wasn't a big deal. I wondered what Missy thought about that.

"So you two really aren't dating?" I pressed.

Braeden sighed and looped his arm across my shoulders again and steered me toward a stack of books. "So innocent," he mused. "Tutor girl, as your man's best friend and your self-appointed big brother, I feel like it's time I teach you about the real world."

"You're my self-appointed big brother?" I asked, looking up at him.

He nodded like it was obvious. "You and Rome… you're an exception to the rule. You two are the real deal, but most guys, guys like me, aren't looking to settle down. They like—"

"To have fun?" I finished for him, slightly amused.

"Exactly."

"But what about the girls?" I asked.

He gave me a clueless look. I sighed. "Maybe it's me who needs to teach you, *brother*."

He lifted an eyebrow.

"Guys might want to have fun," I said, using his words, "but girls have a harder time keeping their feelings from getting involved."

"Relax, tutor girl," Braeden said. "I know how to handle things."

• • •

I didn't know what that meant, but I hoped it meant Missy wouldn't get hurt.

Romeo appeared in front of us, crossed his arms over his wide chest, and stared at me and Braeden. Braeden didn't seem to mind the death glare he was receiving. "You're looking awful cozy over here with my girl."

"I was just schooling our girl here on the ways of the world," Braeden replied smoothly.

"*Our* girl?" Romeo repeated.

"Don't get your panties in a twist." Braeden grinned.

I interrupted their macho talk with some talk of my own. "He was asking about Missy."

Romeo grinned.

Braeden dropped his arm from around me and gave me a look of betrayal. "What happened to brother-sister confidentiality?"

I laughed.

"Dude, there's a hot girl in line over there," Romeo said, motioning with his chin. "Go get in line behind her."

Braeden turned and a slow smile spread across his stubbled jaw. "Day-um," he said. "Good looking out, Rome." He held up his fist and Romeo pounded his against it.

"Tutor girl," Braeden said, and then he was gone. I watched him slip smoothly into the line right behind the girl Romeo just declared hot.

She was the total opposite of me. She looked like some ski bunny who spent all her time lounging by the fire at some exclusive ski lodge. She was dressed in a pair of skintight black leggings, tall white boots, a hot-pink long-sleeved top, and a white vest zipped up over her ample chest. Her ultra-blond hair was pulled up and she had a pair of large black sunglasses on her head.

The only thing that gave away the fact she wasn't on skiing holiday was her arms were full of books and we were all standing in a bookstore.

Braeden said something to her and she turned. I knew by the way her body leaned in toward his that she was interested.

It left a sick feeling in my stomach.

"Hey," Romeo said from beside me.

I pulled my gaze away from Braeden and focused on the list in my hand. "I think the first book I need is right over here," I said and started off in its direction.

Romeo caught me around the elbow and gently pulled me around. "What's wrong?"

"You used to be just like him," I blurted out. Then I slammed my lips together, cursing myself for not thinking before I spoke.

Romeo's brows drew together. "Braeden?"

I nodded. "You liked to have fun. You hit on a different girl every day…" I paused and took a breath. "Pretty girls."

Something very close to anger lit up his eyes and burned there like the hottest part of a flame. Before I could backpedal, his large hands slid beneath my arms and hooked beneath my shoulders. Romeo lifted me off the ground like it was easy, like it didn't even take effort. My feet dangled in the air as he drew me up so we were eye to eye.

"A thousand of those girls"—he made a slight motion with his head toward Braeden—"couldn't even make up one of you."

"Romeo," I whispered, caught up in the molten blue flame flickering in his gaze.

"You know I was like that once. I've never made a secret of it. But you're it for me now, Rim. There's no one else. There never could be."

Even though he spoke softly, I still felt the room around us listening. My neck still prickled with a thousand stares, but I didn't care. His words pierced me. They took the feelings of doubt creeping up inside me and totally vanquished them.

I smiled and something in his eyes relaxed. Worry I hadn't seen until that moment disappeared. He gave me one of his oh so charming lopsided smiles and pulled me closer to kiss me.

It was a fast kiss, but it was more than effective.

Once I was back on my feet, reality began to intrude and I noted just how much of an audience we acquired.

I started to duck my head, but Romeo plucked the list out of my hand and tugged me along toward the nearest section. And just like that, everything seemed to start back up. Everyone began to move again; the room came alive.

My lips were tingling as I reached out for one of the textbooks I needed and began shuffling through the pile, looking for a used one (they cost so much less). Romeo reached around me, helping me look.

A few seconds later, he pulled back, his body stiff.

"Did you find one?" I asked, turning around.

His hands were empty and tension radiated off his body.

"Romeo?" I said, pressing a hand to the small of his back. His muscles reacted, tensing immediately.

I peered around him, wondering what could be causing such a reaction.

I should have known.

It wasn't a *what*, but a *who*.

Zach.

And judging from the half snarl on his lips and the calculating glint in his eyes, I knew he hadn't come for books like the rest of us.

No, he was here for a piece of Romeo.

CHAPTER FOUR

#UhOh
Old habits die hard and it appears so
do some rivalries.
#EveryoneLovesRomeo #ExceptForOne
#BuyingBooksJustGotInteresting
... Alpha BuzzFeed

ROMEO

Fucking Zach.

If there were an award for asshole of the year, he'd
be the reigning champ.

He was so eaten up by his father's reputation, his
father's money, and everything he thought he was that
he never stopped to consider the truth.

He was just a loser with a credit card.

Maybe in the past I never realized that. Hell, maybe
I'd been the kind of guy who thought money equaled

class. Maybe I thought the air of arrogance Zach wore as armor made him superior to others.

And then I fell in love with a girl who was the epitome of the opposite of my world.

She shattered everything I thought I knew. And though she might be the one wearing glasses, it was me who was finally seeing clearly.

Our eyes locked from across the bookstore. His lips were curved like he had something nasty to say, and I partially wanted him to. I'd love an excuse to wipe that look off his face.

The familiar sound of phones beeping was partially distracting, but neither of us looked away. It was like we were locked in a contest of wills to see who would back down first.

Rimmel's small hand slid into mine, her fingers curling against my palm as her thumb curved around and tugged. I still didn't look away from Zach.

"Romeo." Her voice was low and she tugged at my hand again.

Zach's eyes slid to where she was beside me, and a smile split his face. My upper lip curled in response, and

I swiftly turned, putting my back to him and blocking Rimmel from sight.

She held up her phone with a sigh. It was a Buzz about me and Zach. I glanced around and people averted their gazes. I couldn't help but wonder who went running to the BuzzBoss about my staring contest.

People needed to get a life.

"You ever wonder who the BuzzBoss is?" Rimmel asked.

"Nope," I replied truthfully. "I couldn't care less."

She pocketed her phone. "Well, they sure care about you."

"Let's get your books." I wanted to turn back to where Zach had been, but I resisted the urge. I wasn't going to start anything with him here, now. Not when Rimmel was at my side. I didn't like the way he looked at her, like he was a predator and she was prey.

I swear she needed like fifty pounds worth of books. It seemed like every pile we passed she had to add another to her stack. "Damn, if I'd known you needed this much, I could've skipped training this morning," I quipped.

She snorted and turned to say something with a smile on her lips. But the words seemed to catch in her throat and her eyes went over my shoulder, then back to me again.

"Still together, I see," Zach said from behind me.

I drew myself up to my full height and turned fully, angling my body so it completely blocked Rimmel from view. Even though I paid him back for what he did to her in the haunted house, I wasn't going to forget it. I didn't want him anywhere near her.

Behind me, Rimmel tried to peek around my side, and I planted my feet more firmly to the ground and shifted to block her.

Her cute little huff of frustration only made me more determined to keep her out of sight, to keep her protected.

Zach had dark hair that stuck up in the front and was cropped close to his head around his ears and neck. It was a pretty-boy haircut he probably spent thirty minutes on every morning. He was dressed in a pair of jeans and a navy-blue pea coat with too many damn buttons. What the fuck did a guy need so many buttons for? Unless he was overcompensating for other areas in which he was lacking.

The thought made me grin.

"You can stand in front of her all day long, Anderson. But I still know she's there," Zach said, giving me a smirk.

A few whispers went through the store as everyone in the place listened attentively to our exchange. Ever since Zach got dethroned from his presidency of Omega and word got around I was involved, rumors flew around campus faster than the blustery winter wind.

I didn't give two shits about the rumors, though. I continued like I always had. I smiled, I joked, and I played football. If anyone thought my involvement was shady, they never said it to my face or within earshot of any of my friends.

Hell, as far as I was concerned, it was a new semester. Everything that happened with Omega was in the past, old news. I had no interest in dragging it all up again.

Clearly, Zach had other ideas.

"What the hell do you want, Bettinger?" I asked, already bored of him.

"I wanted to let you know I haven't forgotten about what you did."

"What I did?" I kept my voice even, almost conversational. I lifted my eyebrows. "And what was that?"

He stepped closer, a snarl marring his pretty-boy features. "Payback's a bitch," he said low.

"Is that a threat?" All the muscles in my body tightened. My eyes narrowed on his face.

Braeden appeared beside me, planting his feet into the floor and mirroring my position. His arms folded across his chest as he glared at Zach. But he spoke to me. "What's going on, Rome? Trouble in the neighborhood?"

"Nothing I can't handle." I stared directly into Zach's eyes when I replied.

"I don't make threats," Zach replied, looking back at me. "I make promises."

I couldn't help it. I grinned. "What the fuck is this?" I asked. "Some cheesy after school movie?"

A couple snickers floated through the store around us, and Zach stiffened.

"Get the hell out of here, man," Braeden said. "Before you embarrass yourself more."

After another long, charged stare from Zach, he turned. "See ya later, Rimmel," Zach called, making the muscles between my shoulder blades squeeze together.

Braeden put a hand in the center of my chest like he knew I was seconds away from grabbing that bastard by the scruff of his neck and face-planting him into the closest hard surface.

"Forget him," Braeden said low.

I grunted and turned back to Rimmel. She gave me and then Braeden a withering look. "What the hell was that all about?"

Braeden whistled under his breath. "Tutor girl gets pissy."

Rimmel narrowed her eyes.

Braeden spoke quickly. "Gotta jet. Hot girl is holding my place in line." He slapped me on the shoulder and left.

"Coward," I muttered after him, and he laughed.

I put my arm around Rimmel's shoulders and directed her toward the next stack of books she needed. "He's just pissed off he's not Omega president anymore."

"He seems to think you're the reason," she said low.

I didn't tell Rimmel my part in having Zach arrested, which resulted in him losing presidency. She hadn't needed to know all that. I wanted her to have plausible deniability. She'd been through enough on account of me, and I wasn't about to put her through more. Besides, no one needed to know except the couple people involved in helping set him up, and I knew they weren't going to talk. They didn't want to risk Zach's wrath.

Especially since they were still in the same frat house.

Turns out his little "theft" from the dean was enough to get him a night in jail and the loss of the top spot at Omega, but it wasn't enough to get him completely booted out the door. It should have been, but Zach wasn't without connections. His dad pulled some strings, called in some favors, and he was still in the brotherhood.

I wondered how it was for him there since he got knocked down a peg or two.

"Romeo," Rimmel said when I didn't answer right away.

I looked down at her and smiled. "Haters gonna hate."

Her hand slid between my shirt and jacket and she poked me in the ribs. "That's not an answer."

I covered her lips with mine and explored the inside of her mouth with my tongue. Then I drew back slightly and spoke against her lips. "I'm starving. Let's get your books and get out of here." I pulled farther back to look into her eyes. Today there were green flecks in their depths. "I'll take you to lunch."

"What about the snow?" she asked.

I shrugged. "We'll get takeout on the way to my place, then."

If she thought anything more about Zach, it never showed.

'Course, that didn't make me feel any better because he was in the back of my mind and so was the dark way he stared at me when he promised payback.

I no longer felt like I was going to be able to leave last semester where it belonged, in the past.

If today were any indication, Zach was dragging along all of our old baggage into the present.

CHAPTER FIVE

RIMMEL

Girls still watched us.

Or rather, watched Romeo wherever we went. He was practically the sun of the campus universe.

As a result, I got looked at too. First because I was standing beside him, but then the stares turned curious, some envious.

I never got used to it last semester, and I knew now—even just a few moments back on campus—I wasn't going to this semester either. There was a new dimension to the stares now. In addition to the usual curiosity, there was also something more.

Shock.

People were shocked we were still together.

I felt my cheeks heat a little as we walked through the cold, and white flurries coated the dark hair around my shoulders. I knew what they were thinking.

They thought he would get tired of me. That he would get over whatever phase possessed him to date me in the first place. Even though silent stares and evil whispers taunted the back of my mind, I refused to give in.

I walked proudly, carrying my things across the parking lot with my chin held high.

Romeo led the way. Even loaded down with my nearly bursting suitcase and couple extra bags, he was still graceful and athletic. His legs were powerful and lithe as he strode across the ground, his sneakers making dark impressions against the freshly fallen snow coating the asphalt. I marveled at how large those dark shapes appeared and looked over my shoulder, back at where my footprints followed along with his.

My feet were half his size. It was almost comical to see the two prints side by side. One was so much more intimidating than the other. I was so caught up in marveling at the size difference, of course, I was paying no attention to what I was doing.

My booted foot hit the front of the curb and I went flying forward. I let out a little squeal as the bag I was carrying flew out of my hands and off to the right. I fell onto the cold, wet concrete sidewalk. My purse fell off my shoulder and tangled around me and stuff went rolling all over.

People stopped and stared. Some of the girls giggled.

I landed on my side, my hip taking the brunt of the fall. It burned and stung from the hit, but I ignored it and struggled to sit up quickly. There really was no point in hurrying so no one would see.

Everyone already saw.

A pair of jean-clad legs appeared before me, and my suitcase and all my other stuff was dropped nearby.

"Whatcha doing down there?" Romeo drawled, his hands on his hips as he stared down at me with dancing blue eyes.

"Making a snow angel," I quipped. I glanced down at my hands, which were covered with wet snow and bits of salt (to keep the pavement from getting icy).

Clearly, ice wasn't required for me to fall.

A small group of girls just "happened by," and by that I mean they'd been staring at Romeo with puppy dog eyes and giving me the stink eye. When I fell, they took it as an opportunity to descend like buzzards stalking the dead.

Their leader was the girl who approached me the very first day I'd worn Romeo's hoodie around campus and told me he'd get bored. As they stalked closer, looking like clones from the movie *Mean Girls*, I caught the calculating look in her eyes. This wasn't going to be good.

I pushed up off the ground so I wouldn't feel so vulnerable, but the new snow was slick and my hand slid right out from under me and I fell back again.

Romeo was there immediately, the teasing light in his eyes gone as he slid his hand around my back and started to pull me up. "Careful, babe," he said gently.

The girls were behind him so I knew he hadn't seen them approach. They stopped as one unit, and I braced myself for whatever their leader was about to say.

She was wearing painted-on skinny jeans (I mean, really, how did she sit down and still breathe?) and some designer coat with a monogrammed scarf draped fashionably around her neck. Her boots were high-heeled, made of suede and laced up the back with contrasting ribbon.

"Wow," she said, opening her perfectly painted pink lips. "I saw that from way over there. That sure looked like it hurt." She said it fairly amicably, but anyone who could see the twist to her mouth as she said it would know better.

Romeo paused in lifting me to my feet. I felt his eyes on me. Then his lips thinned as he turned and looked over his shoulder.

"Ladies," he said like he was greeting a group of welcomed friends. Annoyance prickled my stomach like tiny needles stabbing me.

It's not that I wanted him to be rude, but did he have to sound so welcoming?

"Romeo," Cruella DeBarbie (I didn't know her real name, but this one fit) purred. "Haven't you grown bored of this clumsy mule yet?"

Unable to stop myself, I gasped and jumped up to my feet. If she wanted to call me a mule, I'd show her just how much of an *ass* I could be.

Romeo brought his arm out and stopped me from marching past. I collided into him, and if his fingers hadn't knowingly grabbed hold to steady me, I'd have fallen again.

"Actually," Romeo said, his voice calm, "I am pretty bored."

Three smirks were sent my way. What a bunch of idiots.

"The view from where I'm standing sure leaves a lot to be desired."

One by one, their eyes rounded when they realized the view he referenced was them. Without another word, he pivoted around and looked down at me, his gaze going soft. "No need to make snow angels, baby," he said loud enough for the slack-jawed buzzards to hear. "You already look like one standing here with all that snow in your hair."

• • •

Before I could say a word, he picked me up and fastened his mouth to mine. My legs wound around his waist without thought, and I kissed him back as gentle snow fell against our faces. His tongue was warm compared to the air, and I drank him in eagerly. Somewhere in the middle of our public display of affection, I heard a few huffs and some boots stomping away.

Slowly, he pulled back and set me carefully on the ground, his forehead touched mine, and he looked at me. "That the girl who said something to you last semester?"

"How'd you know?"

"Thought I was gonna have to restrain ya." He smiled. "You were about to throw down."

"I probably would have embarrassed myself," I confided. I moved so our noses touched as well as our foreheads.

"I'd have bet money on you." He pressed a quick kiss to my lips before bending to the mess I made on the sidewalk.

We worked quickly, shoving everything from my purse back inside. When we were done, Romeo straightened and gave me a wide, cheeky smile. "Maybe I should carry you. It might be safer."

"Ha-ha."

Upstairs in my room, Ivy was already completely unpacked. Well, if by unpacked it meant her clothes were already strewn all over the room.

She squealed when I walked in and rushed toward me like we hadn't seen each other in months instead of weeks. I grinned as Romeo stepped in behind me, blocking Ivy's path. Her eyes followed my giant suitcase as he lugged it by, and I shut the door.

"Your suitcase wasn't that full when you left here," she said. I swear she had some kind of sensor for new clothes.

"I went shopping," I said nonchalantly.

She squealed and I laughed. Poor Romeo was practically mowed over by her attempt to get to the bag, and she was unzipping it before I could toss the rest of my stuff on the bed.

"Ohmigod," she said, her words running together. She stared down into the mess of clothes like it was some holy shrine. "Look at it all!"

Romeo looked at me like he was confused, and I shrugged. Ivy pried herself away from my new fashion haul and flung her arms around me, giving me a big hug. I was a little taken off guard by her easy affection. Having a circle of friends still felt so new to me, but it was nice, so I hugged her back.

"I was starting to think you wouldn't ever get here," she said, turning back to my clothes and holding them all up one by one.

"I've been at Romeo's."

Ivy looked at him. "Aren't you like super busy getting ready for the championship game?"

Apparently, this game was a big deal. It was like the Superbowl of college football. And Romeo was the starting quarterback. He'd spent most of his winter break playing in finals games. He hadn't said much about the game coming up, but I knew how important it was. I knew what it could mean for his career.

He gave her the full-on Romeo treatment, running a hand through his blond hair, smiling, and flashing those baby blues at her. "I've been doing my training."

Ivy seemed dumbstruck for a minute, but then she recovered to say, "Well, you definitely look like you've been training."

"I just hung out with Murphy when he was at practice," I added and moved over to him. His arm wrapped around my middle and tugged me into his side. Automatically, my cheek lay against his chest, and I sighed.

"Speaking of… I gotta go. I need to be at the field." His voice rumbled through his chest and against my ear as he spoke.

I sighed and stepped out of his arms. I was sad that our couple days together were over and I would be here tonight without him. Classes started tomorrow, and I knew we were going to see a lot less of each other now that the semester was starting.

"I'll walk you out," I said and followed him to the door.

Ivy was still digging through my clothes and called out a good-bye.

"Just stay inside," he said, palming the handle. "It's cold and slippery out there. You'll be safer in here."

I grimaced. "You're probably right."

He grinned. "I'll call you later, 'kay?"

I nodded.

He released the door handle and closed the distance between us with one step. The toes of his shoes bumped against my boots and the front of his jacket brushed against me.

My stomach fluttered and my heart rate doubled. The effect he had on me was nothing short of amazing. I tipped my head back so I could look up into his eyes, and the corner of his mouth lifted. He looked at me with so much affection in his gaze that emotion caught in my throat. He didn't have to say anything because I heard everything just by looking in his eyes.

My fingers curled around the hem of his shirt and tangled in the cotton fabric, and at the same time I stretched up, he bent down.

The feel of his lips against me was my favorite sensation. Nothing compared to the way his mouth owned mine. His tongue stretched out, sweeping through my mouth with gentle pressure, and I sighed into him and sagged forward.

A low laugh vibrated his chest and he pulled back.

"Be careful walking to class tomorrow, huh? Don't fall and hurt yourself."

I nodded, barely comprehending his words.

He slipped out the door before reality came flooding back. I rushed forward, caught the closing door, and called out his name.

He stopped and turned. The lopsided, knowing smile on his face was smug. "Good luck at practice," I called, ignoring the few girls who stopped to watch us.

"Thanks, baby."

I swear every girl within earshot sighed.

I couldn't even blame them.

I shut the door and leaned against it.

Ivy put her hands on her hips and looked at me. "I'm gonna need a mega supply of barf bags to put up with you two this semester."

I smiled. "So how was your break?"

"The usual. My brothers picked on me, my mom made too much food, and my grandfather took an hour and a half to eat." The affection in her voice totally negated the way she tried to make it sound like torture.

"Sounds nice," I said and plopped down on her bed. Mine was covered in clothes. I tried to imagine what it would be like to have two brothers, a mother, and a bunch of other family around my table. If my mother hadn't died, our holidays might resemble Ivy's. This year, it had just been me, my dad, and grandparents.

"Did I mention my grandfather smacked his lips constantly while he chewed?" She glanced at me and mock shuddered.

I laughed.

"So is Missy back?" I asked.

"Got back yesterday," she replied, holding up an icy-blue sweater with a white heart on the chest. "This better fit me."

"Braeden asked about her."

Ivy threw the sweater aside and made a dramatic sound. "He didn't call or text her once over break."

"I kinda figured that after I talked to him. Is Missy upset?"

Ivy plopped down in my desk chair. "She says she isn't, says she hadn't expected him to call, but I think deep down it hurt her feelings."

I was afraid of that. "Guys just don't get it." I sighed.

Ivy screwed up her face and reached for the pillow on my bed. Next thing I knew, she launched it and I shrieked as it hit me in the head. "Hey!" I cried and flung myself flat on the bed.

"Guys just don't get it," she mocked with a faux high tone in her voice. "Says the girl with the perfect boyfriend."

"He isn't perfect…" I said, even though he kinda was.

Ivy laughed. "You can't even say that with a straight face."

I flung a pillow across the room at her. She batted it away with her hand. I sat up and adjusted my glasses. "We both know Romeo has quite the past with girls. It wasn't very long ago that he was just like Braeden."

"So what's your secret?" Ivy asked, leaning forward like she was waiting for me to divulge some tremendous bit of information.

I snorted. "Are you serious? You think I know?"

"You're the only girl on this entire campus to have landed Romeo Anderson."

"I didn't land him," I said, a serious note in my tone. "I wasn't even looking for him."

She groaned. "Well, how do you *not* look for a guy?"

I got up from the bed, went over to the mini fridge, and reached in for some bottled water. It was empty. "Ugh. We need supplies."

"We can go now if you want. I'll drive."

I shrugged. "Sure. Why not?" I glanced at the clothes all over my bed and grimaced. It looked just like Ivy's side of the room.

She noticed and laughed. "C'mon."

I snatched up my bag and coat from the bed and followed her out the door.

"So…" She began on our way down to the ground floor. "I think you gave me an idea."

"I did?" I asked, surprised.

The messy blond bun on top her head bounced as she nodded. "I'm going to find a guy by *not* looking for a guy this semester."

"You're looking for a guy?"

She gave me a long stare out of the corner of her eye. "Aren't all girls looking for *the* guy?"

My answer would have been no, but I didn't think that was the one she wanted to hear. "I thought you liked being single."

She shrugged. "I do, but seeing you and Romeo… well, makes me kind of want something like that for myself, you know?"

"Yeah," I agreed. I could understand that. I hadn't even realized I'd wanted it until Romeo gave it to me.

Outside, the sky was closing in on darkness. White flurries still fell as cold wind blew around us. Thank goodness Alpha U had an indoor field, because the thought of Romeo out practicing in this was a terrible thought.

Inside Ivy's little car was no warmer than outside, and I prayed the heater worked fast. I rubbed my hands together and blew into them as Ivy started up the car. Maybe I'd buy a pair of mittens while we were out.

As Ivy backed out of her parking spot, I turned toward her. "I hope you find him," I said. "You know… *the* guy."

"Thanks." She smiled. "And maybe while I'm *not* looking, I can have some fun."

"Be careful," I sang. "You sound like Braeden."

"Hmmm," she mused. "Maybe Braeden has the right idea after all."

We looked at each other and laughed.

CHAPTER SIX

#Randomness
The University of Victoria has a class in
the science of Batman.
#AlphaUFail #MathSucksStudyBatman

... Alpha BuzzFeed

ROMEO

Alpha U had a large indoor field for us to train on during the cold months. It wasn't quite as large as a regular football field, but it was big enough for us to stay conditioned and on top of our game.

The sport of football had an off season—but the players didn't. The Wolves practiced almost all year round. It's what made us so competitive. It's what got us to the championships this year. Most college teams were done with their season. They were enjoying a lighter schedule, but not us.

The entire winter break was filled with training, early morning practices, and traveling to the finals games.

All that preparation, all those wins… they all came down to one thing. The championship.

It was next week, and the Wolves were hungry for it. *I* was hungry for it.

I knew some NFL scouts were at some of the final games, I knew I played well enough to impress them, but the big test was this game. As the quarterback, I felt even more pressure to lead the team to victory, and as a player, I felt pressure to perform for my future.

Since I blew off Omega, it wasn't going to be as easy to snag an in with the NFL. I was going to have to make up for that with hard work.

I worked hard at practice, running drills, throwing passes, and occasionally running the ball. I was a little bulkier than some quarterbacks so I didn't run it as often, but it was still something I practiced because I didn't want my size to deter my ability to run.

When I was out here on the field, it was just me and the lights. Me and the ball. I focused on my breathing, on the sound it made filling up my lungs. I kept my eyes and mind focused on the field, the team, and the plays.

When Coach called practice, I stayed out a little longer with Braeden and practiced throwing down the field. By the time I was done, my shoulder was sore and the muscles in my body shuddered from exhaustion.

When Braeden and I headed off the field, I saw Trent on the sidelines, watching us. He was already changed over, wearing a pair of jeans and an Alpha hoodie.

"Looking good out there," he said when I was within earshot.

"Thanks, man," I said and snagged up my water off the bench. I emptied the bottle and tossed it in a nearby bin.

"You've been pushing yourself," Trent said.

"I want the trophy next week."

"We all want that trophy next week," Braeden said from behind.

"Any luck with the scouts?" Trent asked.

"Not yet," I answered, rubbing a towel over my sweat-drenched head.

"The offer to be an Omega still stands," he replied. "The connection might help."

"Thanks, but I'm gonna do this on my terms."

He nodded. "I can respect that."

We fist-bumped and I grinned. "Speaking of Omega, how's it feel to be president?"

Trent replaced Zach as Omega president almost right after he was carted off in handcuffs.

"Not too shabby." He smirked.

"How is it with Zach still around?"

His expression slipped a little. "Dude, that guy is a complete tool."

I nodded. "He still pretty pissed about last semester or what?"

"Oh yeah," Trent said. "He thought he was still gonna be president after everything. Hell, he wouldn't even still be there if his daddy hadn't stepped in."

"He giving you problems?" I asked, my eyes narrowing.

"Seems to be laying low for right now," Trent answered. "But knowing Zach, that just means he's up to something."

"He threatened me the other day."

Trent straightened, his gaze sharpening on my face. Beside me, Braeden crossed his arms over his chest. "What'd he say?"

I shrugged. "Nothing specific, just that he hadn't forgotten."

Trent swore beneath his breath. "I'll keep an eye on him. Have a couple guys at the house do the same. I'll let you know if I hear anything."

"Appreciate it, man." I grabbed up my gear to go hit the showers. My shoulder was sore and I needed to ice it down.

"Hey," he called out behind me. "We having a team party for the championship or what?"

I laughed. "Hells yeah."

Braeden made a whooping sound. "Might as well plan that bitch now, because the win is in the bag."

I laughed. "We can do it at my place. Team members only and their dates."

"Exclusive," Braeden said. "Me likey."

"Sweet. I'll pass word with the guys." Trent agreed. "BYOB."

I headed off into the locker room and made a mental note to tell Mom about the party. She'd make

* * *

sure it was stocked and that would be one less thing I'd have to deal with. We could have had it somewhere else, but as the team quarterback, I felt like it was my place to do something for my team.

After I yanked off all my gear and tossed it in my locker, I sat down and reached for my bag. I was exhausted and starving. I decided to skip the shower and just take one at home.

"Yo, I'm out!" I called to Braeden.

He came around the corner in nothing but a towel. "Dude, I've told ya before. You're a good-looking guy too. It's just that not many can hold up to all this," he cracked and gestured to himself with his hand. "Sometimes it's lonely being so damn fine."

I grinned and grabbed an ice pack out of the nearby freezer. After kneading it around a minute, I slapped it on my shoulder beneath my jacket and laughed. "Fuck you."

He grinned. "If I had a private shower at home like you, I'd be leaving too."

"Mi casa es su casa," I told him.

"Thanks. You better go ice down that shoulder. Maybe call up your girl for a rub down."

I was exhausted, but just the thought of Rimmel and her hands on me was enough to give me a second wind.

"I'll see ya tomorrow," I called and left.

I could hear the shower running and Braeden singing some lame song at the top of his lungs as I walked down the hallway.

It was well past dinner by the time I walked into my place. I tossed my stuff by the door and went straight to the shower. When I was finished, I threw on some sweats and a T-shirt and wandered over to the main house because I knew they had better food than I did.

The kitchen was dim with only a few pendant lights hanging over the massive marble-topped island. The room lit up a little more when I opened the stainless steel fridge and rummaged around for some grub. There was a container filled with grilled chicken, roasted vegetables, and seasoned rice, and I popped the lid and put the whole thing in the micro to heat. As I was waiting, I adjusted the fresh ice pack on my shoulder.

Rimmel was at the library, working on some paper that wasn't due for like another two weeks. She'd wanted to get a head start she'd said. I'd never done an assignment that far in advance. Hell, if it wasn't for her tutoring me again this semester, I'd probably be on thin ice with my grades. But she would keep me on track.

When my food was finally done heating, I reached in to grab it and spun around to grab a fork. My mother was standing on the other side of the island. Watching me.

"Geez, Mom. Creepy much?" I said. snagging a fork and then leaning against the counter to eat.

"Why are you icing your shoulder?" she asked, her eyes zeroing in on my arm.

"I'm fine," I told her around a huge bite of meat. "It's just sore from practice."

She pulled out one of the upholstered chairs at the island and pointed at it. "Sit when you eat."

I shoved another huge bite in my mouth and made sure I chewed extra loud on my way to the chair.

"Really, Roman." She sighed and put a kettle of water on the stove to boil.

"Thanks for the food, Mom."

"There will always be meals in here for you. I know how hard you work and how busy your schedule is. The last thing you need to do is worry about trying to feed yourself."

I smiled extra toothy-like, making sure she got a glimpse of what I was chewing. She made a tsking sound but smiled fondly and laughed under her breath.

I went back to eating (with better manners), and she went about getting out a white porcelain mug and placing a teabag inside.

When I could hear the hot bubbling of the water inside the kettle, she lifted it off the heat and poured the steaming liquid over her tea.

"Where's dad?" I asked.

"Working late. He has a case."

I grunted. That wasn't much of a surprise. Dad worked long hours. I guess being a sought-after attorney with a good reputation came with a price. Sometimes I wondered if it was my mother who paid most of it. She was here alone more than not, and I knew sometimes it had to get lonely.

"Why didn't you tell me she didn't have a mother?" Her question jarred me out of my thoughts, and my head snapped up. She was rhythmically dunking her tea bag in the water as she awaited an answer.

I was surprised. She could have asked me about my grades, football, or anything else for that matter. Rimmel wasn't really a topic we ever engaged in.

She made it clear how she felt.

And I made it clear I didn't give a fuck.

So it was interesting now that she was coming to me with information I never gave her.

"I didn't realize it mattered." My voice was lazy even though I felt anything but. My mother was poking around in my life. Poking around Rimmel, who she hurt once before with her less-than-gentle attitude. I didn't like it.

"If it concerns you, it matters," she said coolly, abandoning the tea bag.

My mother cared about me. I wouldn't say or think otherwise. The fact is I was her only child, her miracle baby at that, and I knew she loved me more than anyone. And I loved her, but sometimes her fierceness got in the way of my life. The older I got, maybe the less I noticed it. Maybe I told myself it wasn't there, and sometimes it was easy to feel like I was nothing more than a trophy for my socialite parents to display.

But right now, I knew this was about more than her wanting to protect me from a girl she thought only wanted something from me.

And then I understood perfectly.

"You hired a private eye to find out about my girlfriend?" I couldn't hide the cool contempt from my tone. My fork clattered against the dish.

Her eyes widened just a fraction and she cleared her throat. "Of course I did. How else was I to find out anything about her?"

"You could have asked."

She frowned. "I'm not trying to upset you, Roman. It's clear she means a great deal to you."

I sighed. "Yeah, she does. Which is exactly why I'm not getting into this with you." I stood, pushing back the stool, and grabbed up the food. "I'll go finish this at my place."

I left before she could say anything else. She did call out my name behind me, but I kept going. I felt guilty as I walked around the pool with a bowl of food in my hand that I knew she made for me. I felt a little guilty because I'd left her standing there alone instead of keeping her company for a bit.

But then I remembered the look on Rimmel's face the night my mother accused her of only wanting something from me. I remembered how freaked out I was seeing her small frame walking back to campus on a dark street, alone.

I kept walking.

Inside, I set my food on the counter and grabbed a bottle of water out of the fridge. I pulled my phone out of my pocket and thought about texting Rim to see if she was done studying, but the sound of the front door closing had me glancing up.

My mother followed me into the kitchen, carrying her mug of tea in her hands. I leaned against the counter and readjusted the ice on my shoulder and waited.

"That was rude." She lifted her eyebrow.

"Mom," I ground out, barely holding on to my patience. "What kind of reaction did you expect?"

"All I did was make an inquiry. You've been spending a lot of time with her."

As she spoke, Murphy waltzed into the room as if to punctuate Mom's point. She gave the black one-eyed animal a look, and then her eyes flashed to mine as if to say, *See, told you.*

She wasn't too thrilled when she came over one day to find a cat sitting on the kitchen counter. Animals didn't really fit into our lifestyle, and animal hair didn't really go with the décor in the main house.

I expected a fight, for her to tell me to get him out.

She didn't. Mom just told me it was my job to clean up after him, not the housekeeper's.

"So you're saying you had her background checked because you don't trust my judgment?"

Her eyes narrowed. "Don't speak to me like that." She took a sip of tea and a deep breath. "I was merely doing the responsible thing any parent would do. Your father has a very good reputation. We have good standing in this community. Is it so bad that I wanted to make sure she was who she said she was?"

I wasn't going to argue with her. It didn't matter. "And I assume you're satisfied now?"

She sat aside her tea and regarded me with serious, dark eyes. Her blond hair was down around her shoulders today. It was straight and thick. I knew she spent a lot of time and money to keep it looking that way.

I almost grinned because of the stark differences between her and Rimmel.

My mother was so refined and polished, and Rimmel was raw and uncut.

After straightening her cable-knit sweater over her white jeans, she said, "Her mother died when she was just a child." Her brown eyes softened as she spoke.

"She found her body in the pool," I added.

Mom nodded. "I read that in the file the investigator sent over."

My back teeth came together. "So if you already know all of this, why are we talking about it?"

Murphy jumped up on the island with a thump and meowed loudly. Mom jerked in surprise and made a little squealing sound.

I grinned.

She picked up her mug and moved it farther away while eyeing the cat. "I'm not used to animals being around."

"He's harmless, Mom. He just wants a treat."

"A treat?"

I reached into the cabinet and pulled out a large bag of soft cat treats. Rimmel said they were his favorite and fed him way too many of them. "Here," I said, handing her the bag. "Give him one. Rimmel won't be by tonight, so he won't get his usual twenty-five today."

"Twenty-five," she echoed. "That seems a bit excessive."

I laughed. "It is, but Rimmel doesn't care."

She took the bag and opened it gingerly to reach in for a small brown snack. It was tuna flavored. Murphy saw what she was doing and started purring loudly and walked across the counter toward my mother.

She frowned at the sight of him on the surface but didn't tell him to get down. He sat next to her and waited patiently, all the while purring like a small engine.

"He's very loud," she remarked and placed the snack in her palm and held it out. Murphy leaned down and sniffed the treat before gently taking it out of her hand to chew it.

"What happened to his eye?" Mom asked, watching him.

"Not sure. He came to the shelter like that. No one wanted him and he lived there for a year. Rimmel took a special liking to him and they bonded."

"And so you adopted him."

"She couldn't. Not in the dorm. Besides, he's a pretty cool cat." I reached out and scratched Murphy behind the ears. After a few minutes, he hopped down and sauntered from the room.

"Did she ask you to?" she asked me.

"No, Mom. Rimmel's never asked me for anything. I did it because I knew it would make her happy. She didn't even know until she came over and saw him here." I still remembered the look on her face when she saw him. The joy. I'd adopt him all over again if I could, just for that reason.

"You love her, don't you?" It wasn't an accusation; it was more of a statement.

"Yes. I do."

Mom went silent a moment and picked up her mug. The tag fluttered against the porcelain side. "I'd like to get to know her."

That surprised me. I felt my eyebrows shoot halfway up my forehead. "So you can insult her again like the last time you cornered her in the driveway."

"I did not corner her," she said with a disapproving tone. "When you have a child of your own, you will understand why I did what I did."

I wasn't sure if I agreed. The idea of me having a child seemed so far away it didn't even matter. "I doubt Rim's gonna want to talk to you."

"Is she that sensitive, then?" she asked, sipping at her drink.

I bristled even though I knew that's what she wanted. "No. But I am. I'll not have you hurting her. She's been through enough."

She tilted her head. "With her mother's death, you mean?"

I shrugged noncommittally. That was part of it.

But my mother knew how to read people; she wasn't a stupid woman. "I can't imagine her essentially snagging the most eligible bachelor on campus was very easy." She sipped her tea, then added, "Especially for someone like her."

I lifted a brow. "Someone like her?"

Mom rolled her eyes. "Please, Roman. You and I both know she isn't in the same social circle as you."

"Does it matter?" I asked bluntly.

She lowered the mug and looked me right in the eyes. "If you she loves you, then no."

My shoulders relaxed. I knew Rimmel loved me. I wouldn't even have to try and prove it. "I'll see if she wants to meet you and Dad."

Mom nodded. "We'll have dinner next week."

"I'll let you know," I said, not agreeing to anything.

"I'll have it catered in," she called over her shoulder as she carried her cup to the front door. "See you then."

Apparently, she took my maybe as a yes.

I pulled out my phone and texted Rimmel.

PARENTS WANT TO MEET YOU.

I THINK IT'S TIME WE BREAK UP.

I laughed out loud.

UR NOT GETTING OUT OF IT THAT EASY.

When she didn't reply right away, I knew her joke was just a way to cover up how nervous my mother made her.

MOM GAVE MURPHY A TREAT.

A mere second ticked by when my phone vibrated. I smiled.

DID HE EAT IT?

YEP.

OK. WHEN AND WHERE?

DINNER. NEXT WEEK.

I'LL BE ON MY BEST BEHAVIOR.

She signed off with a hashtag and then a heart. For a girl who said she never paid attention to the BuzzBoss, I knew that was where she got that little tag.

I slid my phone into my pocket as I thought about next week's dinner. I wasn't worried how Rimmel would behave, but my mother… that was a different story.

CHAPTER SEVEN

> She's still
> wearing his hoodie. Alpha U's most
> elligible bachelor is officially
> #OffTheMarket.
> Romeo and Rimmel 4eva?
> #NerdIsStillTheNewSexy
> ... Alpha BuzzFeed

RIMMEL

YOU GONNA WEAR IT TODAY?

GOOD MORNING TO YOU TOO.

☺ GOOD MORNING, BEAUTIFUL.

HI ☺

I WANT YOU TO WEAR IT.

I stared down at the phone, equal parts charmed and frustrated. Romeo just had to have his name on me. It was early, the first day of classes this semester, and he wanted to be sure I was going to "represent" him on campus today.

I MISSED YOU NEXT 2 ME LAST NIGHT.

Even though it was way too early in the morning, I melted. I'd missed him too. I woke up more than once and reached for him. It was entirely too easy to get used to his large, warm body beside me, and when it was gone, it felt like something was missing.

ME TOO.

Ivy walked in carrying her little bathroom tote and rolled her eyes at me sitting on the bed with my phone clutched in my hand.

"It is far too early for that," she grumped and set her tote on the end of her bed.

"I made you a coffee," I said and gestured toward the Keurig and her cup of brew.

"You're a saint!" she said and lunged for the cup. After three sips and two grateful sighs, she regarded me over the rim.

"Aren't you going to do your hair?" she asked, eyeing me.

"What's wrong with it?" I asked. I'd pulled it up in a bun.

Okay, so I hadn't used a brush.

Or a mirror.

My phone vibrated in my hand and I forgot about my hair.

WELL?

I was already dressed in a pair of navy-colored leggings and a button-up flannel. It was plaid, navy, red, and white. Grandma said these shirts were back in style. I couldn't care less. I was just happy she'd been trying to convince me to buy something warm, baggy, and that could be worn with leggings.

Snow was still blowing around outside, and I knew I would likely be a human Popsicle by lunch. Adding another layer over my T-shirt and flannel wouldn't be a bad idea.

IS THAT A YES?

I smiled.

YES.

HELLS YEAH.

"Seriously," Ivy said and took the phone from my hand and tossed it on my pillow. "You don't have time for that right now. You have a hair emergency."

"Can't I just wear a hat?"

"Not on the first day back!"

I didn't hear a no. What I heard was wearing a hat was sometimes fashionable. I needed to get a hat.

She took another sip of coffee and then attacked my hair. When she was done, I carefully pulled Romeo's hoodie over my head and looked in the mirror. It was still pulled up in a loose bun on the top of my head. But there was a side braid that started at the front and went all the way around my head to stop above the opposite ear. She finished it off by pulling out a few wispy pieces around my ears and neck.

It looked a lot better than however I'd planned to wear it.

"You should be a hairstylist," I told her.

She grinned. "Now that sounds like a fun career."

I realized I had no idea what she was majoring in, so I asked.

She made a face and took another drink of coffee like she was trying to fortify herself. "I don't know."

Horrified was exactly how I felt. She didn't know! How could she not know what she was even here for!

"I've changed my mind like three times. There's too much to pick from."

"Well, I guess you could just be a college student forever," I said and grinned.

She wagged her eyebrows like it was actually her devious secret plan.

I glanced at the clock and sighed. "Guess I better get to class."

"Wanna meet for lunch at the food court later?" she asked.

"Sure. I'll see you there."

We both had the same time open for lunch, and I wondered if that would become a regular thing. I kind of hoped so.

My course load this semester was full, and I knew it was going to be a lot of work to keep up with it all, but I was committed. On top of doing my full schedule, I was still volunteering at the shelter and I was going to be tutoring Romeo.

Part of me wished I could get a part-time job, but I just didn't have time. My scholarship paid for all my books, my dorm, and my tuition fees. There was a little money left over at the end of each semester that I was able to use for meals and extra things I needed. Honestly, I didn't need much money. I wasn't the kind of girl who went out on the weekends or spent a lot of time at the mall. My dad sent me money every month, and occasionally my grandparents did too, but I never asked for anything unless it was something I really needed.

Still, it would be nice to be able to save some money so when I graduated I could buy myself a car. I still had my scooter, but really, it was useless in this wintry weather.

Of course, there would be plenty of time to save for a car later. I was going to be in school a long time. Becoming a veterinarian was a long commitment. After four years of undergraduate study (I was earning my bachelor's in Science in Veterinary Technology), I would have to apply to a vet school. Once I was accepted, I would have another four years of studying before I would actually finish my degree.

I planned to take summer courses, which would help speed things along, but since I was only a sophomore, I still had quite a ways to go.

I tried not to think about how much I had left. Instead, I tried to take it one semester at a time.

With two lecture/labs this semester, an animal behavior class, and precalculus on my schedule, it was probably a smart plan.

I snuggled down into the hoodie as I walked and blinked against the harsh wind and blowing snow. When my building finally came into view, I almost cheered. My face was numb, my fingers were stiff, and I was beginning to wonder if I'd ever feel my ears again.

I rushed ahead, anticipating the warm rush of heat that would greet me at the door. I kept my head down so my face wouldn't be battered by the wind any more than it had to be.

I should have known better.

The glass door to the building opened and that first rush of heat mingled with the cold and beckoned me closer. I quickened my step and collided with someone in the doorway. I bounced off them. Automatically, my hands came up to steady myself.

I grabbed the closest thing in reach.

My stiff fingers dug into the scratchy wool of a coat, and I looked up, surprised.

"Sorry!" I said, flustered.

And then I realized who it was.

Familiar eyes watched me, turning calculating in an instant.

"Zach." I gasped like I was out of breath. Really, it was just the bad taste in my mouth that he seemed to bring on.

"Well, look who it is," he said, a smile curving his mouth.

I scowled and his smile turned into a full-blown grin. "I see you're having a hard time letting go."

I glanced down.

My hands were still clutching the front of his preppy coat. I let go immediately, falling back a few steps. People rushed around us to get in the building, and I looked after them longingly.

I started to step around Zach, to go inside, but he blocked my path.

"Fancy meeting you here."

"We aren't *meeting*."

"Where's your bodyguard?"

"You mean my boyfriend?" I corrected.

"Could've fooled me. He acts more like you're something he owns."

He was a jackass, and I didn't have time for this. I pushed past him and went inside. My class was on the second floor, so I headed for the set of stairs near the wall off to my right.

Zach fell into step beside me. I glanced at him out of the corner of my eye. "Weren't you on your way out?"

"I just realized I also have class in this building."

Did that mean he'd purposely run into me? He was already inside. The only reason he would be walking out, if not to leave, would be because he saw me.

"I'm going to be late." I quickened my steps up the stairs, ignoring the weight of my bag and pushing myself faster.

I wanted away from him. There was something about Zach that was just so creepy. Even if we didn't have some kind of history that proved he wasn't to be trusted, I would still be creeped out by him.

It was a sixth sense, like the kind animals used to know when someone had bad intentions. I felt that now with him keeping pace beside me. He made my skin crawl. There was just something off about him.

"You know…" He began, and inwardly I cringed. Was he not done talking to me yet? "You never really struck me as the type of girl to be fooled by a charming smile. I thought a girl like you was smarter than that."

My steps faltered a little. "Excuse me?" I asked coolly.

"I get why all the girls on this campus are so hot for Romeo. He's popular and good-looking and he has money. It just surprises me those things pulled you in too."

The door to my class came into view and I was never gladder to arrive at an early morning class than I was in that minute. Before going inside, I stopped and turned to fully face Zach. He had a scarf draped around his neck and his eyes were keen as he tried to bait me.

What the hell he was baiting me for, I had no idea.

"I couldn't care less about Romeo's money and social status," I said. I didn't have to explain myself to him, but in that moment, it sort of felt like I did. It was an insult to Romeo that Zach implied he had nothing else to offer a person besides superficial things. "He's more than that."

Zach grinned. "Yes. I supposed he is."

I blinked. He was agreeing with me? I expected some quick-witted and irritating comeback.

Zach stepped forward and leaned in like he was divulging some big secret. "He's also a liar."

I spun away from him and into the doorway of class, but I didn't make it very far. Zach caught me by the wrist and yanked me back around, his hand squeezing my arm just a little too tight.

I tried to twist free of his grasp, but he only tightened his hold. "Let go," I growled.

He ignored my request and squeezed harder.

"You're hurting me," I ground out, trying once more to twist away.

"Why don't you ask him why I'm not Omega president anymore."

"Everyone knows why," I snapped, still struggling. Someone walking by glanced at us and the way I was being restrained. His eyes snapped up to Zach and then back to me. "Because you got arrested." I ground out.

He jerked me closer. I stumbled and would have fallen if I hadn't hit his chest.

"Hey," the guy watching us intoned. He took a step toward me as I pulled away from Zach.

"Ask your bodyguard why I got arrested," Zach said low in my ear.

He released me then and strode away. I rubbed at the soreness in my throbbing wrist as I watched him disappear into a nearby classroom.

"Are you okay?" the guy asked.

I glanced at him and smiled weakly. "Yeah. I'm fine." I pushed up the too-long sleeve of the hoodie and glanced down at my wrist. It was red and blotchy.

I caught the stranger gazing down at it as well (did he look familiar?) and hurried to cover it back up with the sleeve.

"What was that all about?" He gazed off in the direction Zach disappeared.

"Nothing," I answered. "He was just being a jerk."

He looked like he wanted to argue or ask more questions, so I cut him off with a small smile. "Thanks for stepping in like that. You didn't have to."

His eyes widened and a look of horror crossed his face. "I'm not gonna stand around and watch a woman get manhandled." Then under his breath, he muttered, "Especially you."

"What?" I asked, wondering if I'd heard him right.

"You're gonna be late." He gestured to the class behind me.

I straightened. *Crap!* I'd forgotten about class! I rushed into the room and slipped into a seat near the front.

As the professor started lecture, introducing himself and the objectives for this semester, my eyes and my mind wandered back to the open doorway.

No one was there. Not anymore.

But my wrist was still burning and sore and I couldn't help but wonder about what Zach had said.

CHAPTER EIGHT

ROMEO

I wasn't a book kind of guy.

Sitting in class and listening to professors drone on and on… and on was frankly not my idea of a good time. Half the time, I spaced out and didn't hear what they were saying anyway.

Okay, fine. Not half the time.

All the time.

I was a physical kind of guy. I wanted to be on the move. To be outside. To be doing something that required action.

Needless to say, my morning classes crawled by. I had a thirty-minute lapse between the class I'd just escaped and my final class of the day. Once that was over, I was going to grab some food and then hit the field for some training before practice started. The championship was coming, and I wanted to be as ready as I could get.

The wind was still blowing around, but the sun was out and it felt a little warmer than this morning. I wondered how Rimmel was doing in the cold and if my hoodie was keeping her warm.

I was glad she was wearing it. I caught some of the surprised looks we got yesterday. People thought I would have discarded her by now. I didn't like it.

If she had a hard time when we got together, it would be worse if everyone thought I dropped her. They would taunt her about being used and tossed aside. The thought of that made my hands ball into fists. She was too good for that. Too gentle and naive.

My lips curved into a smile because if she knew I thought of her that way, she'd try to kick my ass. She wouldn't want to be viewed that way, because she was strong. Rimmel had been through a lot in her life and made it through, but that's why I felt so protective of her. She was still gentle and naïve despite all those things. And she was so small. Wanting to shield her was a natural instinct for me.

In a way, my hoodie was a silent shield around her, and today, everyone who didn't already know we were still together would. Hopefully, it would keep some of the vultures away.

I took my time making my way to the building my next class was in. I stopped at a vending machine and grabbed a soda, and then a couple guys from the team walked by and we started talking strategy for the big game.

They were all joking about the party at my place when they walked away. As I uncapped my drink, I noticed Michael was hanging back a bit.

"Got something on your mind?" I called out, gesturing at him with my chin.

He was a good player, he worked hard on the field, and I respected him. I got the feeling, though, that I wasn't going to like what he wanted to say. I could tell by the hesitation in his face and body language. He probably disagreed with some of the plays I wanted to try tonight and didn't want to piss me off in fear I would freeze him out on the field.

But I wasn't like that. I left personal shit in the locker room. There was no room for drama in the game.

He walked back over in front of me as he adjusted the strap on his shoulder. "I'm not sure I should say anything."

"Just say it, man. It's cool."

"I saw your girl this morning." He started, and everything in me went cold.

This wasn't about football. This *was* personal.

"You looking at Rimmel?" I asked, my voice calm and low.

His eyes widened a little, but he shook his head. "No, man. I probably wouldn't have known it was her, but she was wearing your hoodie."

I nodded for him to continue.

"She was in the hall, outside her class," he said, glancing at me.

He needed to get to the fucking point already. I was losing patience.

"That guy Zach was with her. It looked pretty intense."

I jerked upright. "What?" I growled.

What the fuck was Rimmel doing with Zach? Why was he talking to her?

"He was grabbing her arm. Jerking her around pretty good."

Red tinged my vision and adrenaline started pumping in my veins. "What did you just say?"

Michael nodded grimly. "It's why I noticed them. He grabbed her and she cried out. She told him to let go, but he just jerked her more. She almost fell."

A noise rumbled out of my chest and anger so swift and hot that it hurt filled me. "Tell me you pulled him off her," I intoned.

"I was going to. I called out to them and started forward, but that's when he let her go and walked away."

I was going to kill him.

Dead.

"I asked her if she was okay. I don't think she knew I'm on the team with you."

"Probably not," I muttered, still trying to control the anger spiraling out of control inside me.

"She said she was." He continued, but I heard the doubt in his voice.

"But?" The word came out harsher than I intended, but he didn't seem to notice.

"But her wrist was pretty red. Looked like it was going to bruise."

Thought ceased in my head. Rationality evaporated. "Thanks for telling me," I said and rushed away in the opposite direction of my next class.

I checked the time on my cell and knew Rimmel was probably in the food court. She had a break now and mentioned to me this morning about having lunch with Ivy. She never mentioned a word about Zach.

I took the stairs two at a time up to the food court, rushing past people who called out my name without even so much as blinking.

People were everywhere, walking around with trays, sitting around laughing and standing in lines. The scent of coffee and pizza filled the air, and music played over the speakers, fighting with the sounds of everyone talking over each other.

I blocked it all out.

My eyes scanned the room, bouncing around the crowds of people. Searching for Rimmel in a roomful of people might seem like finding a needle in a haystack to some.

But not to me.

I was drawn to her in ways I didn't even understand.

I found her in mere seconds. She was sitting toward the back of the room, across from Ivy at a four-person table. Missy was on the other side of Ivy, and the fourth chair beside Rimmel was empty.

She was smiling at something Ivy was saying, and it pierced my heart.

Without thinking, I strode through the crowd, not slowing my pace when I drew closer. She noticed me. Her face broke into a smile and her eyes lit up.

But then she must have sensed my mood. The dangerous way I was moving. Her eyes widened and the smile slipped from her lips.

I didn't say a word when I stopped at the table. I just picked up her arm and shoved back the sleeve of her hoodie. Her wrist was fine. Creamy smooth skin without a single blemish.

"Romeo," she said, shocked. "What are you doing?"

My movements were jerky and stiff when I dropped that arm and reached for the other. I yanked it up and her body tightened. I glanced up at her face and saw the twinge of pain in her eyes, and instead of feeling sorry for hurting her, I got even more pissed off.

Even though I wanted to rip the sleeve away, I forced myself to push it back gently, knowing—*knowing*—I wasn't going to like what I was about to see.

My back teeth snapped together, making a sharp clicking sound when I saw.

She was bruised. A ring of purple, blotchy bruises circled her slender wrist, and around them the skin was red and irritated. I cradled her palm in mine and turned her hand over to note the same kind of bruising and light swelling underneath as well.

"Oh my God," Ivy said from beside me. "What happened to your wrist?"

Rimmel tried to slip her hand out of mine, but I wouldn't let her. My eyes pierced hers, drilling into them, trying to find an answer.

"Were you going to tell me about this?" I asked, deadly calm.

"I'm fine," she argued, tugging her hand free of mine. I wanted to snatch it back to continue to stare at the marks some other man put on her skin.

But I didn't. I wouldn't hurt her that way.

I made a frustrated sound deep in my throat and shoved my hands through my hair. Then I stacked my hands behind my head and blew out a breath, unable to stand still.

"Damn it, Rimmel," I said, harsh. I felt the stares from several tables nearby.

"Maybe we should talk about this later," she said, her voice almost a whisper.

I laughed. "You think I'm going to wait until later to find out the details of how that fuckwad put *bruises on your body?*"

Missy gasped and Ivy made a sound of distress. I didn't look at them, though. I kept my eyes on my girlfriend as I pulled in fast, shallow breaths.

I felt out of control in that moment. I'd never felt like this before. I was used to being calm and collected, but I couldn't find that part of myself right then. The vision of those bruises, of Michael standing in front of me warily telling me how he witnessed Rimmel being pushed around in a hallway, assaulted me.

The sight of Zach smirking at the bookstore days ago, the sound of his voice when he told me he hadn't forgotten.

One of his "friends" picked that moment to walk by. Judging by the look on his face, I knew he was probably taking notes so he could report back to his buddy later. I moved lightning fast, jerking out my hand and grabbing his shirt right at his neck. He was shorter and smaller than me, and I felt the toes of his shoes dragging across the floor as I brought him right up into my face.

"Where is he?" I asked.

"Who?" he asked, his eyes bulging out of their sockets.

"You know who," I growled.

"Romeo!" Rimmel's voice cut through some of the blinding anger inside me. Her hands slid around my waist and she tried to nudge herself between me and the guy I was interrogating. "Put him down."

I just stood there. I didn't listen.

"Come on, let's go talk." She tugged on my shirt, and I released him.

He scrambled away as people stared after him. I turned toward Rimmel. She grabbed her bag off the seat beside her and looked down at her tray.

"I'll take care of it," Ivy said and slid a glance at me.

She nodded and slipped her hand into mine. "C'mon."

We walked down the stairs away from the prying eyes of our audience and around the corner toward the bookstore. I tugged her past the entrance and we went farther down the hallway where no one but the staff ever went.

When I felt like we were alone enough, I stopped walking. Rimmel dropped her bag on the floor and looked at me. "Don't you have class?"

"I'm gonna be late," I said, my eyes not leaving her face.

She shook her head. "Being late on the first day—"

I cut off her lecture. I swooped forward and caught her around the waist and pushed her back into the wall. My mouth crashed down over hers, and she moaned, stretching up to meet my kiss.

It was desperate and a little bit angry. I kissed her more roughly than I should, but I couldn't stop. She kissed me back just as aggressively. It was as if whatever emotion was rolling around inside me were calling out the very same thing in her.

I pressed forward, pushing my body along hers, and wrapped my arms around her waist.

Some of the intensity of my anger dissipated and drained away. After a very long, steamy kiss, I broke away, breathing hard.

Rimmel's head collapsed against the wall and she stared up at me with unfocused hazel eyes. The flecks of color in the center were green today. "Romeo," she gasped.

I pulled back enough so I could lift her arm and grasp her fingers. She made a sound of protest when I pushed back the material of the shirt once more and stared down at the dark blotches marring her skin.

"How were you going to explain this to me?" I rumbled.

"I wasn't going to lie, if that's what you're implying," she snapped.

"Ah, baby." I groaned and lifted her wrist to press my lips to the marks. "I'm being a jerk."

"You said it…" She agreed, letting the rest of her sentence fall away.

I smiled against her skin and then kissed her inner wrist once more.

"Do you know what it did to me when Michael told me what he saw Zach doing to you?"

"Michael?" she asked, a question in her eyes. Then it cleared away and she whispered, "The guy from the hallway."

My eyes narrowed. I didn't like the thought of any guy coming to her defense if it wasn't me. I held in that little piece of info. I didn't think she'd appreciate it. Besides, I was glad he was there. If he hadn't spoken up, who knew what Zach would have done?

"He's on the team," I explained.

She sighed wearily. "Is there anyone on campus you don't know?"

I smiled but pinned her with a serious stare. "You should have told me."

Behind her glasses, her eyes rolled. She looked adorable standing there squished against the wall, in my shirt, her glasses, and a braid in her hair.

"It's not your job to protect me, Romeo."

"You're wrong," I said, my voice leaving no room for argument. "It is and I will."

"You're my boyfriend. Not my bodyguard." Her words were annoyed, and I felt something behind them. But before I could question her, she kept going. "He was just being a jerk. I tried to walk away, and he stopped me. If I hadn't fought against him, I probably wouldn't have a bruise at all."

I felt my eyes narrow as I spoke dangerously low. "Are you saying it's your fault Zach treated you this way?

Letting her take any responsibility for this was something I would *not* allow.

She sighed. "I'm saying you're being a drama queen."

I laughed and raised my eyebrow. "Do I look like a woman to you?"

A fine pink blush spread across her cheekbones. "No."

I took her face in my hands and tilted it up so I could stare into her eyes. "Listen to me. My reacting to someone putting their hands on you is not me being dramatic; it's me loving you."

"Oh, Romeo," she sighed my name and my cock hardened.

I pulled her into my chest and wrapped my arms around her. "Being an asshole is just part of my charm, baby," I said matter-of-fact, unable to keep the smile out of my voice. "This is just me loving you."

"You love real good," she mumbled against my chest, pushing a little closer.

I palmed the back of her head, holding her tight. It scared me how much I loved her sometimes. Just like the anger I'd felt just moments ago scared me. It was raw and intense. It almost bordered on hate.

And all of it… every single flame of that animosity was directed at one man.

I had been well prepared to leave it all in the past.

But those bruises on Rimmel's body were not in the past.

And I wasn't going to let them go.

CHAPTER NINE

#Spotted
One very disheveled-looking lady made her way out of the Omega House early this morning.
#WalkOfShame #TheBeerMadeHerDoIt

... Alpha BuzzFeed

RIMMEL

I wasn't a football kind of girl.

Learning different kinds of plays, positions, and what the heck the refs were signaling all the time wasn't my strong suit. I'd much rather read a book. Or help an animal.

But dating Romeo opened my eyes to a new world. I didn't so much as know anything about the game or how it was played, but I did enjoy going and watching Romeo and the Wolves on the field.

There was always so much energy at the football games. The cheering fans, the peppy cheerleaders, and the loud music all created a jazzed-up feel in the air. It was fun to go sit in the stands with Ivy and Missy, to sip hot apple cider, and it was pretty fun watching Romeo run around in those tight pants.

Even though my experience with football was limited, I thought I knew what to expect when the championship game rolled around.

But I had no idea.

During the days leading up to the game, the campus was more alive than usual. Signs and banners covered every available space. The school colors (navy and golden yellow) were plastered everywhere. Some people spray-colored their hair in wacky designs.

Girls walked all over campus with Wolves T-shirts and the football players' numbers drawn on their faces with face paint.

More than half those girls wore number twenty-four.

I tried not to let it bother me. I mean, it was basically a school tradition to show support for the team. But why did most of the girls have to show support for *my* player?

But even with the girls displaying their affection for my boyfriend, the energy that crackled through the air was infectious.

The championship was a home game, and that meant it was happening here, on our turf (check me out, talking the lingo like a pro), and I was glad because it meant I could be at the game without having to travel to get there.

I hadn't seen much of Romeo the first week and a half of classes because he was so busy with training, practice, and meetings with the team. In a way, it was good because it gave me a chance to get a good head start on all my classwork. On the first day, the professors usually gave us a course syllabus, and I liked to go through and see if there was anything I could work on in advance. I was a planner that way. I liked to really learn the material from each class, because it was quite possible something I learned now could save an animal's life later. I'd already been able to outline a paper I had due in a couple weeks and get a head start on the research.

It was also good because it kept Romeo distracted. Distracted from Zach. I'd never forget the fiery look in his eyes when he stormed into the food court that first day. I'd never seen him so mad.

I wanted to be mad at his reaction to my not texting or calling him right away, but the truth was I couldn't be mad at him for being who he was. I couldn't be mad at him for loving me and being enraged that someone who caused trouble for him (and us) in the past was causing issues again.

I didn't tell him what Zach said to me. He'd been so enraged at the bruises on my wrist he didn't ask what Zach wanted, and I didn't bother bringing it up. It would only make him angrier.

Besides, Zach was probably lying and just trying to cause trouble anyway.

Romeo needed to stay focused on the game. This could be a stepping-stone to the NFL.

"I think the entire campus is hungover." I laughed as Romeo drove slowly through the parking lot toward my dorm.

The day before the game, all the classes on campus were cancelled. There was a huge pep rally for the team and about a hundred different pre-game parties going on practically all night.

We didn't go to any parties. None of the players did. The game was too big to risk going out the night before and everyone being hungover. I did stay the night at Romeo's place, though. I spent the night in his arms.

Everywhere I looked, people were stumbling around in oversized coats and hoodies. Some of them with sunglasses over their faces and most of them with giant-sized coffee cups clutched in their hands.

Romeo laughed. "Must have been some epic parties."

When he pulled the Hellcat up to the curb next to my dorm, I turned in my seat to face him. "You nervous?"

He leaned the back of his head against his seat and looked at me. "Nah." His lopsided grin was infectious. "I got my good luck charm," he said and pulled the dog tag I gave him out from under his shirt.

"You don't need a good luck charm because you're a great player."

He reached across the car and took my hand. "I know I haven't been around as much," he said, "but after today, my schedule won't be so busy."

"I understand," I said softly. And I did. "Football is your life. It's your dream."

He made a sound. "You're just as important to me."

I smiled. "I have to admit I won't be upset when this game is over and all the girls around here stop wearing your number all over their bodies."

His white teeth flashed. "Is someone jealous?"

I snorted.

His smile grew wider.

"Maybe a little," I admitted.

He lunged forward and in seconds had me in his lap, my legs straddling him so we were face to face. He buried his hands in my tangled disaster of hair.

I admit I hadn't even brushed it when we got out of bed this morning.

"You're my favorite girl," he whispered.

"I better be your only girl."

He smiled. "That too."

Romeo brushed his lips over mine. The first contact sent goose bumps racing across my skin. Our lips met again and again, stroking against each other and creating sizzling friction that brought forth a hungry need deep in my belly.

As we kissed, his thumbs drew lazy circles across the sides of my jaw and I sank farther and farther into his warmth.

Eventually, he pulled back and glanced at the dash. He groaned. "I gotta go. I can't be late to the field. Coach would have a heart attack."

I leaned my forehead against his. "Good luck today."

"Thanks, baby." He stroked the side of my head, and I wished fleetingly that I had brushed my hair so it was silky soft for his hand.

He reached into the center console of the car and pulled out a white envelope. "Here's your ticket into the stadium. Missy and Ivy's too."

I took the envelope and smiled. "Thanks for getting us good seats."

"Thanks for coming and cheering me on."

"You know I wouldn't miss it."

"I'll see you after," he said. "And tonight we'll party at my place."

After one last kiss, I climbed out of his lap and onto the sidewalk. It was freezing outside, and I made a mental note to put on as many layers as I could or I'd be a Popsicle before halftime.

Why they hadn't made the indoor stadium large enough for games was beyond me. Romeo said it was too small so it was just used for practices.

It was still early. I had a few hours before I needed to be at the game, so when I got upstairs to my room, I decided I would shower now and get some studying in while my hair was air-drying. The room was very dim when I walked in. I crept toward my bed and glanced over at Ivy's side of the room.

She was lying tangled in the blankets, one bare leg flung to the side and dangling off the bed, her face was buried in a pillow. All I could see was her blond hair, wild and all over the place. It actually made me feel better about the way mine looked.

She was snoring lightly and the faint smell of alcohol permeated her side of the room.

She was going to be so hungover.

As quietly as I could, I gathered up everything I needed to shower and left the room. Our shared bathroom was at the end of the hall. It was mostly quiet on our floor, with the exception of a couple girls looking a little worse for wear who were clearly stumbling into their rooms after a long night of partying.

The bathroom was large and basically divided into three sections. The toilet stalls were lined off to the right when you first walked in. As I followed the tile hallway past, I heard the unfortunate sound of someone throwing up the contents of their stomach.

"I'm never drinking again," I heard her moan between heaves.

I grimaced and kept moving. All the way back was a section of showers. Just before the showers were a row of wooden benches, some mirrors, and simple tables along one wall.

I went to the very last shower on the end and set my tote and towel on the bench in front of my selection. I pushed back the white shower curtain and reached in to turn the water on. As I was waiting for it to heat, I hung my towel on a small hook just beside the curtain and pulled off my clothes, piling them beside my tote.

I kept a pair of flip-flops on my feet as I stepped under the spray. I'd never used the shower without my shoes. The idea of my bare toes touching this public floor made my skin crawl.

The water was hot, and I sighed in appreciation, ducking my head beneath the spray and letting my hair get saturated. I lingered in the shower longer than usual because it was very rare I had them to myself, but because it was early on a Saturday and everyone else was hungover, I got some privacy.

After I rinsed out my hair one last time, I shut off the spray and reached out to grab my towel. I stood behind the curtain to dry off.

I heard the main door to the bathroom swing closed, and I figured the girl who swore to never drink again had finally barfed up everything she drank last night.

After roughly squeezing the excess water out of my hair, I wrapped the towel around my body and slid open the curtain. The room was steamy from my ultra-hot shower and the air was moist and thick.

I dug around in my tote for a brush and began trying to comb through the tangles in my hair. The sound of a faint scuffle had me glancing around curiously, but I saw no one. I shrugged and went back to brushing.

When most of the tangles were out, I replaced the brush and grabbed up a bottle of moisturizer for my skin. Another sound, kind of like a heavy thump, cut through the silence, and I jumped and turned.

Still no one.

"Hello?" I called out.

Maybe the drunk girl was still here after all. Maybe she'd passed out and hit her head on the toilet.

When no one answered, I still couldn't shake the feeling that something was wrong. Still clutching the bottle of cream, I moved through the shower room to go check on the girl I'd heard earlier.

My flip-flops were still wet from my shower and they made a squeaking sound against the tile. As I walked, I glanced at the mirrors lining the walls. All of them were covered in steam from the heat of my shower. Suddenly, having the place to myself didn't seem so great anymore.

"Are you okay?" I called out to her, not because I expected an answer, but because the sound of my own voice was preferable to the silence.

When the only sound that replied was the dripping of water in one of the nearby sinks, I started to feel like a giant chicken.

I mean, seriously, who got scared while taking a shower in a dorm full of other girls?

I thought about turning back to what I was doing but decided I really should check to make sure that girl wasn't passed out.

The next to last stall's door was closed while the rest were partially ajar. I tugged the towel a little tighter around me as a stray droplet of water ran down the back of my leg and over the back of my knee. I shivered against the creepy feeling it left in its wake.

There was some movement off to my right, and I jumped, gasping a little. I spun all the way toward the motion I'd seen and then laughed.

"Only you would be scared of your own reflection," I muttered.

The mirrors in this room weren't all fogged up from the shower, and the movement I'd noticed was me walking by. I couldn't really make out all my features because I'd left my glasses lying with my clothes.

That would explain the slightly hazy look to everything in here.

Gah, I was losing my mind.

"Get a grip," I said out loud, my voice echoing through the empty room. My feet slapped against the floor as I moved quickly to the stall with the closed door.

"Is anyone in here?" I called out and shoved open the door. It made a banging sound when it hit against the wall and the flimsy stall vibrated from the force of my meager shove.

No one was in there.

I rolled my eyes and stepped back, looking in each stall before I went back to the shower room.

I decided to never tell anyone about this. Talk about embarrassing.

Back in the shower room, the mirrors were still foggy and the air was warmer. My stuff was still piled on the bench where I'd left it and I used my hand on the mirror above the nearby sink to brush away the fog so I could see.

Even though everything was mostly blurry without my glasses, I still could make out enough of my face to apply moisturizer. I pumped some of the white cream onto my fingers and then set the jar on the edge of the sink. After spreading it around on my fingertips, I glanced back up in the mirror and started rubbing it into my face.

And then I froze.

I stood stock still, hands still stuck to my face as I glanced in the mirror at what was behind me.

It was just the shower curtain, I told myself.

Yes, but I didn't close the curtain when I got out.

I'd left it open.

It wasn't open anymore.

The thick, white fabric was stretched all the way across the opening, blocking the entire square of the shower from sight.

I stood there staring into the mirror at that wall of white for endless moments.

Had I shut it and just forgotten?

I'd already checked the bathroom. I was alone in here.

Wasn't I?

And then something behind the curtain moved.

The movement sent ripples of activity through the white fabric, and I watched in horror as it swayed slightly.

Did I just imagine that?

It happened again. This time the curtain swayed more. I thought I saw the dark shape of a shadow behind it.

My heart started pounding so heavily that it was the only sound I could hear. My throat suddenly constricted and it hurt to breathe or swallow. Fear prickled the base of my spine, and I dropped my hands from my face and wiped what was left of the lotion on the towel wrapped around my body.

I was so not up for being attacked today.

While I was wearing only a towel.

I crept forward as silently as I could and reached down for my glasses. If a girl was going to defend herself, she needed to be able to see.

The room came clearly into focus, and I felt slightly more in control. Until the curtain moved again.

With a heavy sigh, I stepped around the bench and approached the shower.

I reached out and gripped the edge of the curtain.

My lungs burned with the need for oxygen, but I just couldn't seem to take in air. I was so scared in that moment that it was all I could do not to run away.

I should totally run away.

Instead, I counted to three.

One.

Two.

Three.

I yanked back the curtain.

Someone lunged at me.

I screamed.

CHAPTER TEN

#GameDay!
Get your hungover asses to the field. We
got a team to support.
#NothingElseMattersToday

... Alpha BuzzFeed

ROMEO

Something didn't feel right.

But I had a game to win.

Everything else was going to have to wait.

CHAPTER ELEVEN

Dorm Room Essentials:
Clothes.
#NoOneWantsToSeeAllThat
#KeepItContained #WaxThatShit

... Alpha BuzzFeed

RIMMEL

A figure dressed in dark clothing shot out of the shower stall and wrapped his arms around me. I screamed and fell backward, my flip-flops not providing very much traction against the slick tile floor.

I grappled for my attacker to keep from falling back, and he grabbed me and righted us as a laugh filled the space.

I felt like my eyes were going to fall out of my head when I glanced up and saw Zach and his devious grin.

I jerked away from him, coming up against the edge of the pedestal sink, clutching the towel (that suddenly seemed way too small) back around me from where it had slipped and almost exposed all my goods to this creep.

"What the hell are you doing!" I yelled.

He chuckled. "You should see your face."

Anger lit me up inside. Anger and indignation. How dare he scare me like that!

The sound of a sharp slap echoed through the room when my open palm connected with his face. Zach's head rocked on his shoulders and his hand came up to cup his jaw and massage his fingers into his reddening cheek.

"I never would have guessed a nerd like you would have so much fire beneath those glasses." His eyes were appraising when he looked me up and down. "Who'd have thought you have a nice little body beneath all those ugly clothes you wear?"

I was going to hit him again.

I felt exposed and vulnerable standing here like this. I wanted my clothes. I wanted to get out of here. He was standing between me and all my things.

"How did you get in here?" I demanded, glancing toward the door.

"Don't you worry," he said, reaching out for a wet strand of my hair. I jerked back and he smiled. "I locked the door so we wouldn't be disturbed."

"I'm gonna start screaming," I warned, shrinking back against the sink even more.

He made a tsking sound. "No, you won't. Because word of you being alone in the girls' bathroom with me—*naked*…" He emphasized that last word like I was in here naked with him because I wanted to be. It made me sick to my stomach. "Would get out faster than you could put on these lacy little panties."

He picked up a pair of navy-blue cotton panties with a lacey waistband that I'd bought to specifically match the Wolves' colors (to support Romeo, of course) and spun them around on his finger.

I was going to have to burn them. He was getting his grimy cooties all over them.

Such a shame. I hadn't even gotten to wear them yet.

"Give me those." I gasped and snatched them out of his hands, clutching them against me.

He laughed.

"Texts would go flying, and Romeo, *oh Romeo...*"—he sighed—"would get wind of this little tête-à-tête, and then his head would be all messed up for the big game."

"You are such an asshole," I growled.

"Imagine his precious little nerd and me... his biggest pet peeve, together naked."

"You're disgusting. He knows I'd never willfully be alone with you."

He smiled. "Maybe. But it would still mess up his game."

I'd had enough, and I moved to shove past him, but he pushed me back.

"What would everyone say about our campus hero when he messed up the biggest game of the year and handed the trophy to the other team? Wonder if he would still be adored by everyone."

He slid his cell phone out of his pocket and held it up. Before I knew what he was doing, he snapped a picture of me standing there in my towel. "Maybe," he said, "I should send this picture out and let everyone know what we're doing. Right. Now."

There is this quote that I read a long time ago. A quote that I loved and made me feel strong. It had stuck with me over the years, like so many of the other words by the author.

And though she be but little, she be fierce.—Shakespeare

I thought about that quote right now.

I might be little. I might be easily intimidated, but I could be fierce.

I *was* fierce.

With a cry, I lunged forward and threw all my weight into Zach. He hadn't expected me to do such a thing, and it threw him off balance. He backed up against the wooden bench lining the center of the room, and it caused him to fall back on his butt. I snatched the phone out of his hand and whipped it at the wall in the back of one of the showers.

The small device crashed into the tiles and shattered, small pieces flying everywhere.

He looked at me with shock on his face.

I shrugged. "Oops."

"That was a five hundred-dollar phone!" he cried and jumped to his feet to examine all the pieces scattered about.

I started to gather up my things and rush toward the door.

"Did you ask him?" he said, his voice halting my footsteps.

I glanced over my shoulder at him. "Of course not."

"I guess you don't care if you're dating a liar, then." He said it like those stupid words would somehow be used as reverse phycology on me. Like I would somehow be tainted against Romeo, against the only man I'd ever loved.

I thought the satisfaction of seeing his phone shatter had been enough to quell my anger. But I realized now that it hadn't been. Renewed anger rose up inside me. I was angry that he would try and taint something special. Something I'd never had with anyone before.

I wouldn't let him take it from me. Or from Romeo.

"You know what?" I said, turning to fully face him. "I don't care."

He lifted an eyebrow.

"I don't care even if you are right. Even if Romeo did lie about something, I'll forgive him. It won't matter. Chances are if he did lie, it was because he thought it would protect me."

This is just me loving you. His words echoed inside me as I sought to defend our love.

I glanced at the pieces of the ruined phone. This was me loving him.

"I don't know why you hate Romeo so much, and I don't care. Do yourself a favor and just let it go. Trying to hurt me to get to him isn't going to work."

His eyes were hard when I spun back around and marched around the corner and to the door.

Sure enough, the lock was thrown from the inside.

I slid it free and yanked the door open and stumbled out in the hall wearing nothing but a towel. Two girls were standing there with all their shower stuff in their hands and confused expressions on their faces, dividing their attention between me and the door.

Even though I was dying inside of embarrassment, I marched down the hallway and let myself in my room.

Once I was there, I dropped everything by the door and ran for my phone.

I grabbed it up and punched in a number I was suddenly glad I had.

It rang and rang, and my stomach began to churn in fear that he wasn't going to answer.

Just when I knew the phone was going to go to voicemail, he picked up. "Rimmel?"

"Braeden," I said with apparent relief in my voice. I sank back against the door and clutched the phone to my ear.

"What's wrong?" he asked, his voice going sharp, and I felt his alarm come across the line.

"I'm fine," I said quickly, trying to keep him from panicking. I didn't want to mess with his head before the game either, but he was the only one I could call. "I just… I need a favor."

"I got your back."

"Having a brother isn't so bad," I said.

The noise in the locker room almost overpowered his chuckle, and I heard the coach in the back, hollering something. "Hey, man, I'll be right back. Cover for me." I heard his muffled voice over the line.

"Sure thing," Romeo replied, and I squeezed my eyes shut.

The noise in the background faded away, and then it was just Braeden. "What's going on, Rim?"

"You didn't tell him it was me," I said.

"Yeah, I kind of figured you called me because there was something you didn't want him to know."

"I need you to keep him away from his phone before the game. And away from anyone other than the team. No gossip."

"What the hell happened?" he demanded. The anger in his tone made me wonder if maybe I shouldn't have involved him.

"It's nothing." I lied. Then I sighed. "Well, it's something. But I don't want anything messing with Romeo's head before the game. That's what he wants."

"He who?" Braeden said sharply. Then he growled. "Is this about Zach?"

"Yes."

"Girl, you better not have any more bruises," he intoned.

I shivered because his voice was just as deadly as Romeo's.

"I don't," I said. I wondered what he would say if I told him there might be a picture of me in nothing but a towel. "Look, I'll explain after the game tonight. Just do this for Romeo."

"Of course I will."

"Braeden?" I said when I thought he hung up.

"Tutor girl?"

I smiled. "Don't worry about this, okay. About me either. Everything's fine. Just go out there and play."

"You got it." The smile in his voice made me relax.

"Good luck today."

"Thanks, little sis. I'll see you tonight."

I hung up the phone and took a steadying breath. Those girls outside the bathroom had to have seen Zach. They would have known I'd been in there with him.

I could only imagine what he would have told them.

Rumors were going to be flying.

I walked farther into the room and glanced down at the bed and Romeo's hoodie. I hoped Braeden could keep the rumors from getting to him.

Before tossing my phone aside, I sent out a quick text to Romeo.

I LOVE YOU.

It beeped immediately with a reply.

I LOVE YOU. TURNING OFF PHONE NOW. BRAEDEN'S ORDERS.

Thank God for Braeden.

On the other side of the room, Ivy stirred and lifted her head. Her hair was all over the place and covering most of her face. She pushed at the tangled nest with her hands and squinted at me.

"God." She groaned. "Is it morning?"

"Yep. It's game day."

Her head fell back on the pillow and she groaned again.

I smiled and rummaged through my drawers to find something to wear. "Wild party last night?"

"You have no idea," she muttered and sat up, leaning against the wall. I watched as she pulled the covers away from her body and glanced down. Her eyes went wide and she pulled the blanket back down. "Where the hell are my clothes?"

I laughed and looked around. "There," I said and pointed at her top. "And there." I pointed somewhere else at her jeans.

She grinned. "Well, I must have had a damn good time."

I laughed and turned back around to get dressed. I couldn't stop thinking about Romeo… and Zach. And the bathroom.

He was going to totally flip when I told him.

But I didn't have a choice.

I just prayed to God I was the one who was able to tell him first.

CHAPTER TWELVE

#Spotted
A very familar #Nerd wearing
nothing but a towel leaving a locked
bathroom. Someone who was not #24
followed.
#Cheater   #NerdGoneWrong
... Alpha BuzzFeed

ROMEO

The massive football field was empty and almost quiet.

The only sounds came from the crew working on the sidelines, making sure everything was in place and ready to go for the game.

It wouldn't be long now that the stands would be filling up with people, music would be pumping through the air, and the sights and smells of a Saturday football game would fill the atmosphere.

In addition to the pre-game energy spilling out of the locker room, there was also an unspoken amount of nerves. This was a huge game for us. A win was a lot more than a trophy.

The school would get more money in grants. The prestige of this university as a whole would rise to the next level. And the Wolves… the Wolves would go down in Alpha U history.

We were ready. I felt it in my bones. We worked our asses off to get ready for this. I knew we could take the game. I wanted it.

I glanced over at the boxed section where I knew some of the NFL scouts would be sitting. I had a lot riding on this personally. Then I glanced down at the section near the field where I knew Rimmel would be sitting. I'd be able to see her from the sidelines.

The sight of her here supporting me meant more to me than she would ever know. My parents would be here too. They had box seats, just like most of my home games. They supported me; they always had. But Rimmel's support was different.

It felt different.

It felt like I wasn't just doing this for me anymore, but for her too.

I wanted to make her proud.

A heavy hand dropped onto my shoulder and Coach moved to stand beside me. We stood silently staring out at the field, which had been expertly cleared of snow. I knew from the fat flakes falling lazily from the sky that all the green stretched before us probably wouldn't stay as pristine as it was now.

"You're ready for this." Coach spoke beside me, not taking his eyes off the green.

"The whole team is." I agreed.

Coach cleared his throat. "You're a damn fine player, Anderson. The respect you have for the game and the determination you show on the field isn't something I see very often among players."

"Thanks," I said, not knowing what else to say to a compliment like that.

"You're the backbone of this team. I just wanted to tell you before the game that I'm proud of you. That won't change even if we don't bring home the trophy today."

Some of the tension and nerves coiled inside me eased. I pulled my eyes from the field and looked at Coach. He was dressed in a pair of golden-yellow pants and a navy Wolves jersey with *Coach O'Connor* across the back. A whistle hung around his neck and a baseball hat with the team logo (slashing claws) was pulled down over his head.

"We're going to bring home that trophy," I said, determined.

He smiled. "I figured you'd say that."

"Guess I better go get everyone riled up."

"You do that," Coach said, turning back to the field. "I'm just gonna stand here a few more minutes. The quiet before a game is a good time to reflect."

I left him in peace and pushed into the locker room. The guys were rowdy and loud, ribbing each other and getting their gear ready.

I took a minute to take it all in just like I'd done out on the field. For some reason, I felt like things were changing, that these kinds of moments were fleeting.

My endgame had always been the NFL, and I would jump at the chance to get there. But even so, the memory of college football would always be a defining time in my life. It was moments like these that made me remember what football was all about.

"Yo, where you at, pretty boy?" Braeden hollered and came around the corner.

I grinned and he laughed. "You ready for today?" he said and hooked me around the neck with his arm and tried to bend me down so he could mess up my hair.

"Hells yeah," I said, dodging his attempt.

The guys that were around us all starting trading insults, so we joined in until the sound of music cut through the laughter.

Some old song about how the guy singing was too sexy burst through the noise, and we all started to laugh. "B-man!" someone shouted a row over. "Phone's ringing."

Braeden sauntered off in the direction of his phone, and I followed along behind him, talking to some of the guys as I went. Trent and I exchanged nods and fist bumps.

When I came around the corner, I zeroed in on the fact that everything about Braeden had changed. He wasn't wearing a shirt and all the muscles in his back were bunched up, tightened. He was hunched around the phone and had a finger pressed in his opposite ear so he could hear better.

Something was wrong.

I walked over to his side and was about to ask what was up when he said, "Hey, man, I'll be right back. Cover for me."

"Sure thing," I said as he walked off with his phone.

It struck me as odd. Who would be calling him right before a big game that he would actually take the call and leave the locker room to speak with?

I hoped nothing was wrong.

It made me think about Rimmel. Maybe I should check up on her. Or at least check my messages.

I rummaged through my jacket pockets and pulled out my phone. Before I could check the screen, a couple guys came over to talk plays with me, and I gave them my full attention. When they were gone, I lifted the phone to light up the screen.

Braeden appeared beside me and grabbed the phone. "Hey, hey," he said. "What's this? No phones before the game. We gotta get in the zone!"

"Says the man who just took a call."

He shrugged. "I had to take a call."

"And I need to check on Rimmel."

Something passed behind his eyes, and I felt my own narrow on his face. My phone went off in his hand, and I reached for it. He held it out and glanced at the screen.

"Speak of the devil."

I took the phone and looked down at the text. The three words she sent made me smile.

"See," Braeden said. "Look at you getting all soft. Turn that thing off before you turn into a diaper-wearing, bottle-sucking pansy ass before the game."

I laughed and shot off a reply to Rim, then hit the power button. "Happy now?"

"Hells yeah," Braeden said and set his phone back in his locker.

I noticed *he* didn't shut his off.

Coach's voice boomed through the locker room. "Suit up. Let's go warm up!"

My stomach jumped with excitement. It was almost game time.

When we were all suited up and everyone was filing out onto the field, I realized I left the dog tag Rimmel gave me in my locker. I rushed back in to pull it over my head and tuck it beneath all my pads.

On my way past Braeden's locker, my footsteps hesitated. Something was up.

Without another thought, I opened his locker and reached for his phone. I pulled up the recent history in his call log and stared down at the most recent call.

It had been Rimmel.

"Yo!" Trent called from the front of the room.

"Coming!" I yelled back and shoved the phone back where it had been.

As I jogged out to join the team on the field, all I could think about was what Braeden hadn't told me.

Why the hell had Rimmel called him?

What didn't I know?

CHAPTER THIRTEEN

RIMMEL

By the third quarter of the game, I started to relax.

Romeo was dominating the field. He was totally in the zone and it was nothing short of amazing to see.

My chest swelled with pride every time I looked at him.

He'd thrown four touchdowns right into the end zone. Perfect straight throws that literally sailed right into his teammates' hands. When he wasn't throwing touchdowns, he was throwing complete passes that gave the Wolves an edge and had them ahead on the scoreboard.

The rest of the team was on fire as well. They worked as a unit, as a whole. It was like they knew each other so well they could anticipate each other's moves before they made them.

I guess all those hours upon hours of practicing and being together was totally paying off.

I had been nothing but a bundle of nerves and anxiety as I was getting ready for the game. I checked my phone constantly for cryptic texts and every Buzz notification. There was one that sent me into a cold sweat, and I prayed Romeo hadn't seen it.

But judging by the way he was playing, he hadn't.

I was able to relax a little during the first half of the game, but when halftime rolled around, I started to worry again. What if someone said something to him in the locker room? What if he turned on his phone and saw the Buzz?

He might not realize it was about me, but what if he did?

Once halftime was over and the team rushed out onto the sidelines, I knew it was okay. Romeo looked over to where my friends and I were sitting and smiled.

I gave him a thumbs-up and smiled.

As the players settled back into the game, I signaled for a new apple cider. The one I'd gotten earlier had grown cold. My stomach had been so knotted I wasn't able to drink it. But as the vendor handed over a new steaming cup, I knew this one I would get to enjoy.

My face was so cold my cheeks had grown numb and even with my fur-lined boots, my toes were cold and feeling a little stiff. I was dressed in a pair of thick black leggings, thick cream-colored socks that came all the way to my knees, a long-sleeved T-shirt, a flannel, and Romeo's hoodie over top.

I'd even added a pair of purple mittens and a purple knit beanie. Beneath it, I wore my hair down, hoping the length would provide an extra layer of warmth. I tried to curl it in those loose curls Ivy made look so easy.

I burned my forehead and my ear before I gave up.

The result was partially curled hair.

It was good I was wearing a hat. It kept my poor attempt at a hairstyle covered. As usual, I was wearing my glasses and not a stitch of makeup (except Chapstick).

Beside me, Ivy and Missy looked as cute as ever in jeans, boots, and trendy coats that looked like capes. Missy was wearing a pair of leopard-print gloves (that girl liked her animal print) and Ivy was wearing a pair of white mittens that looked like sweaters.

Both of them wore expertly applied makeup and looked far too good for two ladies who stayed up most of the night partying.

The crowd began chanting Romeo's number, and I clapped as he ran out on the field with his other teammates.

I glanced up at the large screen that was showing random shots of the people in the stands and close-up shots of the game. Romeo's image filled the picture and people began to cheer. Even on screen and with a helmet on his head, the effect of his blue eyes was absolute.

I couldn't wait to be with him tonight. Even though I stayed with him last night, it still felt like forever since I'd seen him. It made me angry that what was supposed to be an entire night of celebration and fun was going to be interrupted by me having to tell him about Zach.

"You okay?" Ivy said, leaning over to speak into my ear.

I glanced at her. "Of course. Why?"

She shrugged. "You just seem a little off… kind of quiet."

"I'm always quiet," I pointed out and then sipped at the cider.

"I know something's going on," she said pointedly. "I've heard some rumors flying around."

Everyone around us went wild and jumped to their feet. I looked up to see that Romeo had thrown yet another perfect pass right into the end zone.

I jumped to my feet and yelled and screamed along with everyone else. I laughed when Braeden launched himself at Romeo and he caught him. Braeden banged on Romeo's helmet in celebration as the pair showed quite a bit of their bromance out there on the field.

I made a mental note to tease Braeden about it later.

Once the crowd quieted down, Ivy looked at me again.

"I'll explain later," I said, hoping she would let it go.

• • •

"You can tell me at the party tonight."

I half nodded and took another sip of the cider to keep from having to commit.

A few plays later and the Wolves intercepted the ball from the other team, and the crowd went wild again.

My eyes followed the large twenty-four on the back of Romeo's jersey as he ran out on the field to make the offensive play.

A few moments later, the ball was snapped into his capable hands, and I marveled at how it managed to look small when he gripped it.

He held the ball as he scanned for an opening to make the pass. When he found where he was going, he drew his arm back, ready to launch what I knew would be another perfect throw.

I watched the ball spiral through the air, toward its target. The player caught the ball and ran it down the field.

People were yelling and cheering.

And then they weren't.

"Oh my God!" Ivy screamed, and her fingers dug into my arm.

Even though the Wolves just scored another touchdown, the stadium fell eerily quiet.

A sick feeling twisted the pit of my stomach, and my eyes sought out Romeo. But he wasn't where he was supposed to be.

Instead, there was a player lying on the ground, splayed out beneath another player from the opposing team.

My chest tightened when several of the Wolves lunged at the player and pulled him off. Braeden shoved the guy back with so much aggression that he stumbled.

Referees swarmed the situation, and I heard the blowing of several whistles.

Everything slowed for me.

Romeo lay on the field, flat on his back.

Unmoving.

Still.

"What's going on?" I mumbled, my brain unable to process what I was seeing.

"That guy from the other team plowed into Romeo after he threw the ball. It looked deliberate. Like he wanted to take him out of the game."

"Look!" Missy said, grabbing my arm and pulling my attention off the field and up to the giant screen.

They were playing back what had happened.

Tears filled my eyes and blurred my vision as I watched Romeo, who hadn't seen it coming, tackled and roughly shoved into the ground.

"No," I whispered. Why would someone want to hurt him like that?

Because he was too good. He was playing so well that it was embarrassing the other team.

The Wolves, the coach, and one of the refs crowded around Romeo, and when I looked, I could no longer see him. But I knew he was still lying there.

What if he was hurt?

What if something was broken?

Before I knew what I was doing, I was out of my seat and rushing up toward the railing that divided the seats from the field. I had to make sure he was okay. I couldn't just sit here and watch him lie there in pain.

I heard my name called, but I ignored it as I flung my leg over the top railing and prepared to hoist myself over.

One of the guys working security happened to see me and he rushed over and ordered me to stop.

"I can't. That's my…" My voice broke. I couldn't force the word boyfriend between my lips. It just wasn't enough. It just didn't describe how desperate I was to get to him.

"He's my everything," I finished.

The security guard gave me a grim look. "You can't come on the field."

A lone tear tracked its way down my cheek, and I craned my neck. Frustrated, I glanced up at the big screen to see if it was showing a different angle.

But they weren't playing Romeo. They were focused on me.

I blinked at the site of me half straddling the railing and the security guard standing there with a grim look on his face as he stared me down. My cheeks were red, behind my glasses, my eyes wild.

I turned away from the screen, irritated that they weren't focused on Romeo.

I glanced at the guard. "I'm coming over."

He crossed his arms over his chest as if to say, *I dare you.*

I flung my other leg over so I was balanced on the bottom rung.

"This is your last warning," the guard shouted.

The crowd started to cheer and go wild. Romeo's number started filling the air. I looked up.

He was okay!

He was on his feet, helmet in hand, and laughing at something Braeden was saying. Beside him, the coach looked relieved, and all the Wolves were clapping.

The guy who'd mowed him down was being escorted off the field.

Jackass.

Relief made me weak and a sob caught in my throat. I sagged back against the cold metal of the rails. The guard gestured for backup, and a few others that were dressed just like him started my way.

I mean, really. He was being a bit dramatic. I was only one girl. And a small one at that.

Ivy came up behind me and grabbed at my shoulders. "Are you insane?" she shouted. "Get back over here."

"I just wanted to be sure he was okay."

"He is," she replied. "Now come on!"

I started to turn back when the guard grabbed my ankle. "You're going to need to come with me," he intoned.

The crowd started going crazy. Like even crazier than when Romeo got up from the hit. I was clinging to the railing, wondering if I would like prison, when Ivy sighed. "I swear. You have all the luck."

Confused, I glanced around. Romeo was jogging toward us, helmet in his hands.

Quickly, I glanced at the big screen and it was showing a wide shot of me clinging onto the rails and him running toward us.

When he arrived, he slapped the guard on his back and said something in his ear. The guard looked at me and grinned and then walked away.

Romeo stepped up to where I was. At the height I was at on the railing, for once I was taller than him.

"You're killing me, Smalls," he said. "I had to interrupt a championship game to keep you from going to the slammer."

"I was worried. You didn't get up."

"And so you were just going to march out on the field and what?"

God, he looked so… so incredible right then. His uniform stretched out over his wide shoulders and narrow waist. The pads strapped to his body made him look even stronger. He had grass stains on his knees, sweat in his hair, and ornery laughter in his sparkling blue eyes.

I swear I'd never seen anyone equal parts of to-die-for good looks and boy-next-door troublemaker.

"I was going to come out there and kiss it and make it better."

He threw back his head and laughed, and the stadium erupted once more. I was aware that every moment between us was being broadcast like some reality TV show, but for once, I didn't care how many people were staring.

This was our moment.

And I was so damn happy he wasn't hurt.

"So you're okay, then?" I asked.

"Takes a lot more than a shady illegal attack to keep me down."

Behind him, the players were getting back to the game, rushing out onto the field, and the coach was yelling out orders.

"I'll just go back to my seat, then," I said.

He rushed forward and grabbed me off the railing. The crowd cheered when he slid me down his body and pressed his lips to mine.

It wasn't a chaste kiss. It was the kind of kiss that made me blush when I watched it on TV.

But I kissed him anyway. I got lost in him.

When he pulled back, I said, "By the way, you're totally kicking ass out there."

He chuckled and put me back on the railing and kept one hand on my butt as I climbed back over. Back in the stands, I gripped the cold metal and gave him a small wave.

He'd been walking backward toward his team, but then he changed direction and sprinted toward me. In one graceful leap, he was up on the wall and leaning over the railing.

"Love you," he half-growled and pressed a swift kiss to my lips. "Next touchdown's for you."

Behind us, the coach was calling his name, the game resumed.

He hopped down and ran over to the coach, who hit him in the back of the head with his clipboard.

Beside me, Ivy sighed. "I want to be a nerd."

I elbowed her and we both laughed.

The rest of the game went by without any more attempts at removing Romeo from the game. His teammates seemed to rally around him to shut out anyone who even got close.

In the end, Romeo threw another touchdown. The one he said was for me.

And when the clock wound down, the Wolves became college football champions.

Alpha U was getting a new trophy.

CHAPTER FOURTEEN

> #LadiesBeSwoonin
> Forget climbing in through a window.
> Modern day Romeos interupt football
> games and climb over railings.
> #PublicDisplayOfAffection
> ... Alpha BuzzFeed

ROMEO

"That was some shady shit out there, Rome," Braeden said once the total chaos of winning the game had gone down to a considerable roar.

We were finally in the locker room, and I was stripping off my sweat and grass-stained gear.

"Total douche move." I agreed.

It wasn't the first time a team had tried to take me out of a game. It was pretty much common practice, especially when something like a title and championship was at stake. Still, I'd never quite had anyone come at me like that before.

The play was already in progress. Sacking me wouldn't have changed the touchdown I'd just thrown. Except of course to keep me from throwing another one.

That guy deliberately came in like a freight train and plowed me down. I lay there stunned for long moments, waiting for the air to come back in my lungs and for my body to process the shock of the hit.

Thankfully, he wasn't that good at tackling and it did nothing more than stun me.

And it got him thrown out of the game.

It really hadn't been a big deal. Like I said, it happened a lot. But it was the first time it happened in front of Rimmel.

I couldn't help but notice how the large screen on the field had zeroed in on the girl in number twenty-four's hoodie, who was climbing over the railing and preparing to leap down onto the field.

The security guard was yelling at her, but she barely noticed him. Her eyes were trained out on the field, where I was.

It was almost laughable that her tiny ass was going to rush out onto a field full of men more than double her size to make sure I was okay.

Goddamn. I loved her even more just then.

When the guard put his hand on her ankle, trying to stop her from going back to her seat, something happened.

Something that never had in my entire life of playing football.

The game faded away.

For once, I was out on the field and unable to focus on only the game. It took a backseat to the girl teetering on the edge of the railing. I wasn't going to let her get punished for worrying about me. Hell, she didn't know she couldn't just jump onto the field and run out here.

I grinned to myself. I was going to have to give her some rules.

"Dude," Trent said and stopped in front of my locker. I glanced up. "Now every chick within a fifty-mile radius of this place is gonna expect all of us guys to pull some grand romantic crap on the field like you just did."

I laughed. "Nah, man." I disagreed. "No one was even watchin'."

"Fuck," Trent said. "How'd you even say that with a straight face?"

"It's a gift."

Braeden burst into the conversation, his hair sticking up all over the place and a towel slung around his waist. "We getting drunk to-night!" he hollered.

Everyone within in earshot gave a loud whoop.

Braeden gave me a sheepish smile. "So yeah, our exclusive party tonight?"

"What about it?" I asked.

"Well, I might have invited more than one date."

Trent glanced at me. "Yeah, me too."

I groaned. That meant our exclusive party was no longer exclusive. Not that I'd expected anything less.

We were the college champs after all.

And damn if I hadn't played awesome.

"I'm hitting the shower," Braeden said and slammed his locker shut.

"Hey," I said and caught him by the shoulder.

He glanced around at me. "You wanna tell me why Rimmel called you before the game?"

Braeden spun. "Did you go through my phone?"

"Did you lie to me about my girl?" I countered.

He wiped a hand over his face. "Fucking A. Don't put me in the middle, Rome."

"You're my best friend, asshole. There is no middle. It's my side."

"Hey now," he said. "Sisters before misters and all that."

"What the fuck does that even mean?" I drawled, amused.

"It means I've taken her on as my little sister. You're her mister. I'm officially in neutral territory."

"Are you actually telling me you're picking her side?"

He muttered a few curses beneath his breath and sighed. "I'm on your side, Rome. Always. I'm doing this for you. Something's up. That's all I'm saying. And that girl loves you, so you better not fuck it up."

"And how would I do that?"

"Just let her be the one to tell you whatever it is she has to say. Stay off your phone and shit 'til you're with her."

I stared at him for long moments. He didn't back down or cave in at all.

"All right, man. Thanks for the heads-up."

The shouts and laughter of victory didn't let up while everyone showered and changed, but I barely heard them. I knew I wasn't going to like whatever she had to call Braeden for. I tried not to be upset she called him and not me, but the truth was it pissed me off.

At least I knew she wasn't hurt. I'd just seen her on the field. Physically, she was fine.

It seemed like knowing that only made it easier to be mad. I was glad she felt like Braeden was someone she could count on, but I wanted her to come to me. Always.

Getting out of the locker room wasn't a quick thing. There was too much celebrating to do. Part of me itched to find Rimmel, but the other part of me wanted to enjoy this win. We'd worked so damn hard for the trophy we were all drinking beer out of, so I told myself to scratch that itch later.

After the pre-party in the locker room, I gave a couple interviews. The reporters were all waiting outside the lockers in the tunnel that led to the field. They had cameras, pens, and badges clipped to their coats.

I did my thing and turned up the charm. I talked about the game, the team, and I smiled. Hell, half the questions were about the girl I'd stopped the game for. I never realized it would be made such a big deal. I'd only been reacting to the situation, doing what felt natural.

When the coach came out of the locker room, the reporters turned to him, and me and the other team members that were being interviewed were able to escape.

I was still pumped up from the game and our win, but the adrenaline was starting to fade and a little bit of exhaustion was sinking in.

We were heading out toward the parking lot when I turned the corner and a familiar figure snagged my attention.

Rimmel was leaning against the wall with her hands buried in the front pocket of my hoodie.

Braeden, who'd been beside me since we stepped out of the locker room, slapped me on the back. "I'll see ya at the party."

I nodded.

He jogged ahead and Rimmel pushed off the wall and grinned at him. She held up her hand for a high-five and said, "Congratulations!"

Braeden pushed her hand away and crouched low to pick her up and spin her around in a circle. She laughed.

"Thanks, tutor girl." He set her on her feet and then was gone.

Rimmel looked over at me and grinned. I recognized the look on her face, so when she came rushing at me, I was ready and held out my arms. She leapt up into them and wrapped her legs around my waist. Her arms went around my neck and she smiled wide. "I'm so proud of you!"

I gave her a loud, sloppy kiss.

She squealed and then pulled back. "So how's it feel to be the champion, Mr. MVP?"

"Pretty damn good."

She leaned forward and kissed me. It wasn't a sloppy kiss; it was a real one. And it tightened my gut and made me think about skipping the party tonight and just spending it in bed with her.

Behind us, someone cleared his throat.

Rimmel jerked away like she was in trouble, and I tightened my hold on her and lazily turned around so her back was to whoever was there and I was facing him.

He was wearing a National Football League coat over his jeans and boots.

My heart rate jacked up, making my chest feel like it was in danger of exploding. I set Rimmel carefully down beside me and stepped forward. "I'm Roman Anderson. It's nice to meet you."

The man stepped forward and offered his hand, which I shook. "I know who you are, Mr. Anderson."

"I hope you enjoyed tonight's game," I said.

"You played very well," he said.

"Thank you." Suddenly, the charm I usually wore like designer clothes failed me. I felt like I was standing before a judge and jury, and my entire future hung in the balance of the impression I made right here, right now.

"I would have to disagree," Rimmel said, stepping up beside me.

Both of us turned to her. I gave her a wary look, hoping she understood who this was. She ignored me.

Brat.

"You disagree?" the scout said, focusing solely on her.

"Romeo didn't play well. He was awesome." She punctuated her statement by pushing her glasses up on her nose.

The scout chuckled. I let out the breath I'd been holding.

"And who might you be?"

Her eyes widened when she realized she'd called all the attention onto herself, and her cheeks reddened. But she stepped forward and offered her small gloved hand. "Rimmel. I'm Romeo's biggest fan."

The scout shook her hand and tilted his head. "Aren't you the one Mr. Anderson here interrupted the game for?"

Shit. Of course he'd seen that. Talk about unprofessional.

I stepped forward. "This is my girlfriend, sir. She's new to the whole football world, and she hadn't seen me take a hit like that before."

"That was quite the hit." He agreed, looking back at me. "Yet you got up."

"Takes more than that to keep me down," I replied.

His eyes appraised me. "I see that."

He glanced between Rimmel and me. "Stunts like the one you pulled aren't common."

"I—" I started to speak, to tell him it wouldn't happen again. I wanted to kick myself in the ass. But before I could say anything, he spoke over me.

"Stunts like that sell tickets." He looked at Rimmel again, who smiled sweetly. "They pull in a whole new audience to the sport."

I swallowed the excuse I was about to make. He liked it. He liked Rimmel. The charm that failed me earlier came back in one great rush. I grinned and looped an arm across Rimmel's shoulders.

"Nothing like a captive audience."

"Yes," he said and then reached inside his jacket. "You still have a couple years left of college, don't you?"

"Technically." I hedged.

"What's your major?"

"Business management," I answered as he pulled out a small business card and held it at his side.

He smiled. "So you're really just here for the ball."

I relaxed. "The game is all that matters."

"You're young, but you've got talent." He glanced at Rimmel. "You also have a lot of support."

Rimmel nodded enthusiastically.

The scout chuckled.

Damn. My baby was charming the pants right off this guy.

He held out the card in his hand. "I'm Martin Winters of the NFL. That was some good…" Rimmel cleared her throat and he grinned. "Awesome," he corrected, "playing out there. Congrats on your win. I'll be in touch."

I took the card and shook his hand. "I look forward to it."

Rimmel and I stood quietly and watched him walk away. We remained still until he was completely out of sight.

When he was gone, I turned to her.

She opened her mouth in an O shape and jumped up and down.

I let out a whoop so loud it echoed around us. The exhaustion I felt just moments ago was completely erased by brand new adrenaline. I lifted Rimmel off her feet and spun her around until she begged me to stop.

We fell against the wall, and I covered her mouth with mine.

I kissed her hard and deep. Her fingers delved into my still damp hair and massaged at my scalp, making me growl low in my chest. When she started to move against me, I knew it was probably time to cool things off. We were still at the stadium.

"I didn't expect you to wait. I would've hurried."

"That's why I didn't tell you," she said, brushing her fingertips across my cheek. "I want you to enjoy tonight. You earned it. But I also wanted to be here to tell you how happy I am for you."

"Is that the only reason?" I asked, pinning her with a stare.

She sighed and pushed back so I would set her on her feet. I did and we started walking out toward the parking lot. "I really wish this could wait, but I know it can't."

"I know you called Braeden."

Her teeth sank into her lower lip and she glanced at me swiftly. "What did he tell you?"

"Nothing. Sisters before misters, ya know."

She wrinkled her nose. "What?"

"Exactly." I agreed.

The snow was still drifting from the sky when we stepped out into the parking lot. The Hellcat was covered with a fine layer of the white stuff because it'd been parked there for so long. Beside me, Rimmel shivered, and I felt like an ass because she'd been out in this cold half the day and then stood in the drafty tunnel and had to wait on me.

The engine was already purring; I'd hit the electronic start as soon as it came into sight. I pulled off my varsity jacket as we walked around to the passenger side, and I draped it around her shoulders.

"Pretty soon I'm gonna have your entire wardrobe." She smiled and pulled my coat farther around her.

"You can have whatever you want, baby."

I opened the door and ushered her inside. On my way around the hood, I remembered my phone was still off and I powered it on. Inside the car, I turned on the wipers to clear the loose snow off the window.

My phone started beeping with a bunch of notifications. I grinned and picked it up to silence it. "This thing is gonna be going off all night."

Rimmel gave me a tight smile and my eye caught one of the notifications that flashed on the screen. It was a Buzz from a couple hours ago.

It was about a #Nerd in a towel…

Oh, hells no.

I looked up at Rimmel and turned the screen so she could see.

"You better start talking."

CHAPTER FIFTEEN

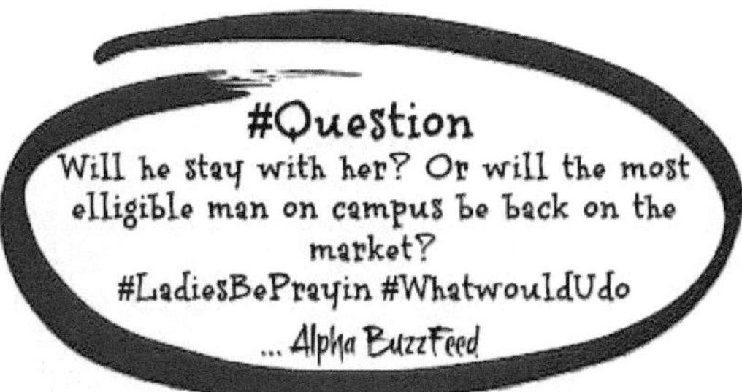

RIMMEL

Silence was not golden.

Silence was scary.

Especially the kind of silence that Romeo was exuding right now.

His silence was so quiet that it was the loudest sound I'd ever heard.

The minute he'd seen the Buzz, he knew it was about me. The BuzzBoss only called one person on this campus a #Nerd. I didn't put him off. I didn't try to downplay what happened or even drama it up.

The truth was bad enough.

So I told him. I told him everything.

Okay.

Not everything.

I left out the part about Zach touching my underwear.

Or the picture I destroyed.

There were some things better left unsaid.

He didn't say anything. Not once. He didn't look at me either. He stared out the windshield and into the dark.

He stared so hard and so long that I turned to stare too. The only thing I saw was the dancing snow in the headlights of the idling Hellcat.

Finally, after what seemed like endless hours of hushed tension in the confined space of his car, he did something.

He reached out and griped the steering wheel so tightly that his hands turned white. I swallowed thickly. I wasn't scared of Romeo. I was scared of what he might do.

I was beginning to realize that Zach wasn't just an asshole. Well, he was. Everyone knew it. But when it came to Romeo, it was more.

It was hate.

In its true form.

It was almost unfathomable. What could cause such wretched animosity? Did Romeo hate Zach in return?

"I really need to teach you how to drive this car," Romeo said, his gravelly voice breaking into my thoughts.

It wasn't at all what I expected him to say. "What?"

He kept his eyes trained out beyond the windshield. "Because if you knew how to drive this car, I'd tell you to leave so I could go find that son of a bitch and beat his ass."

"Gee." I snorted, nerves making me extremely awkward. "Well, if that isn't a reason to learn to drive a stick, I don't know what is."

He glanced at me, his eyes hard. "Did he touch you?"

"I told you he didn't."

His eyes drilled into mine. "I wanna rip off every last layer of clothes on your body right here, right now, just so I can look you over for bruises."

I shivered against the idea of me naked before him, but the thrill quickly vanished. "Are you saying you think I'm lying?"

Something very close to anger bit at the back of my throat.

"Fuck!" he growled and hit the steering wheel. "I'm saying the thought of him near you makes me crazy."

"That's exactly what he wants, you know," I told him. "The only reason he bothers with me is because he wants to get under your skin."

"Well, it's goddamn working."

"Hey," I said softly and reached across the seats to pry his white knuckles off the wheel. "Don't let it. It was stupid. It was nothing."

His fingers tangled with mine and he looked at me, his eyes tortured. "It wasn't nothing. He scared you. He locked himself in a room with you. You were vulnerable. *You were fucking naked.* How the hell did he get in there anyway?" he muttered.

I'd wondered that too, but I didn't voice it because Romeo was already pissed enough.

"Don't let this ruin your night," I pleaded. "I wouldn't even have said anything until tomorrow, but I knew you'd hear something. There were people who saw me come out of the bathroom. I wasn't dressed. And I'm sure he stepped out just moments later."

That was the worst part. People were going to think I cheated on Romeo. People were going to be talking; rumors would spread like wildfire.

"That's why you called Braeden," he said like he was just realizing something. "You told him to get me to turn my phone off."

I nodded, wanting him to understand. "I wasn't going to let anything upset you before the game. This day was too important to you."

The muscles in his jaw worked, and again he said nothing.

"Romeo?" I asked softly, minutes later.

He glanced at me.

"You believe me, don't you? You know I would never…" For some reason, nerves tightened my guts. I felt like there was some Boy Scout in there trying to earn a badge in knot tying.

Romeo moved fast and flung open the driver's side door. Cold air swirled in and mingled with the heat the vents blew out. He leapt out, and I stared after him in shock.

Small white flurries rushed inside and melted against the leather of his now vacant seat.

Did that mean he didn't believe me…?

My car door was forced open. Cold air rushed me from both sides now and my seatbelt was tossed aside. Strong hands lifted me out and pulled me up into the snow.

"I oughtta make you walk home for saying something so stupid," he said, staring down at me.

"It's cold."

He groaned and grabbed me by the shoulders. "Look. At. Me."

I looked up, blinking away the snowflakes that wet my eyes and cheeks.

"There was never a single doubt in my head about you. I never once thought there was any kind of truth to that stupid notification. I know you love me."

"Do you?" I worried, feeling my eyes grow misty. "I know I don't say it that much. I'll say it more—"

He stopped my words with a kiss.

I melted against him like a snowman in the middle of Bermuda.

We kissed so long that snow began to cling to our clothes and in his hair. Whenever I would pause to suck in a breath, the difference between the air and the heat inside me would shock me.

When at last he finally pulled away, I was breathless and forgot what we'd been talking about.

"I fucking love that hat," he murmured, dropping a kiss to my nose.

"You look like a snowman." I smiled, taking in his white-covered hair.

"Honey, if I was a snowman, I'd be a puddle at your feet by now."

"I do love you," I whispered, our conversation coming back.

"I know, baby." He gently guided me back into the car. "I love you, too. Now c'mon. I gotta make an appearance at my party."

Inside the car, the ride was quiet. When we pulled onto his street, I gasped. The entire road was lined with cars. "I thought this was a private party?"

He grinned. "I think word got out."

Even though there was a ton of cars and people were likely everywhere, there was still a clear path up his driveway. Snow coated the pathway like some kind of opulent white carpet. The Hellcat purred up the driveway, and people started cheering and surrounding the car.

It was surreal. Like some kind of movie.

Romeo honked the horn and yelled out the window.

The huge crowd left me feeling a little self-conscious and awkward. All my years of trying to be invisible came rushing back, and I wondered if there was a quiet spot inside I could hide.

Once the car was parked, he gave me a grin. It relaxed some of what I was feeling, but not all of it.

Because I saw.

I saw that beneath that smiling exterior anger still burned.

Romeo wasn't going to let this go.

I grabbed his arm before he could get out of the car and be swallowed by the waiting crowd. "Promise me something," I said.

"What?"

"Promise me you'll just let this go. Promise you won't make it worse."

Slowly, gently, he pulled my hand off his arm and brought it up to his lips to kiss the back of my knuckles. "Now, baby, you know I can't do that."

It took a few moments for his denial to sink in.

By that time, he was already out of the car and the conversation was over.

I leaned my head back against the seat.

I never drank. Alcohol wasn't my thing.

But right about now, a strong drink sounded like a really good idea.

CHAPTER SIXTEEN

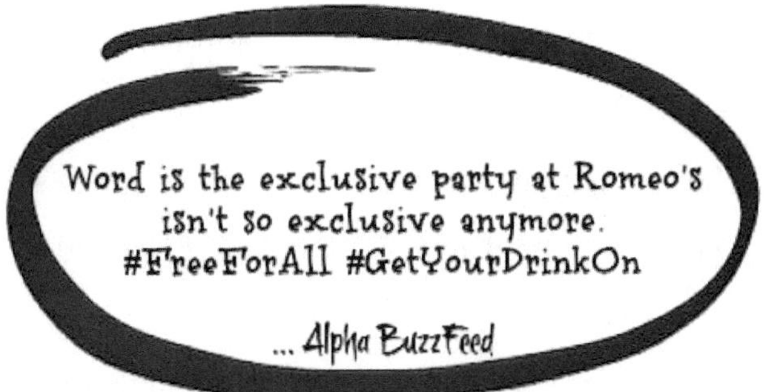

ROMEO

This was my fault.

I should have made him pay the second I saw those bruises on Rimmel.

I'd been too wrapped up in football, in my own life, that I let the first incident with Zach go unpunished for too long.

And now he'd done this.

That little cocksucker attacked her in the bathroom. It was like waving a blood-red flag in front of an already enraged bull.

He was stupid.

He was also gonna pay.

No, she wasn't hurt, but that was the point, wasn't it? He wanted her scared, embarrassed. He wanted to make me look like some lovesick whipped puppy who let his girl cheat on him and still dated her.

He wanted my reputation.

He also wanted to mess with my head and screw with the game.

It backfired. I doubt he expected Rimmel to keep her mouth shut. He probably thought she would run straight to me. Shows what an utter loser he was.

She was stronger than that. Stronger than him. She held it together, did damage control by calling Braeden, and then sat in the stands with her head held high, despite the rumors, and cheered me on.

She'd protected me.

And I'd done a piss poor job of doing the same.

It ended now.

Yeah, he wanted me to come after him. And I was going to play into his hands, but he didn't know which way I was coming.

I threw back my fourth shot of the night and chased it with a chug of beer. "Another!"

Everyone cheered.

We were sitting around the large stone fire pit off to the right of the pool house. People were everywhere, on the patio, near the pool, and spilling out of my house.

My mother was probably inside the main house having a heart attack at the mess everyone was making.

To my left sat Braeden, along with half the team, and to my right was Rimmel, Ivy, and Missy. Rimmel was giggling at something Ivy was saying, and she had a red Solo cup in her hand. I reached out and tilted the cup toward me to see it was empty.

I grabbed her around the waist and lifted her into my lap. "Do a shot with me!"

She laughed. "Okay."

"I was pretty sure she was a little past tipsy. Okay. She was probably drunk. It was the first time I'd seen her like this. But tonight was a celebration. It was the night to get drunk and not remember!

Okay, yeah, I was drunk too.

Braeden produced three shot glasses of clear liquid. Rimmel and I each took one and Braeden held his up. "Fuck the toast! Just drink!"

Everyone cheered and all three of us tossed the alcohol into our throats. Braeden and I watched Rimmel as she screwed up her face and her eyes watered. Then she started coughing. Everyone laughed and I patted her on the back.

"That burns!" she croaked.

"Burns so good!" Braeden sang. He produced another shot and held it out to Rimmel. I took it and tossed it back.

"Dude," he said. "That was hers."

"Dude," I echoed. "She's like a hundred pounds. And she's already drunk."

As if to prove my point, Rimmel collapsed against my chest in a fit of giggles.

"Lightweight," Braeden muttered.

She laughed some more. The way she was wiggling around in my lap was causing my cock to stir. Even drunk, I was still able to get it up for her. Lusty thoughts started crowding my head and I started making plans to escape back into my room with her.

Just as I was about to slip through the crowd with her in my arms, a hushed silence fell over the party.

Beneath his breath, Braeden grunted, "Fuckhead."

"What?" I asked.

He motioned with his beer across the yard.

I glanced over to see Zach walking through the crowd. People parted around him with speculation in their eyes. I could practically hear people smacking their lips for the taste of drama.

Just the sight of him caused my fuse to ignite. My calm, cool demeanor flew out the window. Even drunk, it couldn't be subdued.

"What the fuck is he doing here?" I growled.

In my lap, Rimmel sat up straight and started looking around.

I felt her body stiffen when she saw him.

It only pissed me off more.

"He's here for his ass whooping," Braeden yelled and jumped to his feet.

Behind him, several other Wolves did the same.

That was the thing about being on a team. They didn't even know the full story. Hell, I'd been hearing phones going off all night. I knew people were talking. But these guys didn't care.

They were behind me. They had my back. No matter what.

I stood slowly and deposited Rimmel beside Ivy. "Watch her," I said.

Rimmel huffed and muttered something about not being a dog.

Then she barked.

Ivy laughed.

It probably wasn't my best idea to have one drunk girl look after another, but I had a jaw to punch.

Everyone moved out of the way as I stalked toward Zach. But no one left. They all rushed to get good seats for whatever was about to go down.

"The fuck you doing here?" I spat, strolling over to the wannabe frat president.

"Celebrating the Wolves championship like everyone else," Zach said, a slight sneer on his mouth.

"You aren't welcome here," I said and crossed my arms over my chest in challenge. Most of the team stood behind my back and Braeden was right beside me.

"That was a lowlife move," Braeden said, hard. "Attacking a woman like that."

Zach pretended to look surprised. "Is that what she said?" he asked, amused. Then he nodded. "I guess

I could see why. Imagine what the girls around here would do to her if they knew the girl who managed to take you off the market was getting naked with me in the girls' dorm bathroom."

"You shut the fuck up," I growled. Red was starting to tinge my vision, and I balled my hands into fists. "Get the hell off my property."

"Stop," Rimmel yelled from somewhere behind me. Seconds later, she pushed between Braeden and me.

Zach looked her over appraisingly. "I gotta say, Anderson, she is pretty hot when she's not drowning in clothes."

I lunged forward so fast that no one saw it coming. I jerked him forward by the front of his preppy button-filled coat with so much force his head jerked on his neck.

I brought my free hand back and drove it into his jaw. He slumped forward, but I was still holding him up. I held him out and buried my fist in his midsection.

When I let go, he crumpled onto the ground.

I leaned down to where he was slumped and whispered in his ear. "If you go near her again, this is gonna look like a day at the playground."

Zach's head snapped up and he smiled. Blood was running down the corner of his lip. "Anyone else hear that? That was a threat."

I grabbed him up and slammed him on his feet. "Get out of here."

Zach turned to walk away, but not before I saw the glint in his eye. He came back swinging. When I knocked his fist away, he came in low like he was gonna tackle me.

I planted my feet into the ground and let him rush me. The force of him hitting into me caused my steps to falter, but otherwise, I didn't budge. He wrapped his arms around my waist and shoved.

I grunted and lifted him up by the waist and flipped him over my shoulder. I wanted to pile drive him into the ground, but I held myself back. Instead, I tossed him down.

Everyone was silent as they watched the exchange. Braeden was right there. I could see him itching to come forward and give Zach a piece of him as well. I shook my head subtly. This was my fight. He messed with my girl.

Braeden hung back as Zach stayed down on the ground.

"Asshole," I muttered and turned to walk away.

My eyes sought out Rimmel. She was standing nearby, at the edge of the crowd. Her face was pale and her eyes were round.

"Anyone wanna take out the trash?" I asked and hitched a thumb over my shoulder toward Zach.

Braeden and Trent exchanged a look and nodded grimly.

A scraping sound cut through all the low murmuring in the crowd, and I started to turn at the same moment Rimmel screamed, "No!"

I glanced at her to see what was wrong, but she wasn't there. She was rushing forward with fear on her face.

"Romeo," she cried and zigzagged around me.

Braeden let out a curse, and I spun.

It all happened so fast. Zach was coming at me with a chair. He had it poised in the air, ready to bring it around and take me out.

But Rimmel was in the way.

I shot forward, but it was too late.

Zach brought the chair around and Rimmel jerked away to try and avoid the hit. She ended up slipping on the pavement and fell to the side.

There was a large splash; droplets of water splattered everywhere.

Surprised, Zach dropped the chair and turned to stare at the pool.

The pool Rimmel just plunged into.

The pool she was deathly afraid of.

I watched her small body struggle for a mere second and then she went stiff. She began to sink in the icy cold water.

CHAPTER SEVENTEEN

> A fight. A plunge into icy water. The victory party just got interesting.
> #TheyArentBrokenUp #Yet
> ... Alpha BuzzFeed

RIMMEL

Cold, icy water reached around me like sticky tentacles, trying to claim me. My body was instantly shocked, and my skin stung like a thousand tiny needles pierced my skin.

Over and over again.

I struggled against the frigid prison, even as it sought to lock me up. I reached upward toward the flickering above me...

And then I realized.

I realized where I was.

Something far colder than the near freezing water slammed into me. I felt myself jerk like I'd been shot. I was in the pool.

I'd slipped and fallen in the pool.

Just like my mother.

I opened my mouth to scream, but no sound came out. Instead, my mouth filled with more suffocating water and precious bubbles filled with air burst in front of my face.

Everything was blurry and dark; it seemed to grow darker by the moment.

And then the darkness seemed to fill with a deep shade of red. It swirled around me. The way the color snaked through the water was hauntingly beautiful. Like ribbons blowing in the wind.

I reached out to touch it, but my hand went through like I was touching a cloud.

The red disbursed and the color turned lighter, more of a pinkish shade.

Panic, stark and bleak, rose up in my chest and squeezed until I thought my ribs would crack from the pressure.

"Mom!" I called out, racing through the front door.

My hot-pink backpack was killing my shoulders—I had so much homework!—so I dropped it on the floor as I kicked off my shoes.

"Mom! Where are you?" I called again, wandering out of the foyer and into the open-concept main floor. To the right was a kitchen with an island and directly ahead was the living room with a couch and TV.

She wasn't watching some talk show. There was nothing cooking on the stove. She was probably upstairs and lost track of time.

I backtracked and pounded up the steps. I couldn't wait to tell her what happened today in Home Ec. Not only did Joey burn the English muffin pizzas, but he caught the oven on fire and we had to have a fire drill. Ms. Kostley was so mad!

I rushed into my parents' bedroom, thinking she'd be there. But she wasn't.

"Mom!" I yelled. "I'm home! Where are you?"

Silence greeted me.

"Very funny!" I called out. "You're a terrible hider, and I'm going to find you!" No wonder she wasn't at the bus stop. She was playing tricks on me.

I searched the entire upstairs.

She wasn't there.

I rushed downstairs and checked the pantry, the bathroom, even the laundry room. On my way to look in the cabinet in the living room, I passed by the large windows that overlooked the screened-in backyard pool.

I wrinkled my nose because something didn't seem right.

I opened the slider and stepped outside. The pool water was pink.

I smiled. So that's what she'd been up to! She was turning the pool my favorite color to surprise me. I laughed and walked over to admire the color.

But my laugh turned into a strangled gargling sound.

I stood there completely frozen in horror and disbelief.

"Mommy," I whimpered.

She was floating in the shallow end, her body facedown and near the edge. Her long, dark hair floated out around her head. It moved gently in the water. It sort of looked like a dark halo.

"Mom!" I screamed, her name ripping from my throat as I swallowed back the bile gurgling up.

Without thought, I plunged into the pool. The water was warm like always, and I swam easily over to her side.

"Mom," I sobbed and reached out for her shoulder.

I turned her just enough to see the large gash on her forehead, her blue bloated face, and the way her once beautiful blue eyes stared at me with a milky-white film over them. Her expression of horror.

My entire body began to shake uncontrollably. Convulsions racked through me so hard that my teeth chattered. My eyes went back to the open wound on her head.

The pool wasn't pink on purpose.

The pool was pink because so much of her blood had mixed with the water.

I was standing in a pool of my mother's blood.

I don't remember how I made it out, only that I did. The white cutoff shorts I was wearing were no longer white. They were stained. Tainted.

They were the color of diluted blood.

Something plunged into the water above me. I saw the figure drop down with speed and precision. I barely noticed. At that point, I was too far gone.

I was lost.

Lost in the underwater world of pink death.

Trapped in the memories of the day I'd found my mother drowned.

I still remembered when they zipped the black body bag up over her face. It was the last time I'd seen her. The image of her lying dead in a bag would haunt me forever.

I remembered the sounds of people singing in church the day of her funeral. The pastor speaking in the front had announced her age wrong. He was wrong. And he kept saying the wrong number. Over and over again.

He said she was thirty-one.

She wasn't.

She was thirty.

She was only thirty years old.

It seemed she deserved better than someone getting her age wrong on the day she was being buried.

Something grabbed my arm and towed me upward. The bone-chilling water scraped at me like barren tree branches in the winter's wind as I floated toward the surface of the water.

It was still pink.

Everything in my vision was pink.

I hated the color pink.

My head cleared the water, and a strong arm wrapped around my middle as my lungs automatically sucked in air. I started coughing immediately, water sputtering out of my mouth.

I blinked against my blurred vision as commotion erupted around me.

"Help me, man," a voice said. It was desperate and raw.

Romeo.

"I got her," said another familiar voice, Braeden.

He slid his arms beneath my arms and towed me up out of the water. My legs buckled, and instead of letting me fall, he scooped me up and held me against him.

I dropped my head against his shoulder and wrinkled my nose. He didn't feel right.

The sound of splashing water drifted over, and I flinched against the sound.

"I got her," Romeo said, and I was shifted against a chest I knew very well.

I was home.

I whimpered because he felt so good, and his arms tightened around me.

"Don't let anyone in the house," Romeo said, and I heard Braeden agree.

Behind us there was the sound of scuffling, but it quickly faded away. My body was shivering violently. Just like that day… the day my mother died.

My fingers were so cold they hurt, and even as I tried to bend them, they just didn't obey.

"I got you," Romeo said as he strode swiftly through the house.

He turned on the shower and then stepped inside. I tensed, anticipating the water hitting me, but it didn't. He held me with his back turned against the spray.

"We're gonna warm you up," he murmured. A few seconds later, he said, "Should be warm enough now."

He turned around and gentle, warm droplets of water cascaded over me. It sort of felt like stepping into a summer rainstorm after living in the harsh winter for too long.

I started to cry.

I pushed my face into Romeo's chest and let out deep, gut-wrenching sobs. The memories of that day were still so close to the surface of my mind and they taunted me.

Was that how my mother felt the day she drowned? Had the water seemed like a prison that wanted to pull her farther and farther into darkness until there was nothing left at all?

Romeo held me tight and hunched around me, protecting my face from the shower spray. I think he murmured gentle words to me, but I couldn't hear them over the sound of my own sobs.

Eventually, I quieted and took a shuddering breath.

"We need to get your clothes off. They're still freezing cold," Romeo said. "I'm gonna sit you down."

He stood me in the shower, and I sagged against the wall. I was utterly drained and empty.

Romeo crouched down at my feet to gently tug off my boots. Then he did the same with my thick knee socks. His hands slid up the sides of my hips and he deftly pulled down my panties and leggings in one quick motion.

When those were gone, he stripped the heavy saturated hoodie from my body and went to work on the buttons of my flannel. "How many layers of clothing do you have on?" he whispered, a small smile in his voice.

It ignited something in me. A little flicker of life.

A ray of sunshine in a desolate world.

I focused on him. Everything still seemed blurry, but he was close enough that I could see him.

He was completely soaked. His jeans, shoes, jacket, and shirt. He was just as wet as I was. His normally messy blond hair was darker and flat to his head from the weight of the water.

Dark shadows haunted his eyes and his lips were pale from the cold.

"You jumped in after me," I whispered.

"I'd jump into the pits of hell for you, Rim."

"I'm pretty sure that was the pit of hell," I said, no trace of humor in my tone. I meant it. That pool was my own personal hell.

"I'm so fucking sorry," he said, his voice cracking.

"You're freezing too," I said as he peeled the shirts off my body.

I started tugging at his jacket, and he paused in undressing me long enough so he could toss it on the floor with the rest of our clothes. I unbuttoned his jeans and tried to tug them down, but my fingers were too stiff for the job.

"You first," he murmured and removed the last item of clothing from my body. I stepped beneath the spray as the warm water chased away the worst of the chill. I let it run over my hair, and in the back of my mind I wondered where my hat had gone.

Romeo was watching me when I opened my eyes. He was still dressed. "Your clothes," I said.

"I can wait."

"No," I insisted. "Now."

I watched him as he undressed. Even in my half-drunk, sorrowful, scared-out-of-my-mind condition, I appreciated the way his muscles rippled beneath his skin.

The way the water hit him and ran like streams through the deep cuts of his body made my body heat up from the inside out.

"Your turn," I said and tugged him beneath the water.

Instead of allowing me to back up, he wrapped his arms around me and we stood there together. I laid my head against his chest, listening to the sound of his erratic heartbeat.

I dug my fingers into his back, clinging to him almost desperately. If it hurt, he didn't say a word.

Slowly, he stroked my back, dragging his fingertips along my spine in a soothing motion. The atmosphere around us slowly changed. I began to feel more than just fear running through my insides.

The beat of his heart. The half-smile on his lips. The sound of his voice. It was my entire world just then.

He was life.

I was death.

I wanted more of it. More of him.

My hand slid down his ribcage and I palmed his hip. I felt his lips move against my hair, and I closed my eyes. The feel of us skin to skin was exactly what I needed.

"Romeo," I murmured. My lips brushed his skin, and I moved against him.

He groaned and slipped his fingers into my hair.

"I want you," I whispered, and moved my hand away from his hip and down toward the center of his body. I knew he wanted me too because his length was growing against me.

When I wrapped my hand around him, he made a sound low in his throat. "Now probably isn't the best time, baby," he murmured. "You're drunk and you just—"

I gave his cock a little squeeze and it jerked in my hand. "I'm pretty sure that ice bath cleared up most of my drunkenness. And the other thing… It's exactly why I need you. Right now. I want to be alive again, Romeo. I want to feel you inside me."

He didn't have to be told twice. He picked me up and I wrapped my legs around him. My core was already aching with need, and I rubbed myself against his stomach as he kissed me with such intensity it was almost like I was drowning all over again.

But this was the good kind of drowning.

One of his hands found my breast and kneaded the flesh, and I purred. "Not in here." I gasped, rocking against him. "Not in the water."

He reached around and shut off the spray immediately and stepped out of the shower. On the way into his room, he snagged a towel off the rack and wrapped it around my back. I filled my hands with his wet hair and pulled his mouth to mine.

I took the lead, kissing him with everything I had. I poured every last drop of emotion I had in me into that kiss.

My body started shaking again, my knees entirely weak. But this time it wasn't from trauma; it was from love.

"I love you," I whispered as he laid me across his bed.

"I love you," he replied and climbed between my thighs. He splayed his large palms out over my inner thighs and spread my legs wide, opening me up completely for him.

I reached up between us and took his length in my hand and stroked it lovingly. "I missed you," I confided. Usually, those were words I wouldn't have said, not in such a vulnerable moment as this. I was already giving him so much of me right now, but it wasn't enough.

I wanted him to have everything.

"Fuck, baby. You have no idea. Thank God the season is over," he rushed out as he reached over me for the drawer on his nightstand.

"No," I said, pressing a hand to his middle.

He paused and looked down, a question in his eyes.

"I've been on the pill for weeks now."

"My test results aren't back yet."

I looked him in the eye. "Romeo, are you clean?"

"Yeah, I am."

I believed him. I trusted him more than I trusted anyone.

"I want to feel all of you. Please." The rush of tears filled my eyes, and I blinked them back. My God, how much more emotional was I going to get tonight?

Romeo was going to run for the hills.

"Shh," he said and moved over me. He held his weight on his elbows so he wasn't crushing me, but I could feel his body along mine.

I sighed and stroked a hand along his jaw.

His smooth, hard tip slid against my entrance. I whimpered and bit down on my lip. Romeo's sapphire-blue eyes locked on mine and our gazes held.

Slowly, he slid inside me. Inch by delicious inch, he pushed until he was buried as far as he could go. My eyes rolled back in my head and I arched up against him.

"Hey," he whispered, his voice deep and strained. I felt his fingertips on my jaw, and he brought my head down so he could look into me once more.

He began to move within me, and I couldn't stop the moans filling the room around us. I moved with him. We rocked together until the pressure building within me threatened to consume me.

He whispered my name. It sounded more like a prayer. And he sucked my lower lip into his mouth and suckled it.

Higher and higher we went until the first brush of release griped me. I grabbed hold of his biceps and ground against him. He seemed to know exactly what I needed, and his movements quickened. He pounded into me until there was nothing else but his smooth, rock-hard cock making me quake.

The orgasm rippled through me, and I arched against him, my mouth open but no sound escaping. Oh my God, the sweet release that flowed through my body was like a jolt of electricity to a dead battery.

Just when I thought it couldn't get any better, his entire body tensed and he looked at me swiftly. He started to pull out, alarmed, but I wrapped my legs around him and pushed him deep.

Romeo's groan filled my ears as I felt him jerk inside me as he spilled his hot seed inside my body. I'd never felt anything more intimate in my entire life.

I kissed his shoulder and the inside of his neck when he partially collapsed on top of me.

I let out a sigh, content.

He pulled back and looked at me, his eyes unfocused and droopy. "I had no idea it would feel like that."

"Me either."

"Promise me you won't let anyone ever do this with you. Just me," he demanded. "Only me."

He was so possessive. He was so selfish when it came to me.

I liked it.

Maybe I shouldn't, but my God, I did.

"What about you?" I asked.

"Oh, baby, the thought of dipping my dick into anyone that isn't you does nothing for me."

"Okay." I agreed. "Only you."

• • •

His tongue stroked over mine, mingling and tasting me like he just hadn't had enough.

Loud laughter and music floated in from somewhere outside, and my body tensed slightly. It was so easy to believe we were in our own little world, even though we weren't.

"I need to go back out there." He sighed and nuzzled his face in the crook of my neck.

"I can't." Complete anxiety filled me just at the thought. Not only did I not want to face the people who watched me make an idiot of myself after some guy told everyone I was cheating on Romeo, but I wasn't prepared to look at that pool.

I shuddered at the thought.

"Hey," Romeo said, concern in his tone. "Are you still cold?" His eyes grew worried and he jumped up to move around the room.

I heard the familiar flip of the fireplace switch and seconds later the light whooshing sound of the fire lighting. I sat up and used the towel to dry the rest of my body and clean myself up.

Romeo handed me one of his T-shirts and a Nike hoodie to pull on. Next he tossed me a pair of panties out of the bag I'd left here last night, some socks, and finally the faux fur boot slippers he'd given me for Christmas.

I quickly pulled it all on went to grab my brush.

By the time I brushed out my hair, Romeo was dressed in a pair of jeans and another designer hoodie.

"I've had enough of the party," I said, hoping he wouldn't be upset.

His eyes darkened. "When I saw you fall—"

I held up my hand. I didn't need to relive it. Once was bad enough.

Romeo came forward and grabbed me by the shoulders. "What the hell were you thinking?"

I stared at him blankly.

He blew out a frustrated breath. "You got in between me and a chair, Rimmel."

"He was going to hit you," I said, grim. "I wasn't just going to stand there. I won't let him hurt you."

"I'd rather him hurt me than you." His voice was gentle. Then he smirked. "That chair wouldn't have hurt me anyway."

I shook my head. There was so much emotion swirling around inside me that it was all bunched up.

Sorting it all out into sentences seemed like it would take more effort than running a marathon.

"We'll talk later." Romeo leaned down and kissed me on the forehead. "Hang out in bed with Murphy. Get under the covers and warm up."

There was a knock on the bedroom door and Romeo stiffened. "What!" he yelled.

"I hope no one's naked, 'cause I'm coming in!" Braeden hollered. A few seconds later, the door opened and he stepped inside. One of his hands covered his eyes.

"Is it safe?" he asked.

I giggled. "Is that a no for tacos?"

Romeo shook his head and rolled his eyes. "We're dressed, man."

Braeden dropped the hand over his eyes and he zeroed in on me. It took everything in me not to shrink back from embarrassment. He came across the carpeting and held out my glasses. "Here," he said. "I figured you might need these."

Ah, that explained why everything still looked so blurry.

I slid them on and smiled as my sight adjusted back to normal. I noticed Braeden was soaking wet.

"Oh!" I exclaimed. "You have to be freezing!"

I rushed around the room, pulling out clothes and socks and tossing them at Braeden's feet. "Here! Put this stuff on."

"She's giving away your clothes, man," Braeden said to Romeo.

"Chicks." He sighed.

Braeden shook his head.

"You're dripping on the carpet!" I reminded him.

He laughed and went in the bathroom to get dressed.

"Just leave your clothes with ours. I'll wash them for you," I yelled through the door.

He laughed. "Laundry service? Damn! I'm moving in."

Romeo shook his head.

I yawned. This entire day was catching up to me. Romeo frowned. "I'll make everyone leave…" He began.

"No!" I exclaimed. "This is your victory party! Go enjoy it. I'll stay here."

He seemed torn on what to do. Braeden came out wearing Romeo's clothes (they fit him pretty well) and ran his eyes over me in concern. "You okay?"

I nodded. "Did you jump in the pool to get my glasses?"

He nodded.

"Actually, he jumped in the pool right after I did. In case I needed help towing you out." Romeo corrected.

I glanced at Braeden for confirmation. He shrugged. "What kind of brother would I be if I let you drown?"

Without thought, I walked over and wrapped my arms around him. He seemed a little taken aback by my display of affection, but after a minute, he hugged me back. "Thank you," I whispered.

"Anytime, tutor girl." His voice was soft and his arms tightened around me just slightly. For all his witty humor, sarcastic one-liners, and jokes, Braeden was a really good guy. "We need to teach you to swim." He observed.

I shuddered. "I know how to swim."

"Well, you sank to the bottom like an anchor," he grumbled.

"Must have been the alcohol," I mumbled and pulled away. I didn't want to talk about why I froze up, why I wasn't able to swim.

"Where's the trash?" Romeo asked, his voice flat and hard.

I stiffened, and Braeden patted my back. "Escorted out by several Wolves," he answered.

"Dude," Romeo said, and it sounded like a veiled threat.

Braeden glanced at me and held up his hand. "I know. It's taken care of."

"What does that mean?" I asked, nerves filling me up.

They pretended I wasn't there.

"It isn't good enough," Romeo vowed.

Braeden nodded, his eyes grim.

Romeo came to me, pressed his lips against my forehead, and then pulled away. "I have to go out there. I'll come back as soon as I can."

"You don't have to hurry," I said and gave him a smile. I so did not feel like smiling.

"Tell Ivy and Missy I'm okay."

Once he and Braeden were gone, I made myself a cup of steaming apple cider and carried it into the bedroom. Once the blankets where piled high and Murphy was snuggled up beside me, I settled against the pillows and watched the dancing flames in the fireplace.

But it wasn't the flames I saw.

All I could see was pink-tinted water.

CHAPTER EIGHTEEN

> #WinterSurvivalTip
> Don't eat yellow snow.
> #DrunkGuysPeeEverywhere
>
> ... Alpha BuzzFeed

ROMEO

As soon as the front door closed behind us, I looked at Braeden. "He's gonna pay."

Braeden nodded. "I'm with ya."

Some guy I hardly knew tried to slide around us to go in the house. I grabbed him by the shoulder. "House is off-limits."

"I gotta piss, man."

I pointed to some landscaping on the side of the yard. "There's some bushes over there."

"They're covered in snow," the guy muttered, but he didn't argue.

"What's up with her and the pool, man?" Braeden asked.

I rubbed a hand over my face. "Her mom drowned, man. She found her body floating in a pool."

Braeden swore beneath his breath. "What the fuck is up with Zach? He followed her in the bathroom on campus?"

A sound rumbled low in my chest. Trent joined the two of us and looked at me as if he wanted an answer too.

I shook my head. "He's pissed I got him arrested. Pissed I got him dethroned at Omega. But he's taking things too far. If he wants to come at me, then he should. He shouldn't take it out on Rimmel."

"She's your weak spot," Trent said. "He's using her to get to you."

"How the fuck can you stand to have that guy in your frat, man?" I accused.

Trent grimaced. "No one wants him there. I'm quietly building a case to take to the dean to get him tossed out completely. No call from his father will be able to sweep an entire folder of shitty things he's done under the rug."

"Well, you can add attacking a defenseless woman in the bathroom and trying to hit her with a chair to the list," I snapped. "Not to mention the bruises he left on her wrist the first day of classes."

"Your dad's a lawyer," Braeden said. "Have him get a restraining order on him. Keep him away from tutor girl."

I nodded. That was a good idea. Why the hell hadn't I thought of that?

"That would really force the dean's hand as far as getting rid of him at Omega," Trent added.

"Consider it done," I said. I'd talk to my dad first thing in the morning. I blew out a breath. "I'm tempted to go find him and pound him into the ground right now." I cracked my knuckles as I thought about how good it would feel to break Zach's face.

"I'd say he's already hurting from the hits you delivered," Braeden said. Then he cleared his throat. "And I might have got in a couple of my own when I tossed him off the property."

Hells yeah. I grinned.

It was for the best anyway. I needed to stay here where Rimmel was. I'd take care of Zach later. I just wasn't sure how yet.

"Let's get a beer," Braeden said. I followed him and Trent toward the keg but was intercepted by Ivy and Missy.

"Is she okay?" Ivy asked. "Where is she?"

"She's in the house. Not coming back out. She's trying to get warm."

Missy nodded gravely. "Tell her we'll call her tomorrow."

"I will."

I joined the team by the fire, and no one said a word about what happened. It was like it never even happened. The party continued and people drank and celebrated the Wolves' win.

I stayed out a little longer, more because I felt like I had to and less because I wanted to be there. Mostly, I worried about Rimmel—if she was okay inside alone, what that dunk in the pool had done to her.

The look in her eyes when I first towed her in the house scared me. It was empty, vacant… like she was shutting down. After we made love, she seemed better, more like herself. Still, I wanted to be with her. I wanted to be sure she was okay.

When I couldn't take it anymore, I slapped Braeden on the back. "I'm going in."

He nodded.

"When you want to crash, just take the couch. No driving."

"Thanks, man," he replied.

Inside, the house was warm, the fire was still burning bright, and Rimmel was barely visible in the center of my bed. As I was tossing aside my clothes, Murphy blinked his one eye open and stared at me but didn't bother moving.

I slid beneath the covers, filling the space beside Rimmel so she was sandwiched between the cat and me.

In her sleep, she shifted toward me, rolling over and tucking her cheek against my chest. I gathered her close and she sighed.

I lay there for a long time, plotting ways to make Zach suffer, before I finally allowed myself to sleep.

The next morning, I awoke to feather-light kisses trailing over my abdomen and teasing the waistband of my boxers.

Beneath the covers, Rimmel moved lower, slipping the fabric down low to allow certain already excited parts free.

Clearly, those certain parts woke up a lot faster than the rest of me.

I smiled in satisfaction as her tongue tasted my cock and licked at me like I was a giant dessert. With a low moan, my hand fished beneath the covers to tangle in her hair at the back of her head.

This was my favorite way to wake up. With Rimmel in my bed and her mouth on me. One of her hands rubbed at my inner thigh, massaging the muscles there, and I opened my legs a little more for better access. Her mouth worked me at varying speeds, sliding up and down my shaft while one of her hands held the base of my rod, keeping it exactly where she wanted it.

I groaned at the feel of her soft lips gliding over me and reveled in the way she sucked. She was entirely thorough, almost diligent. It gave me pleasure I'd never really experienced before.

I mean, really, there was no such thing as a bad blowjob.

But there was such a thing as the best fucking one ever.

And every single one of those best fucking ones ever was courtesy of Rimmel (and her mouth).

My abs started to quiver and I knew I was close. I untangled my hand from her hair to try and pull her up, thinking of burying myself deep inside her body, but she made a sound of protest and lightly dragged her teeth along the tip of my shaft.

My hand fell to my side and I shuddered.

The next thing I knew, her lips were wrapped back around me at the perfect angle, applying the perfect pressure, and a wild orgasm ripped through me.

Even while I jerked and spilled into her mouth, she continued to move. Rimmel milked my release until I fell back on the mattress, completely satiated and spent. Goddamn, she was like the fucking cock whisperer.

When at last she let go, she didn't move away or slip up my body to kiss me. Instead, she worked my boxers down my legs and pulled them free. Then she shimmied back up to my waist and used the fabric to totally clean me up, massaging me gently as she worked.

I purred like a damn cat.

When she was done, her dark head cleared the blankets and she collapsed beside me, her hair wild and uncombed. I rolled over and pinned her into the pillows. Her arms slid around me and she sighed.

I kissed her, sweeping my tongue into her mouth. The inside of her mouth was slightly salty and I knew it was from me. Most guys probably had no desire to taste themselves on their woman's lips, but not me.

I liked it.

There wasn't anything about being intimate with Rimmel that I didn't like. Besides, everyone knew how much I liked my name to be on her… Well, I liked to know there was part of me *in* her too.

"What did I do to earn that kind of wakeup, and how do I do it again?" I drawled when I pulled back from her lips.

She smiled, her eyes closed. "Just keeping my Mr. MVP happy," she murmured.

"Hey." I gently grabbed her chin so her eyes would open. They were bloodshot and a little fuzzy. "You could never do that again and I would still be happy with you."

"Is that so?" Her voice was a little raspy this morning as well.

"Yeah, but don't get any ideas."

She giggled, but it turned into a groan.

I grinned. "Someone is hungover."

She groaned again. "Make it go away."

I chuckled and jumped out of bed. I pulled on a loose pair of sweats because I wasn't sure who was out in the living room and then left the room.

I expected to see Braeden on the couch, but he wasn't there. The indent of his head was on one of the pillows and there were a couple blankets tossed at the bottom, but he was gone. I'd never known him to get up and leave so early before.

No one else was in the house, thankfully, so I went into the kitchen and grabbed a bottle of water and some pain reliever from the cabinet.

"Here," I told Rimmel back in the room. She sat up and I gave her the pills and water. She swallowed them appreciatively.

She looked a little pale, and I frowned. "Your stomach okay?"

She nodded. "I think so. Just a little queasy. Mostly I just have a headache and feel fuzzy."

"You'll be okay, babe. Drink that water." I leaned down to kiss her forehead.

Out in the other room, the front door slammed. "Coffee!" Braeden yelled.

So that was where he'd gone. "B must really like ya, Rim," I said. "He never goes and gets coffee for me."

She groaned.

I chuckled and headed toward the door. "I'll let you wallow in peace."

"Aren't you even hungover?" she yelled after me.

Out in the kitchen, Braeden laughed. "I told you she was a lightweight!"

"Nah, baby. I'm a big boy. I can handle my liquor," I teased.

Out in the kitchen, Braeden was still wearing a pair of my jeans, and the hoodie Rimmel had given him to wear was off and draped over one of the chairs. He was looking a little bleary-eyed as he sat at the table drinking what looked like a giant-sized coffee. In the center of the table was a huge box of donuts.

He pointed at the coffee and I went to lift one up. He shook his head. "That one's Rim's."

"You know her coffee order?" I asked suspiciously.

He waved away my irritation. "She's a girl. All girls like those frilly frou-frou drinks."

I grunted because he had me there.

I lifted the other coffee out of the holder and took a sip. It was black. I might not drink those frilly girl drinks, but I didn't take my coffee black either.

I reached into the fridge and pulled out some creamer and dumped some in my cup.

I held it out to Braeden and he shook his head. "I already used it."

"How bad is the mess outside?" I asked, taking a seat across from him.

He lifted the lid to the donut box and grabbed a glazed and shoved half of it in his mouth. "The usual party mess."

Rimmel appeared in the doorway of the kitchen. Her hair was a wreck, her glasses were crooked, and she wasn't wearing any pants.

"Umm, I think you forgot something," I told her.

She wrinkled her nose. "I did not forget to comb my hair. I just don't feel like it," she grumped.

Braeden laughed. "What about your pants?"

Her eyes went wide and she looked down at her bare legs. Then she shrugged. "This shirt is so long you can barely see my knees."

We both watched her as she pulled out a chair and sank into it. Her slippers were in her hands so she pulled them on, giving me a flash of panties when she lifted her leg.

I glanced at Braeden to make sure he wasn't looking, but he was busy inhaling another donut. I snagged her coffee off the counter and sat it in front of her.

She sighed in appreciation and wrapped her hands around the cup. She took a sip and glanced at Braeden. "How did you know I like mocha?"

"Because you're a girl."

"Oh," she said and went back to her coffee.

Braeden pushed the donuts toward her and she made a face. "Coffee, yes. Donuts, no. I'm still not sure if my stomach won't revolt."

I grabbed a blueberry cake donut out of the box and took a huge bite. Braeden followed my lead. Rimmel watched us and said, "I don't understand how you two stay so fit."

"Season's over," Braeden explained.

The front door opened and closed again, and I glanced up as my mother swept into the kitchen. Beside me, Rimmel stiffened and sat up a little straighter in her chair.

"Mrs. A!" Braeden said.

"Hello, Braeden," she said, glancing at him with a hint of a smile on her lips.

My mother loved Braeden. She always had, ever since we were kids.

"What's up, Mom?" I said, knowing I was going to get a lecture about how big the party was last night.

"I wanted to tell you there is no need to attempt to clean up from last night. I have a cleaning crew coming over. They should be here any minute now."

Sweet.

"You're a peach," Braeden said and kicked out the empty seat beside him. "I got you a donut."

"You know I don't eat donuts, Braeden," she said, exasperated. But there was also affection in her tone.

"It has sprinkles."

"Well, I guess since I'm here and I have coffee…" She motioned at the mug in her hand.

Rimmel's eyes about fell out of her head when my mother sat in the chair Braeden pushed out for her. He reached out and put a sprinkled donut on a napkin and slid it across the table.

Rimmel looked at me in shock.

I winked at her.

"Dad home?" I asked.

"Yes, he is."

"I need to talk to him today."

I felt Rimmel's eyes again, but this time I didn't act like I noticed. I wasn't about to tell her in front of my mother about the restraining order I wanted .

"I also came over to remind you about our dinner tonight," Mom said.

Fuck. I'd completely forgotten tonight was the night for our dinner.

"We'll celebrate your win last night." Then her eyes drifted beside me. "Do you still plan on coming, Rimmel?"

Rimmel nodded. "Yes, thank you."

"Dinner with the 'rents," Braeden cracked. "Go easy on my little sis, Mrs. A."

Mrs. Anderson glanced at Braeden. "Little sis?" She seemed surprised.

He nodded. "She's family now."

Mom turned thoughtful and set down her coffee. "So you like her?"

Rimmel stiffened, and I wanted to groan. "Mom," I warned harshly.

Braeden laughed. "Hells yeah." He glanced at me. "Rim's cool."

Mom glanced at Rimmel again, her eyes softening a little. Maybe a ringing endorsement from Braeden would help get rid of some of her attitude toward my girlfriend.

"Okay, then. I will see you two at dinner tonight." She took her mug and stood. "Braeden, you know you're always welcome anytime. We're having Italian from the place up the street."

"My fave," Braeden said. "But I can't. I got dinner with my other family."

"Well, say hello to your mother for me." Before leaving the room, she glanced at Rimmel. "Maybe comb your hair before we eat."

"Mom!" I snapped.

Rimmel looked like she wanted to climb under the table and hide. I groaned when the front door closed.

Braeden laughed and turned to Rimmel. "Don't worry, tutor girl. She only gives you that hard'a time because she knows you're the real deal."

"You think so?" she asked hopefully.

He nodded.

I hoped the hell he was right because I wasn't about to let my mother treat Rimmel like shit. Tonight's dinner could either go two ways:

1.) It could be the start of a relationship between my parents and the woman I loved.

or

2.) It could be a trip straight into hell.

CHAPTER NINETEEN

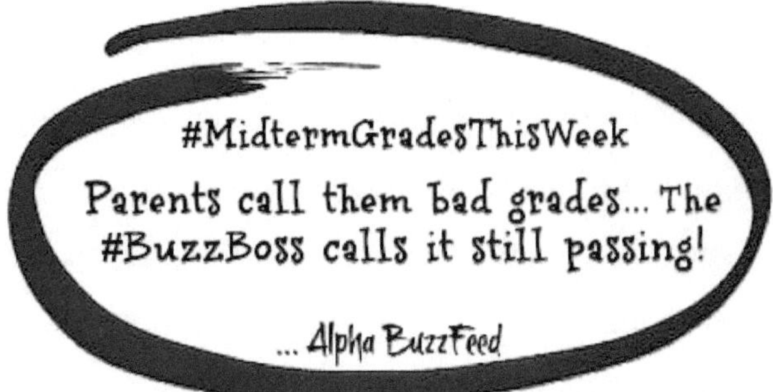

RIMMEL

After Romeo's mother saw me this morning *without any pants* and then told me to comb my hair, I knew I had to bring out the big guns.

Or rather, the *stylish* guns.

So I threw myself on the mercy of Ivy and begged her to make me look good enough to pass the dreaded mother test.

Of course she was thrilled. I was like a human Barbie to her. She basically could do me up however she wanted, and I didn't say anything because I didn't care.

After this morning's reminder of dinner tonight, I hung out with Braeden and Romeo for part of the day and chugged water, trying to flush what was left of the alcohol out of my system. Being hungover wasn't something I cared to repeat. It felt like someone was drilling into my skull with a power tool.

Once I felt marginally better, I took advantage of the fact Romeo had his own bathroom and showered there. After I blow-dried my hair, I had him drive me back to my room so Ivy could help me.

He tried to tell me I didn't need to dress up.

He clearly didn't get it.

I was like a book sitting in a high-end bookshop. A bookshop where his mother shopped. She was going to judge me by my cover. If my cover looked frumpy and out of place, then she wouldn't bother trying to read inside.

My pages were pretty damn good.

Now I needed a matching cover.

At least for tonight.

Damn if I was going to do this every single day.

Being a girl was entirely too much work.

"You are way too nervous," Ivy said, pausing as she flat-ironed my hair. I thought she was going to curl it like the night I went to my first frat party with Romeo. But she announced that tonight's look called for sleek and straight. A style that would shine and reflect the light.

"Have you met his mother?" I muttered.

Ivy laughed. "Momzilla?"

I snorted. "She makes Momzilla look like a friendly grandma."

"Don't do that at dinner," she instructed and patted me on the shoulder.

"Maybe I should just cancel."

"Are you kidding?" Ivy said as she continued to work on my hair. "You better show his mom that you aren't going anywhere."

"Oh, is that all?" I mused.

"Okay." She sighed. "I've been waiting all day. It's become clear you aren't going to say anything."

I glanced up in the mirror. "Say anything about what?"

"The fact that there are rumors all over the place about you cheating on Romeo." She paused for effect and then leaned down in my ear. "*Romeo*."

I rolled my eyes. "Yes, I'm aware of who he is."

Ivy straightened. "And then there's the little episode from last night. When Romeo pounded Zach into the ground, but then Zach got up and tried to take him out with a chair." She took a breath and kept going. "But! You got in the way and fell into the pool!"

"Wow," I said, dry. "It's a good thing you recapped all the drama in my life. I would have forgotten."

"Ugh!" Ivy said in disgust. "And yet there you sit, so… so… bored by it all."

"I'm sorry if all the upheaval in my life doesn't thrill me."

"Girl," she drawled with her sassy attitude. She held up a brush. "Don't make me beat it out of you."

"Zach's been using me to get to Romeo." It sounded so simple when I said it that way. But it was anything but. Zach was crazy. He was starting to scare me. I was beginning to wonder if maybe he had a couple screws loose in his head.

"Why does Zach hate Romeo so much?" Ivy asked.

"I don't know. It all started last semester with rush."

Ivy nodded. I'd told her about everything. The initiation, the fact that Romeo turned down a place at Omega because he refused to use me and do what Zach wanted.

"It's like he's jealous or something." I sighed.

"What happened in the bathroom?"

I groaned. "He must have followed me in there yesterday morning." Had it really only been yesterday? So much had happened since then. "He locked us in there, alone. And he hid behind the shower curtain like some creepy stalker."

Ivy mock shuddered.

"He took a picture of me in just my towel."

Ivy gasped. "He didn't!"

"Yep."

"Romeo is going to fly off the handle if that gets out."

"I didn't tell him. And it won't," I said in a way that relayed the unspoken message for her to keep her mouth shut.

"How can you be so sure?" she asked.

"I broke his phone."

"Nice!"

"But then I ran out still mostly naked, and a couple girls were at the door. They must have seen Zach come out of the bathroom."

"That would explain the Buzz notification." Ivy nodded.

"He did that hoping Romeo would find out before the game. He wanted him to play bad. He was trying to sabotage the game and Romeo's good stats." It infuriated me still.

"Not to mention now everyone thinks he's letting you cheat on him," Ivy added.

I groaned. "Like I would ever sleep with Zach." I shuddered. "Ugh. The thought of him touching me makes my skin crawl."

Ivy continued on my hair and said nothing.

"I wonder how he even got in the building." I deliberated aloud. "Where was he that he saw me go into the bathroom?"

Still, Ivy fell silent. In fact, she suddenly seemed *very* focused on my hair.

"Ivy," I said, a note of warning in my tone.

She glanced up.

"What aren't you telling me?"

"What?" She stalled. "Nothing. I'm just focused on your hair."

I snorted. "You could do my hair in your sleep, and we both know it."

Her shoulders slumped forward. "I'm so embarrassed."

I turned and looked up at her. "Why?"

"IsleptwithZach." She rushed the words out so it was one long word.

"What!" I gasped. My hand flew up to my lips. "Ew!"

"I know!" she whined and paced away from me. She flung herself on the bed. "I'm the worst friend in the history of friends!"

After I recovered from the shock (and the unfortunate mental image of Zach and Ivy in her bed together… *ewwww*), I said, "Tell me what happened."

Ivy sat up and hung her head. "We were at the pre-game party, you know, at the Omega house?"

I nodded. Romeo and I hadn't gone because of the game the next day.

"I got really drunk. Like really. I have no idea what the hell they put in that punch that night," she said, grimacing. "The next thing I knew, I was back here in the room with Zach. I don't remember much, but I do know we… *you know*."

I felt sick for her. Like physically sick. Zach basically took advantage of her inebriated state. Then on his way out the next morning, he probably saw me enter the building and decided to have a little fun, at Romeo's expense.

"I'm so sorry," Ivy said, desperate. "I swear, I never meant to sleep with him. I know how much Romeo hates him. I know he's a douche and he hurt you last semester. I never would have done that if I was sober."

"Maybe you should stop drinking so much at parties," I suggested. Who else had she slept with that she regretted?

She nodded sagely. "I am. I will. That night was a wakeup call. No more getting so drunk I can't think straight. No more casual sex. No more."

I really hoped she meant it. Not for my sake, but for her own.

"Can you forgive me?"

"For having a drunken one-night stand with a douche?" I asked. "Of course."

"But if it wasn't for me, he wouldn't have been in the building. He wouldn't have been able to corner you in the bathroom."

I sighed. "He just would have found some other way to piss Romeo off."

Ivy got up and came over to finish my hair. "He's pretty pissed, huh?"

"Pissed is an understatement," I muttered.

"What's he gonna do?"

"Hopefully nothing. Hopefully, he got it out of his system last night."

Ivy looked at me with clear doubt in her eyes. My stomach knotted. I didn't want to think about this anymore. I didn't want to think about Zach or the shitty things he'd done.

So I changed the subject. To clothes and makeup. I let her rattle on with lessons on how to make the most of my eyes and full lips. I even let her put some makeup on my face. It was the first time I'd worn makeup in almost seven years.

I didn't like the way it felt on my skin, but I didn't say anything. I also didn't tell Ivy that I had no intention of wearing makeup for another seven years.

Once my face was done, she talked me in to putting on a long-sleeved black dress with a white-and-black horizontally striped skirt that bloomed out around my hips and ended way too far above the knee. I was going to refuse to wear it until she handed me a pair of black tights to wear beneath. I slid them on (they were basically glorified pantyhose and it took me like ten minutes to get the stupid things on—and yes, I fell over while trying) and stepped into a pair of black heels that she told me I could borrow.

I wore the bracelet Romeo gave me (I never took it off) and added my mother's long gold necklace with a large cameo pendant on the end.

"Your hair should be completely cool by now," Ivy said, nodding in approval at my outfit. I sat down and she put a little shiny stuff on her fingers and worked it through the straight, long length. It felt heavy and thick down like this. It hung well into the center of my back, almost touching my waist.

After she ran her fingers through it a couple times, she sprayed it with hairspray and moved around to coat my lips with some kind of slick gloss.

When she was done, she stepped back to admire her handiwork. "Damn. I'm good."

I smiled at her. "Am I going to pass the mother test?"

"If you don't, then that woman really is a momzilla."

"I wanna see." I jumped up and moved around to the mirror.

I looked totally different. Like I had to step closer just to be sure it was me. My hair was pin straight and ultra sleek. I didn't even know it was possible for my hair to lie so perfectly. It hung down over my shoulders like a waterfall of dark water. Some of the strands in the front were a bit shorter and they seemed to frame my face and make it pop.

Or maybe that was the makeup. It was subtle and barely there, but it completely changed the way I looked.

It was like me. But so much better.

My eyes were wide and round; the hazel looked almost golden with the shadow and mascara on my eyes. My cheek's looked flushed and healthy and my lips added the perfect amount of color to the rest.

"Thank you," I said, turning from the mirror and rushing to hug Ivy.

She hugged me back but then pulled away. "Don't mess up your makeup!"

I laughed.

"That dress looks better on you than it does me."

"No way," I said. "You fill it out much better."

But even so, the dress did compliment me. The full skirt gave the illusion I had more curves than I did. It flared out from my narrow waist and my stocking-covered legs stretched out from beneath it, looking extra long because of the heels and short skirt.

"You're really not mad at me?" Ivy said and sank down on her bed.

"No."

"I swear I'll never go near him again."

"Well, that's good to hear because you deserve so much better than him."

Ivy looked like she might cry, so I changed the subject. "What are you doing tonight?"

"Studying." She made a face. "I have a lot of reading to catch up on."

There was knock on the door and I knew it was Romeo. Butterflies took flight in my stomach as I went to answer. I was so nervous about tonight.

Romeo's eyes widened when I pulled back the door. He whistled beneath his breath. "Holy shit, Smalls."

"Do I look okay?" I worried. "Think your mother will approve?"

Romeo reached out and grabbed me by the waist. "You don't have to impress her. I don't want or need her approval. You're my girl. The end."

"No take backs?" I whispered.

He smiled. "No take backs."

I turned back to Ivy. "I might not be back 'til morning. You gonna be okay?"

"Yep. Just me and my biology book."

"Text me if you need anything." I grabbed my coat off the bed.

"Thanks," she said sincerely.

I smiled. "And thanks for making me look presentable."

"You look hot," Romeo corrected loudly.

A couple girls who were walking by the room giggled.

Ivy waved me away, and I shut the door behind us. Romeo dropped his arm across my shoulders as we exited the building.

My hair floated out around me with the evening breeze, and Romeo caught a strand of it before he opened the door to the car. "You really do look beautiful," he murmured, dipping his head low.

"Thanks," I said against his lips.

His kiss ignited instant desire inside me. Even though I spent last night with him, and the night before, I missed him terribly. I felt like we hadn't had enough alone time. I wanted more. I wanted so much more.

He groaned and pulled back. "Let's get this dinner over with," he said grumpily. "I want to spend some time alone with you."

"You read my mind."

"Now that the season is over, we'll have more time together."

"Want to just go to Taco Bell and hide at your place?" I asked when he slid into the driver's seat.

He laughed. The sound filled the interior of the car. "Why, Rimmel,"—he pressed a hand to his chest like he was scandalized—"are you suggesting we stand up my mother?"

I giggled.

"I knew it," he drawled. "Underneath that sweet exterior lies the heart of a baddie baddie."

I laughed out loud. "A baddie baddie?"

"Like totally," he said in a valley girl voice and pretended to flip the long hair he didn't have.

God, I loved him.

• • •

"So what do you say?" I taunted as I smiled. "Want to play hookie?"

He groaned. "I'd love to, baby, but we can't."

I stuck out my tongue.

"Watch what you do with that thing, baby girl."

"Yeah? Or what?" I challenged.

"Or we might be late and I might mess up the perfect hair and makeup you got going on." His eyes twinkled and he fake gasped as he put the car in gear. "Just what would mother say?"

As we got closer to his place, my lighthearted mood began to slip away. The headache I fought so gallantly this morning threatened to reappear.

I worried my "cover" wasn't going to be good enough. I worried that whatever I did tonight, no matter how good, wouldn't be enough.

I had a feeling she'd already formed her opinion of me and she wouldn't be swayed.

If that were the case, it didn't matter how I styled my hair or what I wore.

I would never get the approval of Romeo's mother.

CHAPTER TWENTY

ROMEO

My protective instincts were roaring again.

I took a deep breath and told myself to get control.

She was so nervous sitting there in the passenger seat of the Hellcat, twisting her hands in her lap and bouncing her leg. The thought that a dinner with my parents made her like this pissed me off. I shouldn't have to protect her from my mother. I shouldn't have to protect her from rich douchebags who stalk women in private bathrooms and spread rumors around about their honor.

When I thought of all this shit and drama I brought into her life, it twisted my guts. I was surprised she even wanted to still be with me. I was surprised she wasn't running as far away as she could get.

Just the thought of it made me crazy.

I loved her so damn much. More than I ever thought I could love anyone.

I was going to protect her from that. From anyone and anything who even hinted at trying to destroy it.

I reached across the seat and threaded my fingers through hers. She looked at me and smiled. I'd never seen her hair so straight or smooth before. Usually, it was all wild and unruly. I loved it, though, but I loved this too. It was like I peeled back a layer of her I hadn't known existed.

I couldn't wait to see what layer I would uncover next.

When I parked in the driveway, she fidgeted with her glasses. Rimmel adjusted them on her nose and ran her fingers through the length of her hair.

"If this dinner sucks, we'll leave and go to Taco Bell."

She laughed. "Promise?"

"Hey," I murmured and tucked a silky strand of hair behind her ear. "They're gonna love you. There's no way they won't."

She nodded.

The inside of my parents' house was quiet and warm. Soft jazz music and their low voices floated from the direction of the kitchen, and before we followed it, I took her coat and hung it by the door.

I looked underdressed beside her, in a pair of jeans and a long-sleeved waffle-knit tee.

"Roman," my mom called. "Is that you?"

"No. It's Santa Claus," I called back.

Rimmel didn't even crack a smile. I took her hand and she squeezed it in a death grip. We walked toward the kitchen together, and I could feel her taking in the cool-toned walls, rich furnishings, and all the details of this house that I probably never noticed. It made me curious about where she grew up, what her home looked like.

My mother was standing at the island and my father was pouring them each a glass of wine. They both looked up when we walked in, and my mother's eyes went right to Rimmel. They widened a little as she took in Rim's appearance, and I smiled.

My father was much less obvious in his inspection. In fact, if I didn't know him, I would think he barely glanced at her before turning to me.

But I knew better.

Anthony Anderson gave the appearance of seeing nothing, when in reality, he noticed everything.

"Roman," my father said, abandoning the wine and coming forward. "And this must be Rimmel."

He stopped in front of us and held out his hand. Rimmel took it immediately and gave it a good shake. "I can certainly see why Roman is so taken with you," Dad said. "You're quite the beauty."

Rimmel smiled. "Thank you, sir. You have a lovely home."

"None of that sir business!" Dad said and smiled. His blue eyes twinkled. "You can call me Tony."

Tony. I lifted an eyebrow at him in question. He merely winked at me. He never told anyone to call him Tony. My mother didn't even call him that.

At my side, Rimmel relaxed and a genuine smile replaced the polite one.

"You're not some lame vegetarian, are you?" my dad asked her.

She laughed. "What if I was?"

He huffed. "Then I'd have to tell you to go back to calling me sir."

"Good thing I'm not a lame vegetarian, then."

Dad chuckled and I grinned. He was pulling out all the Anderson charm tonight. I glanced at Mom and wondered if he was going overboard to maybe make up for whatever my mother was going to say.

"Roman tells us you're studying to be a veterinarian." Dad continued. "That takes almost as much school as being a lawyer." He held out his arm to her. "Come over here and tell me about the program."

Rimmel slid her hand in the crook of his elbow and they went over to the island where she went into full detail about her chosen career path. The passion and love she had for animals was so evident that my chest swelled with pride.

My mother listened quietly, sipping her wine. She studied Rimmel like she was some painting in a museum. It was like she was looking at her from every angle, gauging her depth and hidden meaning.

When I'd had enough, I caught her eye and shook my head imperceptibly.

"Are we ready to eat?" she said, actually listening to me.

"Is there anything I can do to help?" Rimmel asked politely.

"No. It's all already in the dining room."

Dad commandeered Rimmel once more and guided her into the dining room. He was talking animatedly about some case he was working on, and Rimmel listened aptly.

"Well," Mom said when we were alone, "she seems to have won over your father."

"Maybe you should give her a chance," I said.

"Perhaps," she allowed.

This was a big house and my parents were very comfortable in their finances, but the house wasn't austere. It didn't have that untouchable quality that made people nervous when they were standing inside.

The dining room was basically a large square with windows on one side. They looked out over the landscaping and then on to the pool. The floors were dark hardwood and in the center was a large area rug in varying shades of green. Sitting on top of the rug was an oak table that sat ten. Instead of chairs, on the one side there was an upholstered bench in a light-colored fabric. The two end chairs were high-backed and tufted in dark, mossy-green velvet. On the other side of the table were more chairs, but these were simple and in the same fabric as the bench.

There were platters filled with several dishes already on the table. All of them were in classy-looking serving dishes that Mom removed the lids from as we all sat down. Salads were already placed at our seats, and each of us had a glass of water. In addition to the four different Italian dishes to choose from, there was garlic bread and a platter of stuffed mushrooms, which I snagged and popped one into my mouth.

Dad took a seat at the head of the table and I slid across the bench and patted the seat next to me for Rimmel. Mom sat across from us in one of the other chairs.

The conversation was pretty light. Dad and I talked about the game most of the time and about how epically I played. I told my parents about my brief meeting with the NFL scout, and Dad launched into a detailed plan to get the man on the phone and get some kind of offer drafted up. Mom behaved herself, and the more time that passed, Rimmel relaxed and was able to be more like herself.

"So, Rimmel…" Mom began, turning all her attention on Rim. "Tell us about your father. What does he do?"

I prayed this wasn't the beginning of a freaking inquisition.

Rimmel set down her glass of water and replied. "He works in construction. He's been doing it my whole life. It keeps him busy."

Dad nodded. "I'm sure with the weather in Florida, he's always busy. Without all the snow, construction season is probably every season."

Rimmel smiled at him and nodded. "Yeah, pretty much. He even worked over the winter break when I was home."

I glanced at her. She never mentioned that. I was under the impression that he took off to spend time with her. It made me wonder how much time she spent alone. The thought of her sitting around alone during the holidays wasn't an image I wanted sticking in my brain.

"That must have been lonely," my mother said, almost as if she could read my thoughts. I glanced at her, but she wasn't even looking at me. She was looking at Rim, her eyes soft.

"Oh, no," she said quickly. "It wasn't. I spent a lot of time with my grandmother."

"You're close with her, then?" Mom asked casually.

I finished what was on my plate and sat back, making sure to tuck my arm around Rimmel's waist. I hoped it sent a silent message to Mom that I wasn't going to put up with the questioning.

"Oh, yes," Rimmel answered. There was clear affection in her tone. "Her and my grandpa. After my mother died…" As soon as the words left her mouth, she slammed her lips closed and her eyes widened. I felt her shock in the stiffness of her body. Her surprise at how she just brought that up in conversation. It wasn't something she liked to talk about with anyone.

She cleared her throat and said, "I'm sorry, I—"

I tightened my arm around her. "They know, Rim. I told them your mom passed away when you were eleven."

Her body relaxed a little. "Oh." She smiled up at my mother. "Well then, I guess that didn't catch you off guard."

"Not like it did you," my mother replied.

My eyes narrowed.

Rimmel didn't bat an eye. She chuckled. "Yes. Well, my mother's death isn't something I bring up in casual conversation. Especially not with people…" She paused and then said, "With people I don't know very well."

"It's quite all right, my dear," Dad said, understanding in his tone.

Rimmel smiled at him. "I guess that just means I'm comfortable around your family and feel I can tell you about myself without any kind of judgment."

Her eyes swung to my mother and didn't waiver.

Point for my girl.

I picked up my water and drank some, not wanting Mom to see the smirk on my face.

"Of course not," my mother replied smoothly.

Rimmel continued like she hadn't missed a beat. "Anyway, after my mother passed, I spent a lot of time with my grandparents."

"Romeo tells us you have a scholarship to Alpha U," Dad said, changing the subject.

She nodded. "Yes. Why else would I move here from the warm Florida climate to freeze in the snow?"

Dad laughed heartily and his blue eyes twinkled.

Rimmel gazed up at me and smiled. "I see where you get the blue eyes."

I wanted to grab her and kiss the shit out of her. I didn't think my mother would agree that was good dinnertime behavior. So I settled for giving her a lopsided smile.

"Who wants cheesecake?" Mom asked, getting up from the table. She glanced at Rimmel with a little bit of haughtiness in her stare. "Cheesecake is Romeo's favorite."

Seriously? She was trying to one-up my girlfriend by proving she knew what dessert I liked best?

"Well, I can understand why," Rimmel said and smiled. "Can I give you a hand?"

The look in Mom's eyes cleared. "No, thank you. I'll just get it and be right back."

I squeezed her hip. I didn't know why I'd been nervous. Rimmel could handle my mother all by herself.

While she was in the kitchen, Dad turned the subject again. "That was some party last night," he said.

I grimaced. "I hope it didn't keep you and Mom up all night."

He waved away my words. "Nonsense. I can sleep like the dead. We used to have parties like that every weekend when I was in Omega."

The mention of Omega made me think of Zach. The muscles in the back of my neck tightened. "Speaking of… There's something I need to talk to you about."

Rimmel gazed at me with a question in her eyes, but I pretended not to see. I hadn't spoken to her about this yet. But it didn't matter. She didn't have a choice.

Mom reappeared carrying a huge round cheesecake with chocolate ribbons on top. She set it down beside my father and began cutting thick slices and transferring them onto plates. When she handed me my piece, I set it down and ignored it.

Dad sensed whatever I wanted to say was serious, so he gave me his full attention.

"I need you to take out a restraining order on someone."

My mother gasped and Rimmel shot straight up on the bench. "A restraining order!" Mom exclaimed. "What on earth do you need one of those for?"

"It's not for me," I said. "It's for Rimmel."

Rimmel groaned beside me. "That isn't necessary."

"Yes. It is."

Dad stared at me without displaying much of a reaction. "You know," he said and took a bite of his dessert, "I can't get a restraining order unless the person filing the complaint has been physically threatened or harmed in some way."

"I'm well aware of that, Dad."

He glanced at Rimmel. "Has someone harmed you?"

"It really isn't that big of a deal. I don't think a restraining order is necessary." Her hand went under the table and landed on my thigh and squeezed.

I knew she wanted me to take it back, but I wasn't going to. This was about her safety.

"Who is this person?" Mom demanded.

I sighed. They weren't going to like this. "It's Zach."

"Richard Bettinger's son?" Dad asked, surprise in his tone.

"Yeah."

"You know Richard is a colleague of mine," he said, his doubt clear.

"I'm on a couple charities with his mother," my mom added.

"Yeah, well, he's a complete douche," I said, flat.

"Roman!" My mother gasped.

I turned away from her completely. "I can't prove it, but last semester, he attacked her in the haunted house. He physically pinned her to the floor."

My dad started shaking his head like it wasn't enough, but I was relentless. "More recently, he's put bruises on her. On her wrist and arm. He grabbed her and was jerking her around even after she told him to stop."

Dad frowned, and I knew I had Mom's attention.

"Someone on the team was a witness to this." I glanced at Rimmel, knowing she was going to be pissed. "I have photos of the bruises."

"What!" she exclaimed.

"I took them while you were sleeping."

"You've got to be kidding me." Her voice was low and even.

"Then just yesterday, he followed her into the girls' bathroom at her dorm. He locked himself in there and hid while she was taking a shower." I had to pause to drag in a breath and control the anger inside me. "When she got out, he attacked her."

My mother gasped and Rimmel hurried to tell her, "Not like that. He didn't touch me."

"When she went running out of the bathroom in nothing but a towel, he used the little scene he set up to make everyone think she was cheating on me. He wanted to mess with my head before the game."

"And last night?" Dad said. "When someone fell in the pool."

"Yeah, that was him too. He had the nerve to show his face here last night. So I decked him. He deserved it. Then I told him to get the hell off the property."

"Did he?" Dad questioned, sensing there was more to the story.

"He came after me with a chair."

"He did what!" Mom demanded.

I ground my teeth together. "Yeah. But Rimmel got in the way. She ended up in the damn pool. In the freezing water."

"Why would you get in the way?" Mom asked, clear confusion in her voice.

"I wasn't going to stand there and watch Zach attack Romeo when he wasn't even looking. He could have been hurt," Rimmel replied. The indignation in her tone had me hiding another smile.

"You stepped in the middle of two grown men fighting to protect my son?" Mom's eyes were wide as she stared at Rim.

"Of course," Rimmel said without pause.

"You need to get a cover on that pool, Dad," I ground out. "She could have drowned."

Once again, my mother gasped. I glanced at her and knew she was realizing what a plunge into the pool probably did to Rimmel. After all, thanks to the PI, she knew how her mother died.

"Of course. I'll call tomorrow," Dad said. His lips turned down as he digested all that information. "Why would Zach do all this?"

"He hates me. He's jealous. He blames me for losing his presidency at Omega. He's the reason I dropped out of rush last semester."

Realization dawned in my father's eyes. He had been disappointed when I told him I'd changed my mind about Omega. I never told him why, though.

"This has been going on for a while, then."

"Yes. And now he's starting in on Rimmel. I won't have it."

Rimmel made a frustrated sound. "You are not my babysitter. You can't just announce that I'm getting a restraining order and expect me to go along with you. You didn't even talk to me about this."

"It's the best thing," I told her.

"Says who?" she shot out, her voice rising. "You do not get to tell me what to do, Roman Anderson."

"He shoved you in the pool," I growled.

"I fell."

"Because he was going to hit you with a goddamned chair!"

"Don't you talk to me like that." She matched my tone. The stubborn glint in her eye frustrated me.

"If I hadn't jumped in that pool after you, you would have drowned," I said, harsh, trying to make her understand how serious this was.

Too late I realized what I'd said.

Her face paled like I'd thrown ice water on her.

"Roman," my mother said quietly, admonishment in her tone.

Rimmel's eyes widened and she looked between my parents like she'd forgotten where we were. Her cheeks turned red and she lifted the napkin off her lap and laid it beside her plate. "I'm terribly sorry," she apologized. "You shouldn't have had to see that. I'll just go."

"Rimmel." I grabbed her arm, but she pulled away from me and stood.

Fuck.

"I'll wait for you outside so you can drive me back to campus." She put some distance between us. A few steps, a couple feet.

It felt like one hundred miles.

"Thank you so much for the lovely dinner," she said politely. "It was nice to meet you."

She started for the door, and I shoved away from the table.

"Rimmel," my mother said without getting up.

I could have called for her a thousand times and I would have been ignored.

But my mother wasn't someone to be ignored.

Rimmel stopped and turned.

"Would you mind helping me in the kitchen before you go?"

I knew she didn't want to. She didn't even look at me once. It felt like someone kicked me in the nads.

"Of course," she replied politely. She was too nice to say no.

There was a heavy and awkward silence as they gathered up the plates they could carry and then went into the kitchen.

I was tempted to go after her, but in the end, I decided maybe it was better if I let us both cool off first.

I glanced at my father. "I want that restraining order."

He nodded. "She has a case. I'm fairly certain I can have one put in place. Text me the pictures you took."

I nodded. "Do it."

"Sounds like she doesn't want one."

"She needs it." I shoved a hand through my hair. "He put his hands on her, Dad. Bruises. Do you see how small she is? How fragile?"

Dad smiled. "She didn't seem so fragile a minute ago."

I grunted, then cracked a smile. "She's pretty pissed."

"Son," he mused, "let me give you a little advice."

I nodded.

"Women don't like to be told what to do. They like to be the ones telling us what to do. You want her to do something, you're gonna have to go about it a different way."

"Is that why Mom has so much jewelry?" I wondered.

He laughed. "Partly." Then he paused. "But she doesn't strike me as the jewelry type."

"She isn't." But she did like honesty. I'd probably rather buy her a diamond than tell her what it was like for me knowing that he'd been lurking in that bathroom with her.

"I'll get the paperwork in place. She's going to need to sign it."

"She will." I didn't care what it took.

Dad shook his head and sighed. "Richard's going to be livid."

"Zach's got some screws loose. He's pissed at me and using my only weakness to get revenge."

"What's he need revenge for?"

I sighed. "I might be partly responsible for getting him dethroned at Omega."

"I know you want to protect your girlfriend, son, but you can't be getting involved in those kinds of situations. You need to keep yourself clean. Your future in the NFL depends on it."

I nodded like I agreed. And I guess I did. But there was no way in hell I was going to stand by and let Rimmel get hurt. "That's why we need that restraining order."

"Consider it done," he said, getting up from the table.

"Thanks, Dad."

"Don't thank me yet," he said. "She still has to sign it."

Before leaving the room, Dad turned to me. "I like her, son. And despite how your mother acts, she likes her too. Now you better go do some groveling, because she's a keeper."

I glanced toward the kitchen where Rimmel had gone. She was upset with me. And she had a reason to be. I wondered what it was going to take to set things right.

CHAPTER TWENTY-ONE

> #FYI
> Everyone wants to know who the
> #BuzzBoss is. I'm not telling.
> #Mystery #SecretIdentity
>
> ... Alpha BuzzFeed

RIMMEL

Oh no, he didn't.

(But yes. In fact, *he did*).

Of all the nerve.

I loved Romeo. More than anything.

But sometimes when he opened his mouth, pure stupidity fell out.

I don't know what possessed him to up and announce at dinner that I was getting a restraining order. Then he went as far as to tell his father to draw up the papers.

I was not a puppet on a string.

I admit I was timid and sometimes awkward, but I wouldn't be controlled.

It wasn't even so much that I hated the idea of the restraining order. I actually thought it might be a good idea. Zach *was* scaring me. And after last night…

I closed my eyes against the memories that assaulted me when I plunged into the frigid water.

But I wouldn't be bossed.

And then when I told him that, he yelled at me! And expected me to take it.

And then.

And then…

He brought up my mother. He practically threw it in my face that I froze when I hit the water and he had to come in to save me.

I wanted to leave. I wanted to go home and seethe in anger. I would have.

But she stopped me.

Of all the times his mother decides she wants to have a conversation with me, it was that moment. Hell.

She probably wanted to give me the third degree about yelling at her son.

Well, bring it on, lady. I was in a piss poor mood and I'd yell at her too.

Okay. I probably wouldn't.

I set the plates filling my hands on the large beautiful island and turned to go back for more.

"Wait," she said. "I wanted to speak to you."

I knew it was coming so I just nodded.

"I apologize."

That wasn't what I was expecting to hear. In fact, I was convinced I heard wrong.

She must have realized by the expression on my face that I was confused, because she smiled. "I haven't been very welcoming to you, and for that I am sorry."

"It's okay," I said carefully. "You were just worried about Romeo."

"Yes. I was." Her brown eyes were sincere. "But I should have been nicer."

I stood there awkwardly, not really knowing what to say. Just moments ago, I'd been mad as hell, but now I was speechless. "I don't understand why," I blurted out. "Why did you suddenly change your mind?"

"Last night at the game."

"The game," I echoed, not understanding.

"You were going to jump onto the field because you thought he was hurt."

Why was that such a big deal to everyone? I mean, sheesh. I probably would have fallen down and hurt myself the second I jumped. Then I would have been carted away like a criminal.

"You didn't think. You acted. Just like tonight."

I was so embarrassed. "I apologize for yelling. He just caught me off guard."

She smiled. "He's like his father that way. Decides what he wants and that's that."

"Oh, I don't know. I think he might have gotten that from you." Actually, I didn't think that. I knew it.

"I saw the same thing again just a few minutes ago. You reacted. You didn't even think and you didn't take his crap." The fondness in her eyes for her son was unmistakable. "Only a girl who is truly in love would react so quickly without thought to her actions."

Again, I was embarrassed.

She might as well ask me if I was raised by wolves.

I started to apologize once more, but she held up her hand. "And the fact that you got in between my son and a chair, well, that speaks volumes."

I shrugged. "I love him. I don't want to see him hurt."

"You know," she said, stepping around the island and placing some dishes in the sink as she talked, "the doctors told me I'd never have children. We tried for years to get pregnant and it never happened. I went to four doctors and every single one of them told me the same thing. I'd never be able to have a child of my own."

"That must have been very difficult," I said. Even though that was over twenty years ago, I could still hear the anguish in her tone.

"I was devastated. I knew Anthony was too, he just never said it out loud. But then I got pregnant. We were all shocked. It was a miracle." Her voice was hushed, like she was recalling something sacred. "I was on bed rest the whole pregnancy. The doctors didn't think I'd even be able to carry a baby to term. But I was determined. I did everything humanly possible to bring that boy into the world."

I moved over and sank down on a barstool, completely enthralled in the tale of how Romeo came to be.

"I knew he was going to be special. From the second I was pregnant, I knew he was going to be. Even before he was born, he was strong. He was a fighter."

I smiled because Romeo definitely was all those things.

"I devoted myself to him, my little miracle baby. How I enjoyed those days when he was small. They go by so quickly," she mused, then blinked, seeming to come back into the present. "What I'm trying to say is that when you spend years trying to live with the fact you will never have a child of your own, but then by some miracle you're given one, the perfect one, a mother will do anything to protect them."

I nodded my understanding.

"It's hard to let go, to stand back and watch them live while you hold your breath and pray to God you did a good enough job raising them."

"You did," I whispered.

She smiled. "It's no excuse for my behavior, but it's the truth."

"You know…" I said, deciding right then that I was going to be honest, just the way she was. I wasn't just going to nod my head. I was going to really talk to her, even if it made me uncomfortable.

Especially after everything she'd just said.

Someone who loved Romeo—her son—that much deserved it.

"I never asked you to let go. Maybe just loosen your grip a little."

Valerie laughed.

"I think Romeo is lucky to have a mother like you. I wish my mother was still here, and I'd like to think if she was, she'd give Romeo the third degree just like you've given me."

"I don't know," his mother mused. "He's very charming."

"Well, there is that," I allowed.

She turned back to the dishes.

"I'm not going to take him away." My softly spoken statement had her pausing at the sink. "I wouldn't even try. A mother holds a special place in a child's heart that no one else can fill. Even after they're all grown up."

"I'm beginning to like you," she said without turning around.

I grinned at her back. "Well, Braeden did give me his stamp of approval."

"That boy." She chuckled. "He's just as charming as Roman."

"He's definitely a ladies' man." I agreed.

"He just hasn't met the right girl yet. He will. He'll find someone, just like Roman has found you. And then everything will change."

Was she saying she thought I was the girl that changed everything for Romeo? And if she was, was that acceptance in her tone? Was I winning her over?

Of course, the happiness I felt at that was dampened by the fact that I was so angry with Romeo right now.

"Now, about this situation with Zach," Valerie said. She turned to face me and a frown pulled at her perfectly made-up face. She really was a beautiful woman, the kind of beauty that was ageless.

"With all due respect, it's really not your business."

"It is my business. It concerns my son." She pinned me with a look. "It concerns you."

"I really don't think a restraining order is necessary."

"I think you know one would be sensible. I just think you're mad at Roman." I started to disagree and she held up her hand. "You have every right to be upset with him. He should have spoken to you about this and not just ordered you do it."

My stomach flipped thinking about the argument we'd just had. We'd never really argued before, over anything. He was probably really angry that I'd yelled at him in front of his parents.

"I'm going to give you my advice. You can do with it what you want," Valerie said.

I nodded.

"Get the order. If not for your own piece of mind, for Roman's. He doesn't get worked up very often, and he's worked up about this. He's only trying to protect you. You make an easy target because it's so clear how my son feels about you; it's written all over his face. Perhaps if you do this, it will send a clear message to Zach and he will back off."

She was right and I knew it. But I was still beyond mad. I mean, he took photos of me without my knowledge. That was taking my trust a little too far.

Romeo appeared in the doorway of the kitchen, his hands tucked into the front pockets of his jeans. "Is it safe to come in?"

"Of course," Valerie replied.

I avoided looking at him. When he stepped farther into the room, the tension in the air became noticeably thicker.

"Why don't you two go?" Valerie said. "I'll take care of the dishes."

"Oh no. I said I would help." I argued.

"And I appreciate the offer, but it's not necessary."

"Come on, Rim. We should talk." Romeo put a hand on my arm, and I stiffened. He pulled back immediately, but the action caused a prick of regret in my chest.

"Thank you again, for dinner," I said.

"Maybe next time we can get through dessert without a yelling match."

I grimaced, but she just laughed.

"See ya later, Mom. Thanks for the chow." Romeo moved forward and kissed her on the cheek, and she smiled.

I followed him back through the house and toward the door. I didn't see his father anywhere. Before going outside, I pulled on my coat and zipped it all the way up. Outside was freezing, and my breath puffed out around me in a great white cloud.

I headed in the direction of his car, figuring he was going to drive me back to campus.

"Where do you think you're going?" he said from behind.

I looked over my shoulder. He was standing there looking adorably kissable with a sheepish look in his eyes.

"Back to the dorm?" I said.

He shook his head and the look on his face was replaced with something much more intense. My blood heated despite the chill in the air, and I swallowed down my immediate desire as he prowled toward me.

"Oh no, you aren't." He took my hand and tugged me gently toward his house. "You aren't going anywhere."

CHAPTER TWENTY-TWO

ROMEO

The distance between us was getting wider.

She thought I would just drive her back to campus, that I would just let her walk away mad.

Hell to the no.

I still remembered the night she got out of the Hellcat and walked away from me. The night I had to tell her getting close to her had only been a bet. The hurt in her eyes still cut me to the core.

I didn't want a repeat of that night. Not ever again.

Zach had been the cause of that night, and he was pretty much the cause of the space between us now.

He was a hater. Plain and simple.

I couldn't. I *wouldn't* let the hate he spewed so willingly overshadow everything I had with Rimmel. I agreed with my dad.

She was a keeper.

Her hand was stiff as I pulled her along toward my place, but she still allowed me to lead her. When we got close to the pool, she moved closer to my side, and I angled my body in front of her to block the sight.

Once inside, we didn't speak. She took off her heels and coat, and I went to turn on the fire in the bedroom. When I came back, she was crouched down in the living room, petting Murphy, who was zigzagging around her feet.

"You took pictures of me when I was sleeping." Her voice was calm and quiet, but it filled the room.

"Yeah, I did." I wasn't going to apologize for that. Deep down, I must have known things might come to this. I was a lawyer's son after all. I knew things needed to be documented.

"You could have just asked." She straightened up from Murphy and looked at me. "Instead, you took advantage of me and never said a word."

"I didn't take advantage of you. I was just doing what I thought was best."

"Well, you don't get to decide what's best for me!" Her voice rose, and Murphy paused in purring to look up at her.

"I don't get a say?" I shot back, trying to hold on to my temper.

She took a deep breath. "Of course you do. But you didn't *say* anything. You just did. Just like at dinner. You just announced I was getting a restraining order. There was no conversation."

I opened my mouth, but she kept talking.

"How am I supposed to trust you when you do things like this without me knowing?"

"You don't trust me anymore?" I said the words with quiet calm. Surely this wasn't enough to ruin the trust between us.

She blew out a breath and paced across the room. "I didn't say that." She spun away from me and looked at the wall. "I'm just upset."

I strode across the room. It was darker where she was. The lights were off in here, and from this position in the room, the crackling fire in the bedroom didn't cast much light.

My feet stopped when I was directly behind her. Usually, I would touch her without thought. But right then I paused.

Fuck. That.

I wrapped my hands around her wrists, then loosened my grip to slide my palms up her arms to rest at her shoulders. I felt her exhale, and I wrapped one of my arms across her chest and pulled her back against my front.

"I could tell you I'm sorry," I whispered in her ear. "I could whisper how much I love you and that I won't ever do something like this again."

The back of her head hit my chest as I spoke. The silky strands of her perfectly straight hair tickled my lips as I talked, and the scent of her shampoo enticed me closer.

"But I'm not going to apologize."

She stiffened, but I strengthened my hold, unwilling to let her pull away. I kept my voice whisper soft and my lips right beside her ear.

"I'd do it again, in a friggin' heartbeat if that's what I thought you needed."

The frustration in her body was evident, but I ignored it.

"Do you know how much I love you?" I whispered. "I love you so goddamned much that it scares the shit out of me. You have no idea the kind of power you wield, how much of me you own. Knowing you were completely vulnerable, that you were locked unknowingly in a bathroom with someone who literally lurked around while you were naked, while you were washing yourself, makes me sick. He could have raped you." My voice broke on the last part because I had to force the words out of my mouth.

"He didn't," she said quickly and tried to turn to face me.

I wouldn't let her. I liked her where she was. It was easier to bare my heart when she wasn't staring into me with her eyes.

"No, he didn't. But he's put bruises on you. The way you looked in that pool last night. The way your body just kind of stopped. You sank to the bottom with a dark cloud of hair obscuring your face. I knew you had to be reliving what happened. It broke me, Rim. Loving me has cost you so fucking much. Too much."

This time, she wouldn't let me hold her. She spun around and tipped her chin up to look at me. I let her see. I let her see the bleakness in my eyes.

"Loving you has *given* me way more than I imagined." She reached up and brushed the backs of her knuckles across my cheek. I dragged my fingers through her hair.

"It scares me too," Rimmel whispered. "How much I love you."

"I'm going to protect you. I'm going to protect us," I said. "I won't ever stop."

"Next time, talk to me. Nine times out of ten, I'll probably do what you ask just because you ask me to. I know you want to shield me, but I can't be *beside* you if you're always pushing me *behind* you."

"Deal."

Rimmel leaned forward to kiss me, but I lifted my lips, denying her. Her eyes narrowed, and I smiled. "One more thing."

"What?" she asked suspiciously.

"Do not get in between me and a chair. Me and *any* fight ever again."

"We'll see," she replied noncommittally.

I growled my displeasure, but she only smiled.

"Kiss me, Romeo."

I pushed my face down to hers. Our lips melded together like they were one and the same. To me, her lips felt like velvet, the softest touch I'd ever known.

I hunched around her, wanting closer, gathering her against me until there wasn't even enough space for air between our bodies. My tongue slipped into her mouth and licked against hers, the slightly rough texture a direct contrast to the softness of the rest of her.

I groaned, but the sound echoed into her mouth.

My face bumped against her glasses, and I pulled them off quickly and tossed them onto the couch.

Her hands began to wander over my body and slipped beneath the hem of my shirt. Her touch was light as it danced across my abs and up over my chest.

When her hands brushed the dog tag lying against my chest, she retreated to push my shirt up to reveal the expanse of my stomach and part of my chest.

Her lips were warm and moist as she pressed them against my skin and then slipped over to press a kiss against the metal of the necklace.

"Baby," I murmured and grabbed a handful of hair at the back of her neck. Gently, I tilted up her head and her eyes fluttered open to look at me. "I'm not sorry for what I did. But I am sorry if it hurt you."

"I love you," she whispered.

The words pierced my soul.

We walked through the dark house, nothing but two shadows in the night, until we stepped into the bedroom and our bodies were cast in the orange glow of the firelight.

I brought her around to kiss her again. This time it was lazy and slow as I backed her up toward the bed. As we moved, she unbuttoned my jeans and then shoved her hands down the waistband, reaching into the back of my boxers, and cupped my ass.

My cock was already throbbing, already jealous that she was touching the rest of me. I pulled back so I could quickly rip off my clothes, and when I looked back, I noted she was doing the same.

When she was standing in front of me in nothing but a pair of black panties and a black lacy bra, I sank down on my knees before her. Her nipples were erect beneath the cups of her bra, and I wrapped my lips around them, moistening the fabric and using my tongue to rub against it, creating friction against her already sensitized skin.

Her hands delved into my hair, fisting in the thickness, and her back arched. I lavished attention on both her breasts until the fabric was wet and she was panting. Her hips twisted around like they were searching for something, and I smiled.

I kissed down her flat stomach and then buried my face in the center of her panties.

Rimmel's groan filled the bedroom, and I felt like a superhero. The fabric between us was too much so I pulled it down her legs and she kicked it away.

Her body swayed on her feet when I licked up her center with one long stroke. My hands wrapped around her narrow hips and pushed her back so she would sit on the bed. I stood to lift her farther back, but she grabbed hold of my jutting cock and slid her mouth down over it.

I jerked in the tight space of her mouth and she took me as deep as she could. I let her stroke and lick me until my knees started to feel weak and I knew I wouldn't be able to pull her off if she went any further.

I pulled back and she looked up. Rimmel's little pink tongue darted out to lick across her lips, as if she were tasting every last bit of me.

A low growl rumbled the center of my chest, and she smiled. She moved quickly, turning so her bare ass was in perfect sight, and crawled up toward the head of the bed to lie down. Before she turned over from her hands and knees, she looked back at me over her shoulder.

I lunged forward, grabbing her hips and pulling them toward the center of my body.

She made a sound of appreciation, and I smoothed my hands over her hips and naked ass. My hand dipped between her legs and slipped in her already flowing juices. I rocked against her without thought, and she pushed her tight little butt into me.

I didn't give it a second thought. I pushed the tip of my swollen head inside her. She shuddered, and I looked down at her narrow waist that gave way to softly curved hips.

I plunged the rest of the way in, and she collapsed onto her elbows. It changed the angle, and I went even deeper into her. My pelvis rocked against her and I rotated my hips in a circle.

She was so tight. So wet and so fucking perfect.

My eyes slid closed as I rode her from behind. In and out, in and out I thrust. I could see her hands fisted in the blankets and hear her ragged breathing. I bent at the waist, bringing my chest against her front, and filled my hand with her breast. Gently, I pinched the nipple and rolled it around in my fingers.

Rimmel ground against me and started rocking her hips. I knew she was close. Her inner muscles squeezed around me. My free hand slid lower, and I pressed my thumb against her swollen clit.

She came apart in my arms. When she would have collapsed completely onto the bed, I held her up and kept riding her. My own release came hard and fast. I pulsed and emptied myself into her body while bliss stole over every last part of me.

I collapsed onto the bed beside her and lifted her boneless body across my chest.

I hated fighting with her. *But damn.* The make-up sex was awesome.

We were both so satisfied that neither of us moved. I thought briefly about pulling back the bedding to cover her, but with the fire going and our body heat, it really wasn't necessary.

I thought she'd gone to sleep, but a long time later, her quiet voice filled the room.

"Romeo?"

"Hmm?" I asked and dragged a hand up the length of her spine.

"He kept telling me to ask you why he was so mad."

I knew who she was talking about, and I was glad she hadn't said his name. I didn't want it in this bed with us.

"I'm the one who got him arrested. I had the nameplate put in his room. I had the dean search it. I knew what he would find."

"He lost presidency because of you."

"No. He lost presidency because he's an asshole and because the members of Omega just needed an excuse to dethrone him. He was supposed to be out of the house completely, but his daddy made some calls."

She fell silent again. It wasn't an uncomfortable silence, but silence all the same. I knew she was awake by the way she would occasionally stroke her thumb across my bicep.

"You pissed again?" I finally asked.

"No. He deserved it."

"Damn."

She lifted her head and rested her chin on my chest. "You wanted me to be mad?"

I gave her a lopsided smile. "I was hoping for more make-up sex."

She laughed. But then her eyes turned serious and she tucked her hand beneath her chin. "You need to stay away from him. No more games."

I stared at her levelly without saying a word.

"I mean it, Romeo. I know you want to pay him back for everything he's done, but it only makes things worse."

"Sign the restraining order."

"Okay."

I lifted an eyebrow. "Just like that?"

"I'll sign it if you stay away from him."

"No."

She twisted my nipple.

"Ow!" I hollered.

She laugh and I rolled to pin her beneath me.

"Say it," she demanded.

"Or what?"

"Or I won't kiss you anymore."

I grinned and lowered my head to do just that. She turned her face so my lips brushed her ear.

"I have ways," I said darkly, "of getting what I want."

"So do I." She matched my tone.

I made a frustrated sound and rolled off her. She sat up and all her hair fell over her shoulders, creating a curtain over her bare chest.

"Please, Romeo," she said sincerely. "No more of this. I'll get the restraining order and that will be the end of it."

I could tell she wasn't going to give in. I wanted that protective order in place. I couldn't be with her twenty-four-seven, but that paper would be. "Fine." I agreed grudgingly.

Rimmel smiled brilliantly and leaned over to kiss me. "Thank you."

Somewhere in the room, my phone went off. I jumped up and fished it out of the pocket of my jeans. It was a text from my father.

PAPERWORK IS DRAFTED. NEEDS SIGNED. WE'LL BE RIGHT OVER.

I tossed the phone on the bed. "Paperwork is ready."

Her eyebrows shot up. "That was fast."

"I told him we'd be over."

She frowned.

Shit. Did she seriously change her mind already? "What is it?" I asked, slightly irritated.

"I don't want to put that dress back on."

I threw back my head and laughed.

She glared at me. "Do you have any idea how uncomfortable those stupid tights are?"

"Well, you looked hot."

"Who cares?"

I chuckled. "I sure as hell don't. You look good in anything." Then I realized I was wrong. "Well, except that lesbian sweater you have. That's not attractive on anyone."

She threw a pillow at me. I caught it.

"C'mon, you can wear one of my shirts."

That seemed to make her happy, and she quickly pulled on a pair of fuzzy pajama pants, the slippers I gave her, and one of my shirts. I dressed in a pair of sweats and a T-shirt. At the door, I crouched down and pointed at my back.

She jumped on and I lifted her with ease. God, she weighed practically nothing at all. Her legs wound around my waist and her arms hooked around my neck.

I carried her between the houses and into my father's office.

He grinned when I walked in with her on my back. From behind his desk, he turned the paperwork toward us, and I handed a black pen over my shoulder.

When Rimmel patted my back to put her down, I didn't listen. Instead, I bent over so she could reach the papers. She laughed but put the pen to paper. After she signed her name, I stood.

"Thank you for doing this, Mr. Anderson," Rimmel said.

"Tony," he corrected.

"Tony," she echoed.

"My pleasure," he replied. Then he glanced at me. "These will be served in the morning."

I knew that was his way of warning me in front of Rimmel.

He wanted me to be prepared, because we both knew Zach—and Zach's father—wasn't going to be happy.

CHAPTER TWENTY-THREE

> To the student doing donuts in the parking lot: the faculty is NOT amused.
> #ButIAm #BlackIceCanBeFun
> ... Alpha BuzzFeed

RIMMEL

He wouldn't stop laughing.

My death glare was so not working.

In fact, it was only making him laugh more.

I crossed my arms over my chest and climbed out.

"Smalls!" he yelled after me, then started laughing all over again.

"I'll show you Smalls," I muttered. I walked over to the nearby grassy area and bent, scooping up some of the snow that was piled on the side of the pavement.

I ignored the sting in my fingers as I packed the frigid mush into a tight ball.

"Baby," Romeo said, coming up behind me. "C'mon, I'm sorry."

I stood up and launched the snowball as I was turning. It hit him between his neck and shoulder. White ice burst apart and some of it slid down the inside of his jacket.

I started laughing.

He didn't look amused.

I admit it made me laugh harder.

Calmly, Romeo reached up and brushed away the remaining snow that was sticking to his shoulder.

I snorted.

He lunged at me, and I squealed. Before I could dodge him, he picked me up by the waist and flipped me over so my head was facing the ground. I had to press a hand to my glasses to keep them on my face.

It seemed like the easiest thing in the world for him to walk while I dangled above the ground. He stopped beside the very snow pile from which I made my snowball. He stretched out his arms so I dangled over it and then lowered me down.

I began wiggling and fighting, trying to get free. "No!" I screeched. "That's cold!"

"You mean you don't want me to dunk your face in this here bank of snow?"

"Romeo," I warned.

"Payback is only fair," he sang.

"You had it coming and you know it!" The blood was rushing to my head and making me feel funny. "Put me down!"

He chuckled and swung me up so I was back on my feet.

"You suck," I said and stuck my tongue out at him.

"Usually, that tongue would distract me, like I know you want it to, but not today. We're busy." He draped an arm across my shoulder and steered me back in the direction of the idling Hellcat.

It was spotless. The lime-green exterior barely had a spot on it. Romeo washed it constantly. He hated how the snow and salt on the roads got it so dirty all the time.

"This really isn't necessary." I tried for like the five millionth time.

"Yes, it is. Knowing how to drive a stick shift is something every girl needs to know."

"I'm not every girl," I grumped.

"No. You're *my* girl. And my girl needs to know how to drive a Hellcat."

"Why couldn't you have gotten an automatic like everyone else in the country?"

"Real men drive stick shifts."

I snorted.

"Come on," he said, a smile already creeping back onto his face.

"Stop making fun of me!"

"I can't help it, Smalls. It's the first time anyone has ever needed a stack of books to see over the dashboard in this car."

I gave him a scornful look. "It has bucket seats."

He nodded gravely. "I knew my textbooks would come in good use sometime."

I rolled my eyes and he gently pushed me toward the driver's seat. With a sigh, I gave in and sat down on my stack of books.

Frankly, I thought this was a crime against the written word.

I might as well dog ear the pages and write notes in the margins while I was at it.

Once I was in, Romeo jogged around and got in the passenger seat. We were sitting in an empty parking lot of some business that had shut down. The asphalt was cleared of snow, and Romeo had come here earlier in the day to throw salt around just to make sure there wasn't any ice. There wasn't a ton of snow on the ground, just enough to cover the grass completely.

I knew any day now we were likely going to get a huge storm that would make the few inches out there now look like nothing.

As if he could read my thoughts, Romeo said, "I need to teach you now before the roads gets too bad and we have to wait 'til spring."

It was almost enough to make me wish for snow.

Almost.

"Fine," I muttered. "Let's do it."

He bit back another smile as he explained how I needed to drive with two feet. Frankly, I was amazed he was teaching me this. I could barely walk without falling, let alone drive a car with both my feet at the same time.

I was a disaster waiting to happen, and he was letting me learn on his precious baby the Hellcat.

"This is the gear shift." He went on, taking my hand and placing it on the thing that stuck up between the seats. "Start out in one," he said and then went on to explain the rest. I listened, because the faster I learned, the faster we could be done.

Even though I listened, it was confusing.

"Okay," Romeo said when he was done. "Now you try."

"What if I wreck?" I worried.

"There's nothing here to wreck into, Rim."

I gave him a look that promised I could find something to run over.

He laughed but then shook his head. "Let's go."

With a sigh, I pushed in the clutch and brake at the same time. I turned the engine over and put my hand on the gear. The car lurched forward, then stalled out.

"It's okay," he said patiently. "Try again."

I tried again.

And again.

On the fifth try, I got the car to move a couple feet before it stalled out.

Romeo was holding on to his patience, but I wasn't. "I'm a failure," I said.

He smiled. "Nah. You just need more practice."

"What I need is the number of a good cab company."

He grinned. "Don't try and go anywhere," he quipped and jumped out of the car.

"Ha-ha," I muttered.

He pulled open the driver's side door and leaned down. "Get out."

"With pleasure."

I stood back as he threw all the textbooks I'd been sitting on in the passenger seat and slid in. He adjusted the seat and then patted his lap.

I looked at him like he was insane.

"Let's try it this way."

I snorted. "You just want me to sit on your lap."

"Hells yeah." He winked. "Come on."

How he thought we were going to drive with me sitting in his lap was beyond me, but I did it anyway.

Maybe I just wanted to sit in his lap.

"All right," he said, his voice close to my ear, "put your feet over mine."

I did, but they barely reached so I scooted forward on the edge of the seat between his legs and put my feet over his. Then he took my hand and put it on the stick shift.

Little shivers of electricity raced up my arm and down my spine when his large, warm hand covered mine.

"I'm gonna start out. You can feel how the car moves beneath us, get a feel for how your feet work."

"'Kay," I replied, breathless.

I felt his leg muscles work as he pressed in the pedals and started the car. With ease, he pushed the car into first gear and let off the brake slowly. The car rolled forward. His foot moved over and touched on the gas. The car responded and purred to life, going forward.

He shifted again, my hand sandwiched between his and the gear shaft. He spoke quietly as he drove and shifted, explaining everything as we went. We circled around the lot more times than I could count, and eventually, I got into the rhythm with the car.

"Are you ready to try by yourself again?" he asked as the car rolled to a stop.

"Maybe," I said, settling back against him. He was so warm and so strong. Maybe car lessons weren't so bad after all.

His arm slid around my waist and he pulled me tightly against him. His teeth scraped over my earlobe, and I groaned.

"You trying to distract me?" he asked.

"Says the boy with my earlobe in his mouth."

"You like it," he whispered.

"Oh yes," I whispered back.

I could feel him stirring against my backside, and the inside of the car was filled with lusty desire. Romeo groaned. "C'mon. One last try before we go."

"Fine."

Once he was settled in the passenger seat and I was back on my stack of books, I tried again, remembering how it was when he was driving and trying to match that.

I got halfway through the parking lot before the Hellcat stuttered and shut off.

"I did it!" I exclaimed and threw my arms around his neck.

He chuckled and tugged on the ends of my hair. "Wanna drive yourself to the shelter?"

I made a face. "You really want me to drive out on the road with other people?" I asked and tilted my head to the side.

He grimaced. "Maybe I should drive. Besides, the poor transmission is probably screaming for a break."

I had no idea what a transmission was, but I agreed just so I didn't have to drive anymore.

Outside the shelter, I turned to him. "Wanna come in for a while?"

"Can't. I'm meeting Braeden at the gym," he said and leaned forward to kiss me.

"If you need a ride back to campus when you're done, call me."

"I can walk. It's only a couple blocks."

He frowned. "It's cold out."

"It's not so bad," I replied. I wasn't going to call him to stop what he was doing just for a ride. I used to walk all the time when Michelle couldn't give me a ride.

"It's probably gonna be dark. I don't want you out walking at night. It isn't safe."

That made me think of Zach. "Do you think they served him by now?" I whispered.

Romeo's face hardened. "I sure as hell hope so."

It was supposed to be done first thing yesterday, but he wasn't there when the courier went to the frat house. They tried again later, but he still hadn't been there. Romeo was convinced he somehow got tipped off about the order and was purposely avoiding the frat house so he couldn't be served.

As far as we knew, he'd yet to be served today either. It was making me a little nervous. Zach was sort of like a loose cannon. I had no idea what he was going to do, and if he really did know about the restraining order, he might be really mad.

"You know what?" Romeo said. "Just wait for me tonight. I'll pick you up."

"I'll get a ride from Michelle."

"Rim," he half growled.

I sighed. "Fine."

There was no use in arguing. Until we knew what's Zach's reaction was going to be, we couldn't be too cautious.

CHAPTER TWENTY-FOUR

> #StalkerAlert
> Someone just got served a restraining
> order. The #BuzzBoss knew the #Nerd
> was too smart to cheat.
> #SorryLadies
> ... Alpha BuzzFeed

ROMEO

"I thought we were going to the gym," Braeden said from the passenger seat as I slowed the Hellcat and parked it across the street from the Omega House.

"Yeah, we are," I said, cutting the engine and staring at the house.

"He still not been served?" Braeden surmised.

"Fuck no. Little bastard's laying low. Meanwhile, Rim's out walking around with a goddamned target on her back."

"Or maybe this time he's coming for you."

I glanced at Braeden. "Good. Let him. He needs to stop taking shots at my girl." I blew out a breath. "What kind of punk bitch goes after a woman?"

Braeden shook his head. "Wanna go find him?"

That thought hadn't really occurred to me. I'd been too busy thinking about Rimmel and making sure she was safe and busy with me. But I could only find so many ways to keep her at my side until we both had to get back to life.

It's the reason she was at the shelter right now and I was supposed to be working out.

"Yeah," I said. "Let's see if we can find him."

"Hide and seek college style." Braeden grinned and rubbed his hands together. "This is gonna be fun."

I grinned. "I wanna talk to Trent first, see what the word is around the house."

"Let's do it." Braeden threw open the door of the car, and I did the same.

Just as I was about to get out, a car drove up to the frat and parked along the side in the members' lot. It was a silver BMW. Zach.

"Hey," I said and slipped back in the car and shut the door. "He's here."

"Aw, man," Braeden complained and got back in the car. "I was looking forward to hunting him down."

I smiled. I kind of was too, but I was glad I knew where he was.

I grabbed my cell to call my dad and tell him Zach was here and to get the messenger over pronto, but Braeden slapped me on the shoulder.

"Check it out," he said in hushed tones.

I glanced up to see an unmarked sedan appear at the curb. A man in dress pants and a button-down shirt got out immediately. He was carrying a yellow envelope.

"That's gotta be the court guy or whatever," he said.

Zach was walking toward the front of the house from the parking lot. He looked like he didn't have a care in the world. God, his ego was the size of a freaking small country. Anger still swirled within me. I wondered if I would ever be able to look at him and see anything other than the bruises on Rimmel's arm or the way he must have looked lurking when she was showering.

"Ah, shit." Braeden laughed. "Karma is coming, asshole."

His running commentary came courtesy of the fact Zach finally noticed the man headed for him on the sidewalk. Zach paused and gave the man a hateful stare. It proved he knew people were looking for him.

The man with the envelope called out to Zach, and he stiffened. Then he drew himself up tall and stepped up closer.

The man said something short. Zach nodded and then he was given the envelope. The man turned and walked away. Zach stared after him with anger in his face.

Once the official was gone, Zach glanced at the envelope. He tore off the seal and pulled out a stack of papers. Papers I knew had Rimmel's signature on the bottom.

Zach flipped through them once. Then twice.

A look of pure hatred crossed his features, and he bunched the papers up in his fist before holding them at his side and stalking toward the front door of Omega.

"That dude is a class-A douche nozzle," Braeden said.

I had to agree.

As Zach was pulling out his keys for the front door, it swung open. He looked up and so did Braeden and I. No one stepped out, but there was movement in the doorway. A large suitcase and an equally large duffle were tossed out onto the concrete porch.

I reached over and turned the key in the ignition just enough so I could hit the button and roll down my window a bit. We were pretty far away, but if he started yelling, we would be able to hear.

"From hide and seek to college-style stake out." Braeden laughed and held out his fist in the center of the seats.

I couldn't leave him hanging, so I pounded it out.

"What the fuck is this!" Zach yelled. His voice was low, but I still heard him.

Trent appeared on the steps, firmly closing the door to the house behind him. He was a big guy, tall with wide shoulders. He worked out hard just like the rest of the team, and I knew he could wipe the pavement with Zach.

He was dressed in a navy T-shirt with the Omega symbol stretched out across his chest. He didn't say anything at first, just crossed his arms and stared Zach down as he gaped incredulously at what I assumed was his shit on the steps.

Trent's lips moved, but I couldn't hear him. It didn't matter. I knew what he was doing.

He was giving Zachy boy the boot.

Zach lunged forward and shoved his face up in Trent's. To his credit, Trent didn't move. His eyes only followed an angry Zach.

"You can't kick me out of here!" he yelled.

Trent said something again, low and calm enough that I couldn't hear. Then he gestured to the crumpled restraining order still clutched in Zach's fist.

"This is a fucking joke!" Zach said and threw the papers on the ground.

Braeden shook his head and sighed dramatically. "No respect for the law."

I grunted and kept my eyes trained on Zach.

Trent said something else. His face held a note of warning and a note of finality.

"That bitch is just being dramatic!" he yelled.

I stiffened and Braeden laid a hand on my arm.

Trent stepped forward and lowered his face until it was right up in Zach's. I saw his lips moving but heard nothing. Zach's face grew red with anger, but Trent ignored it. Then without another word, he turned and went back in the house.

Zach was left staring at the closed door with his belongings and the papers of the restraining order littering the ground around him.

It was done. He was out of Omega and he wasn't getting back in. And if he even stepped close to Rimmel, I would make sure he was hauled off to jail.

"You feel better now?" Braeden asked.

At the same time, Zach spun and his eyes found my car. Even with the distance, I knew he knew I was watching. Through the windshield, our eyes met.

There was unspoken animosity seething into the winter air around him.

I didn't look away.

I wasn't going to back down.

Braeden didn't bother asking his question again. He knew the answer.

No.

I didn't feel better.

If anything, I was afraid things were going to get worse.

CHAPTER TWENTY-FIVE

> A man can be judged by his actions toward other men. But being an asshole to a woman... that just makes you a dick.
>
> #ThisBuzzIsForUZach
>
> ... Alpha BuzzFeed

RIMMEL

The shelter was still one of my most favorite places. A lot of people thought of these places as depressing and sad. A place where lonely animals sat in cages all day, forgotten and unloved.

And yes, some days it was sad.

I wished every animal had a loving home, but wishing something didn't make it true.

But there were more good days at the shelter than sad ones. The animals here were not forgotten and unloved.

I loved them.

And so did everyone else who worked here.

Everyone here gave their time and care to these animals. We were a no-kill shelter and that meant we were overcrowded. But even still, we didn't turn away an animal in need.

Michelle, the woman who was in charge around here, worked closely with several local pet rescue and fostering places to help keep the crowding down and to find loving homes.

Today was a happy day at the shelter. One of the animals, a long-haired four-year-old Chihuahua was being adopted. He'd been here for several months, sometimes looked over for some of the larger more popular breeds. I called him Sailor, for reasons I didn't know other than I liked the name.

He was a brown dog with brown eyes and a pink nose. I knew he was going to make a great companion and the people who adopted him were going to give him a great home.

Since his new family was coming to pick him up at any moment, I finished getting him ready. I brushed through his soft hair and folded the blanket he'd taken a liking to. I wanted him to have it. It was familiar to him.

I reached into my bag and pulled out a little blue sweater with an anchor on it and smiled. "It's cold out there, Sailor," I told him and ripped off the tags. "I got you a little going away present."

He was patient as I pulled it on over his head and his furry brown ears popped out. Once he was dressed, I stood back and admired how cute he looked.

"Good boy," I told him, and his tail wagged back and forth.

Michelle came into the back and looked at us and shook her head with a smile on her face. "You bought him a sweater?"

"I couldn't resist," I said sheepishly.

"Well, I can see why." She smiled and scooped up the dog to love him. "Good luck at your new home, boy," she said and scratched him behind the ears.

After she put him down, she looked at me. "Can you make sure he gets off okay? I have to run and get some food for the dogs. We're low. Again."

I frowned. "We're low already?"

Michelle nodded. "With all the cold weather, we have more animals than usual. It's really draining our supplies."

"Next time I'm out I'll pick up some too."

"You don't have to do that."

"I know," I said. "But I want to."

"Most college students go shopping or buy beer with their money."

I rolled my eyes. I'd rather help the animals here. Besides, most of us here at the shelter donated supplies whenever possible because the truth was there was never enough.

"Becky will be in later," Michelle said, grabbing her coat and bag. "You won't be here long by yourself."

"I'll be fine," I said.

When she was gone, I finished getting Sailor's paperwork ready, then took him and his things out front to wait for his family.

I sat at the front desk and put him on the surface. He sat expectantly and waited like a little gentleman. I laughed and scratched his ears.

The front door opened and I made an excited face at Sailor. "Here they are!"

I glanced up and did a double take.

It wasn't Sailor's new family.

It was Valerie Anderson.

"Mrs. Anderson," I said, shocked, standing up. "I wasn't expecting you."

"Please, call me Valerie."

I nodded even though I probably wasn't going to.

"Romeo isn't here," I said. "He's with Braeden." I figured the only reason she would be here would be to see her son.

"I wasn't looking for Roman. I came to see you."

"Me?" I couldn't hide the shock in my tone.

She smiled slightly. "Yes. I wanted to see where you volunteered."

"Oh," I replied.

She gave me a knowing smile. "I know you're surprised. But you're my son's girlfriend and I'd like to get to know you better."

Did this mean she approved of her son and me?

"And I have to admit I'm impressed you spend so much of your time volunteering." She glanced around the room, and I tried to see it through her eyes.

She probably just saw a no-nonsense building without much style. Oh, and it smelled like animal in here too.

"Well, I do get credit for all the hours I spend here. It counts as clinical hours. I need to have between five and six hundred when I apply to veterinarian school. The more I have, the better I'll look."

"Something tells me that isn't the only reason you come here."

"No." I shrugged. "I like it here."

Sailor pushed against my hand, and I smiled. "I know you're there." I giggled and picked him up.

"Who is this?" Valerie asked.

I walked around the desk so she could see him better. "Sailor. He's being adopted today."

"Well, that's an awfully cute sweater," she said, eyeing the dog. It was clear she had little to no experience with animals.

"I couldn't resist." I grinned.

"You bought it for him?"

"Yes. Kind of a going away present."

She glanced around, her eyes taking in the room. "Where is everyone else?"

"I'm the only one here right now. Michelle went out to buy some food. We're running low."

"Does the shelter pay for that?" she asked.

"Well, usually. But sometimes we run out so we all pitch in."

"Do you get paid for your work here?"

"Oh, no. It's volunteer. But I have a little leftover every semester from my scholarship. And also my dad sends me money." I frowned.

"Is something wrong?" she asked.

"Uh, no." I smiled. I just realized my father hadn't sent me a check since I'd been back from break. "So do you want me to show you around?" I asked, not really sure what else to do.

"That would be lovely," she said.

I smiled. Our relationship (if you could call it that) was so new, but it really touched me that she was making an effort to try and get to know me better.

Just as I was about to start the tour, the family adopting Sailor came bounding in the door. They were led by a boy who looked to be about eight or nine.

"There he is!" the boy said and skidded to a stop in front of me. Sailor began wiggling in my arms, and I felt his tail beating against my side.

I laughed. "He's been waiting for you!" I exclaimed.

The little boy reached out for the dog, and I handed over Sailor.

"We would have been here sooner," his mother said, "but we stopped off at the pet store to get some supplies."

"No problem at all." I smiled. I glanced at Valerie. "I'll be right with you."

She nodded, and I walked around the desk so Sailor's new family could sign the paperwork and make it official. As we were going over the details, the boy set Sailor down and produced a toy out of his coat pocket.

The boy and dog began to play, and I was momentarily distracted watching them. My heart swelled. I was so grateful that these people were going to be taking care of Sailor.

Once the papers were filled out, I tore my eyes away from the dog and made sure everything was in order. "I think that's it!" I said. "Oh." I grabbed up the blanket. "He really likes this blanket. It was his favorite while he was here. I thought he might like to have it."

"That's really sweet of you," the woman said, taking the blanket. She had short, dark hair and blue eyes. "We'll take good care of him."

"I know, and I couldn't be more thankful."

The man with the woman and boy whistled, and the dog rushed toward the door. The boy went rushing after them and scooped him up. "Let's go!"

Before they left, I gave Sailor one last ear scratch, and he licked me on the nose. I laughed. "Good boy."

I watched the family walk down the sidewalk to their car, Sailor in tow. I knew he was going to have a great life.

I felt Valerie's eyes on me, and I turned from the door and smiled. "It's always a good day when one of our animals finds a home. Come on," I said, leading her toward the back. "I'll show you around."

I showed her everything (even the animals). She was a lot more interested than I originally thought. She asked questions and seemed genuinely interested in not just what I did, but what the shelter was really about.

As we went through the rooms, I did things as I saw they needed done, refreshing water, giving out treats and scratches behind the ears.

"So that's pretty much everything." I led her out to the main room again. "It's not very big, but it's effective."

"I'm very impressed with you," Valerie said.

"Oh, well, this wasn't me. I just volunteer here. A lot of the credit goes to Michelle. She runs the place."

"I don't mean the place, though it is impressive as well. I meant you."

I was confused and slightly uncomfortable with the compliment. I wasn't used to it.

"You're clearly very dedicated to what you do. And you keep up your grades, work here, and tutor Roman to help him stay on the team."

"Well, thank you."

Michelle came in the front, carrying several bags of food. "There's more in the car," she called out and then noticed I wasn't alone.

"Michelle, this is Valerie Anderson. She's Romeo's mother."

Michelle smiled wide and dropped the bags on the floor. "Nice to meet you! Romeo is great. We all love him around here."

"Does he spend much time here?" she asked.

"Sometimes," I answered. "But he picks me up a lot and drives me back to campus. He doesn't want me to walk," I said with a grimace.

"That sounds like Roman," she mused.

"Speaking of… Once we get this food brought in, you can go for the night if you want," Michelle said.

I nodded. "Everything is done in the back. Sailor went home. The finalized paperwork is on the desk for your files."

"Is Roman picking you up?" Valerie asked.

"I'm supposed to call him."

"Well, I'd be happy to drive you over to campus if you want."

I tried not to show on my face the shock I felt. Instead, I smiled and nodded. I couldn't very well say no. I'd probably offend her.

Besides, I didn't want Romeo to drop what he was doing to come here and get me.

"Thank you. I'll just be a couple minutes. Let me help, Michelle." I jogged out into the cold and over to the car parked nearby. I grabbed up a large bag of food and spun.

Valerie was standing there, and I jumped in surprise.

"What can I carry?"

"Oh, you don't have—"

But Michelle cut me off by shoving a large bag filled with cans of cat food at her. "This please."

Valerie took the bag and all three of us carried the rest of the supplies into the store.

Once it was all in the back (Valerie helped with that too), I gathered up my coat and bag.

"Michelle," Valerie said as I moved around, "do you do any fundraising here for the shelter?"

"We do what we can. Most of the things we've tried in the past haven't been very successful."

"I'd like to help change that."

My bag fell to the floor when I dropped it. Both women glanced at me, and I blushed furiously.

Why was she doing this?

"Well, that would be wonderful, but I have to warn you. Fundraising is a lot of work and it's hard to get interest in the shelter."

She smiled. "Yes, I'm well aware of the work of fundraising. I'm on several charities and boards. I do this kind of thing quite often."

"Oh, well, I didn't mean to offend you," Michelle hurried to say. She glanced at me, and I smiled. At least I wasn't the only one that found Romeo's mother intimidating.

"You didn't. You wouldn't know what I'm involved in. But I'd like to put together a charity event for the shelter. Rimmel can help me with the details."

Both ladies looked at me. I swallowed thickly. "Of course." I agreed. "I'd be happy to help. Anything for the animals."

I wondered how it was going to be working with Valerie. I wondered how much time we would have to spend together.

"Great! Just let me know what you need and when you need it. I'll help as much as I can."

"Wonderful." Valerie smiled. "I'll be in touch." She looked over at me. "Ready?"

"Yes, ma'am," I said.

I followed her to the door, and on my way out, I glanced back at Michelle. She gave me a thumbs-up.

Valerie drove an Audi SUV. The seats were leather and the interior of the car smelled like vanilla. Once I was settled in the seat, I pulled out my phone to text Romeo.

I GOT A RIDE BACK TO CAMPUS.

He replied a few seconds later.

WHO?

YOUR MOTHER.

WTF?

I suppressed the urge to laugh and replied.

CALL ME LATER.

WILL DO.

It was a fast ride to campus, and we didn't have much time to talk. Mostly, she threw out ideas for the fundraiser event, and I agreed with everything because I knew nothing about this stuff. I directed her to my dorm, and she parked at the curb.

"Thank you for the ride," I said, unhooking my seatbelt.

"Thank you for giving me a tour of the shelter."

"Sure. It was fun." Awkward. But fun.

I started to climb out of the SUV, but she said my name. When I looked back, I read on her face that there was something she wanted to say. I came back in the vehicle and looked at her expectantly.

"I know I haven't been the easiest to get along with." She began. "But I'd like to change that. I'd like to make up for the way I treated you when you first started dating my son."

"You don't have to make up for anything. I understand. It's forgotten."

"I appreciate that. But I'd still like to spend time with you."

An immediate rush of emotion burned the back of my throat. I hadn't expected it, but it was there all the same. I swallowed several times, trying to be certain I would be able to speak over it. "I'd like that," I said. The words didn't come out sounding like they usually would have. Instead, they were slightly high-pitched and a little cracked.

She smiled. I didn't know if she was just being polite about my sudden emotion or if she really just hadn't noticed. "Wonderful. I'll get some ideas and plans together for the event and then we can meet to discuss it. Maybe we could have lunch?"

I cleared my throat. "Um, yeah, sure."

"I haven't had a real girls' lunch in forever," she said, her voice warming. It reminded me more now of how she sounded when she talked to Braeden.

I could only smile. Mrs. Anderson was a mother figure to me. She was Romeo's mom. She had the whole maternal thing down to a science. I guess it shouldn't surprise me that I had the sudden longing for my own mother. That I suddenly became acutely aware of all the mother-daughter "girl" time we'd missed out on over the years.

And now here was Romeo's mom, offering me a version of the very thing I didn't have.

I wanted it so badly that it hurt my chest. It scared me. It scared me so much I just wanted to get away.

"Great!" I said brightly, maybe too brightly, but it was too late to take it back. "Thanks again for the ride. I'll see you later."

I didn't wait for her to reply. Instead, I bolted. I rushed into the dorm and didn't stop until I was safely inside my room.

From her position on her bed, Ivy looked up from the homework she was doing. "Everything okay?"

"Yeah, great." I lied. "It's freezing out there."

"It's supposed to snow."

"Big surprise there," I said, tossing all my stuff on the bed.

"What do you have going on the rest of the night?" she asked.

"Studying. I have a paper to finish."

"Ugh," she said. "Homework sucks."

Out loud, I agreed with her, but on the inside, I was glad for the homework tonight. I was glad for the distraction. I didn't want Romeo's mom to hate me, but I wasn't sure I wanted a relationship with her either.

I'd already lost my mother. I didn't want to risk losing another.

CHAPTER TWENTY-SIX

#BadPickUpLineAlert
Is your body from McDonald's?
Because I'm loving it.
#ThisWillNotGetYouLaid
... Alpha BuzzFeed

ROMEO

"Think I can get in without calling Rim down to open the door?" I asked, grinning at Braeden.

"Please," he replied. "Do women have tits?"

"Dude. That was wrong."

Braeden looked at me with a *what the hell?* expression. "What?"

I chuckled, got out of the Hellcat, and leaned in the door. "I'll be right back."

"Oh, hells no," Braeden replied and got out. "You think you can waltz into a dorm full of chicks and tell me to wait in the car? Dude. I thought we were BFFs for life!"

I laughed. "C'mon, then."

"Besides, I gotta make sure Rim survived the freak visit from your mom."

I glanced at Braeden as we approached the entrance. "You like her, huh?"

"Your mom?" he replied, knowing damn well I wasn't talking about my mother. "She's cool."

"B." I gave him a level look.

"You know I do, Rome. I've liked her since the day she didn't want to wear your hoodie and be associated with you." He cackled.

"Well, she's associated with me now." She was mine. Everyone knew it.

"Chill, bro." Braeden sighed as he checked out a pair of girls walking by. They flashed us their smiles and Braeden grinned. "She's like the little sister I never had."

"You mean it?"

Braeden turned all his attention away from the girls and gave me a serious look. "What's going on? Why you asking?"

I blew out a breath. I hadn't expected all this to come out of me, not tonight. I guess seeing Zach earlier and the look in his eyes… it scared me. It scared me that pushing her into getting this restraining order would only make things worse.

I just wanted to know she had more than me, that Braeden would have her back when I wasn't able to.

"Fuck, man," I muttered. "I guess I'm just worried Zach's gonna try something else. I don't want her getting hurt."

Braeden nodded. "He'd be stupid to pull anything else. But I get it. You know I'll watch out for her, Rome. I got her back. And yours."

"Dude." I held out my fist. He bumped his against mine. "Thanks."

"Ladies," Braeden called to the pair he was staring at before. He jogged over to them as they were opening the dorm entrance. "Let me get that for ya," he said, holding open the door.

One of the girls laughed and went ahead. The other one looked at him suspiciously. "You trying to get in the building, Braeden?"

"She knows my name," he said and put a hand over his heart like he'd been shot.

I shook my head and suppressed a laugh.

"Everyone knows your name," she muttered.

Braeden grinned. "Yeah, we need an in."

"You have a girlfriend in here?" the other girl said from inside, her voice pouty.

"Hells no," Braeden said. "I'm open for business."

Both the girls giggled, and I stepped forward. Both of them looked away from him and at me. "Romeo," said the girl questioning Braeden.

"Ladies." I gave them my charming smile. "I was just on my way in to see my girl. It's a surprise." I grinned a little wider.

Someone inside the building sighed.

"She's so lucky," the girl at the door said. "Come on in."

On the steps to the second floor, Braeden punched me in the arm. "Damn, man. You had to steal my thunder."

I chuckled. "Are you kidding? No one steals your thunder."

"Mm-hmm," he drawled. "Even taken, you still get the attention."

"What can I say? It's a gift."

We drew lots of stares and giggles as we stood outside Rimmel's door and knocked. Braeden ate up the attention, but I was focused on the girl inside.

The door swung open, and Ivy's blond head appeared. Her eyes widened when she took in both Braeden and me. "It's for you!" Ivy called behind her, then pulled the door all the way open so I could see inside.

"Me?" Rimmel grumbled, sitting on her bed with her laptop in her lap. The glowing screen reflected off her glasses and her hair was in this massive pile on her head and it looked like there were several pencils sticking out.

She was a hot mess.

And I fucking loved every inch of it.

"Sis!" Braeden called loudly and pushed past me to walk in.

Rimmel made a strangled sound and looked up, surprised. "Braeden?" Her eyes went behind him to me and she smiled.

"Hey, baby."

She moved the laptop off her lap and slid off the bed. She was wearing a loose pair of sweats and my hoodie. Braeden scooped her up off the floor and hugged her. She laughed when he spun her around. "Damn, girl," he said. "You need a steak."

Then he looked over at me. "How the hell have you not broken her by now?"

Rimmel gasped and Ivy burst out laughing. Braeden turned to smile at her, but when Ivy saw him looking, her laughter stopped and she looked away.

Braeden looked at me and lifted an eyebrow in silent question.

"You done?" I asked, pointedly staring at him with Rimmel in his arms.

"Sure, man," he said and held her out to me like a ragdoll. Her feet dangled over the floor, and she gave me a withering look.

I ignored it and reached for her. Her frown was pronounced when I pressed my lips to hers, but the second we made contact, she melted and kissed me back.

"What are you doing here?" she asked when I pulled back.

"I told you I'd call," I said and sat on the bed, pulling her into my lap.

"We had to make sure you were still in once piece after Mrs. A came to see ya," Braeden said.

Ivy gave Rimmel a curious look. "You never told me that."

"It wasn't a big deal," Rimmel replied quickly. "Nothing to tell."

Braeden pulled the desk chair around and sank into it. Then he propped his feet on her bed. "I knew you could handle it," he said and gestured with his chin at me. "This guy's been worrying like a damn woman."

Rimmel glanced around at me with an amused expression on her face. "You were worried?"

"Not really," I said. *Not about that anyway.*

"Well," Ivy said, getting up from her bed and shooting Braeden a look. "You two take up way too much space in here. I'm gonna hit the showers."

"Want some company?" Braeden asked.

"As if," Ivy muttered.

"Icy," Braeden muttered.

Rimmel shot him a dirty look.

"You know, no," Ivy said, drawing all our attention. Then she smacked Braeden in the shoulder.

"Ow!" he yelled. "What's wrong with you, woman?"

"That's for what you did to Missy."

"Shit," he muttered.

"Ivy is upset about what happened between you and Missy," Rimmel explained. I mean, really, I think Ivy made the point without her saying, but maybe she thought Braeden needed it spelled out.

"Nothing happened." Braeden groaned.

"Exactly," Rimmel and Ivy said at the same time.

"Aw, shit, B. They tag-teaming ya now." I grinned. I liked seeing Braeden in the hot seat.

"I expected better, baby sis." He gave Rimmel the stink eye.

She laughed.

"Seriously, though," Ivy said. "Why didn't you ever call her?"

Braeden rubbed a hand over his face. "Because I was getting the feels."

"You didn't call her because you were having feelings for her?" Rimmel asked, confused. I gave her a little squeeze around the waist.

"No, he meant *she* was getting the feels," I said.

"Was that so bad? Someone actually wanting you for more than sex?" Ivy demanded.

Braeden frowned. "No."

Then he looked over at Ivy. "I said we were just having fun. I was upfront about it. I never promised her more than that. Then I started getting the feels from her. I didn't want to hurt her, so I walked away."

"Dropping someone so abruptly is kind of wrong," Rimmel said.

Ivy snorted. "She's being nice. You acted like a dick."

Braeden's eyes flickered with anger. "No. A dick would have been someone who let her think I was interested, toyed with her feelings, and then dropped her."

Rimmel tensed against me. I didn't think she'd ever seen Braeden angry. He had a temper. He wasn't all cool like me.

"Dude," I said, throwing some ice on his heat. "You did the right thing."

"I'm going to shower," Ivy said. She picked up her stuff and was gone seconds later.

I couldn't help but wonder if anyone was lurking in the bathroom like some creep, waiting to watch her.

"Chicks." Braeden sighed when Ivy was gone.

"I'm a chick," Rimmel said.

"Nah, you're different." Braeden grinned.

"So what did my mom want?" I asked.

She looked up at me. "She wanted to see the shelter, wanted to know more about it. She's offered to put together a fundraiser to help us."

"I knew she'd come around." I patted her leg.

"Yeah." She agreed, but her voice was off and she seemed a lot less thrilled about my mother's sudden acceptance.

"What's wrong?" I asked.

"Nothing." She was a terrible liar.

I was about to make her tell me when Braeden interrupted. "Rome tell you the good news yet?"

"What news?" She looked between us.

"Zach was served. He can't come near you now," I said. Why did it not seem like such a great thing anymore?

"He got thrown out of Omega too," Braeden said. "We had front row seats."

Rimmel glanced at me and I nodded. "He's done."

"Well, I can't say I'm sorry," she said, leaning into me.

Braeden snorted. "Fucker deserved it."

Silently, I agreed.

"Hey, man, give us a minute?" I asked.

He nodded and dropped his feet off the bed. "Of course. I saw some fine-looking ladies in the hall."

Rimmel laughed.

"Hey." He looked at her. "How come you aren't pissed at me about Missy? You two still friends?"

"Yeah, we are." She nodded. "I guess I kind of think you did the right thing."

Braeden smiled. "Yeah?"

"Better to end it now before her feelings really got hurt."

He nodded. "Missy is a cool girl. But I don't do relationships."

"People change," I told him, thinking of a time not that long ago when I felt the very same way.

"Nah. You two are just freaks," Braeden cracked. Then he reached out and ruffled Rimmel's already messy hair.

"Ow!" he yelled and jerked his hand back. "What the hell! You packing weapons?"

She laughed and pulled a pencil out of the mess. "Yep."

"Girl…" He shook his head. "You ain't right."

"Feels pretty right to me," I said, and she grinned.

"See?" Braeden shook his head. "Freaks."

He opened the door and stepped into the hall. "Ladies!" he called out as the door shut behind him.

"I didn't think he'd ever leave," I said and gathered her close. She laid her cheek against my chest and I rested my chin on top her head.

"I'm glad you're here," she whispered and wrapped her hand around my bicep.

"You gonna tell me what's wrong?" I asked after just a few minutes of nothing but her in my arms.

"Hadn't planned on it."

"Rim," I growled.

She sighed. "It's stupid."

"Did my mother say something?" I knew she said things with Mom had gone fine, but I wouldn't be surprised if she was just saying that.

"No. Yes," she said. Then she blew out a breath. "I don't know."

"You're gonna have to help me here, baby. I don't speak woman."

She giggled and the sound tightened my gut and stirred my desire.

"She wants me to help plan the fundraiser. She wants to have *girl* time."

"I'm not seeing how this is bad." Sometimes women confused the shit out of me. Didn't she want my mother to like her?

"I haven't really done that since my mom…" Her voice faded away and everything clicked.

Ah, shit. My mother was reminding her of her mother and all the things she was missing. "You miss your mom."

"Every day," she whispered, and my chest tightened.

This was a kind of hurt I couldn't make go away. This wasn't something I could punch or have served papers. Grief and loss wasn't something I knew how to deal with. I pulled her closer and she snuggled in. One of the pencils in her hair poked me.

I reached up and pulled it out. Then another one.

"Sorry," she mused.

I kissed her on the forehead. "You know my mom could never take the place of yours."

"Sounds like something I said to your mom about you," she mused.

"Oh yeah?" I smiled against her.

She nodded. "And I know. It's just… hard. I want to spend time with her. I do. It's just…"

"You feel like you're betraying your mom?"

She glanced up. "No, not at all."

I frowned. "Then?"

"What happens if we break up?" She rushed the words out so fast I stumbled to keep up.

"You think we're going to break up?" Just the thought gave me chest pains.

"Not everything lasts forever."

And then I understood.

I understood exactly why spending time with my mother scared her.

"Baby," I murmured and lifted her off my lap. Her open laptop was nearby, and I moved it onto the floor. She was looking at me with shadows in her eyes when I turned back, and they haunted me.

I cupped her face in my hands and stared at her intently. "You can let them in. I'm not going anywhere."

Behind her glasses, she squeezed her eyes shut.

I kissed the tip of her nose. "I love you so much. I'm keeping you. My family is your family now. I won't let anyone take that away from you."

"It hurts," she whispered.

Something in my chest constricted. The pain in her voice was unmistakable.

"You were inevitable. I know that now. The minute I was handed that paper with your name on it for tutoring, it was like somehow cast in stone that you would get inside here," Rimmel said as she pressed a hand to her heart.

Her eyes met mine. "I love you, more than anyone. Anything. And the thought of losing you keeps me up at night. You don't know what it's like to lose someone."

"No, I don't," I said gently.

"I can't let her in too. I can't risk loving anyone else and losing them."

"Come here." I reached for her and her arms locked around my neck. I stretched out on the mattress, pulling her with me. Her body was pressed along mine and her face was buried in my neck. I held her without saying a word.

There really wasn't anything I could say. Not really. It killed me that she hurt like this. It killed me that I didn't know how to stop it. All I could do was love her. Love her and never leave.

"You know," I said, trying to lighten the mood. "My mother is a control freak. She's not as lovable as me."

The laugh that bubbled out of her eased some of the tension in my shoulders.

She looked up. Tears filled her eyes. "No one is as lovable as you."

I pulled her glasses off and set them aside. When I rolled on top of her, she sighed and hooked one of her legs around mine. I kissed her deeply, swirling my tongue inside her mouth, and pulled her lip into mine to suck gently on the fullness. Rimmel's hands slid into my hair, and she tugged me closer.

I kissed her with all the love I had inside me, trying to push out some of that darkness, some of that loss. I knew that feeling would never go away for her, but I wanted to at least make it smaller. I wanted my love to be bigger, to overpower that doubt.

She arched up off the bed into me. Even through our clothes, I could feel the erect pebbles of her nipples. She spread her thighs and I settled between her legs, growling in frustration at the layers of clothes keeping me from her skin.

I pushed my hips against her and she met me with a thrust of her own. I tore my mouth away from hers and kissed down her neck, nipping at the exposed skin with my teeth.

She sighed my name, and I ground my hard length into her. She moved restlessly and reached for the hem of my shirt.

Desire pumped through me so hard and fast that I didn't even hear the door open. I just kept kissing her, trying to get closer.

Rimmel's tongue slipped into my mouth, and I groaned.

"Yo, dude!" Braeden hollered. "You're not alone anymore."

Beneath me, Rimmel stiffened. Her hands that had found their way to the button of my jeans went rigid.

I lifted my head and blinked, trying to bring my sight back into focus. Braeden was standing down by my feet, staring at us with an amused expression on his face. "Did you not even hear Ivy come in the room?"

"No," I growled. The desire was still pumping through me, and I was irritated that he was talking.

"Well, you gave her a show."

Rimmel buried her face in my neck with a little squeal.

"I'll be right out."

"C'mon, blondie. Let's give them a few." Braeden tossed his arm around Ivy, who was standing right there and I hadn't even seen her.

When the door closed behind them, I dropped my forehead down on the mattress beside Rimmel's face and sucked in a shuddering breath.

"Stay at my place tonight," I said, my voice hoarse.

"I have class in the morning."

"I'll drive you back." I'd get up in the middle of the night if I had to.

"I have to finish this paper. My laptop is running really slow lately, and it's due tomorrow." As she made excuses, her fingers slid into the waistband of my jeans.

"You can use my laptop. It's new. Hell, you can fucking have the thing."

She laughed.

I groaned. "Please, baby. I can't just leave you here."

My lips found hers again, and they did a better job convincing than any words ever would.

"Promise you'll let me finish the paper?" she asked and ripped her mouth free.

"On my honor," I said solemnly and pushed up off her to place a hand over my heart.

Her eyes went to my crotch and the massive tent in my jeans. Her tongue darted out and licked her bottom lip. I groaned.

"'Kay. Let's go."

I jumped up and gathered her laptop and power cord. "Get some clothes for the morning."

She needed some closet space at my house. I was too impatient for her to pack a bag. "I need my book bag," she said as she stuffed clothes into a duffle.

I tossed it over my shoulder and tucked the computer under my arm. Rimmel finished packing her bag and pushed her glasses back on her face. "Done."

I took her hand and towed her out into the hall. Braeden saw us and burst out laughing.

"I'll see you tomorrow," Rimmel said to Ivy, who was standing right beside Braeden.

After we dropped Braeden at his dorm, I grabbed her face and kissed her again. Long. Slow. Deep.

"You promised I could finish my paper," she reminded me, her voice husky.

"Yes, but I never promised anything about sleep."

"I don't need sleep. Just you."

I didn't think about Zach, football, or my mother the rest of the night. It was only her.

CHAPTER TWENTY-SEVEN

> #BreakingBuzz
> Sources say our favorite player is in
> talks with the NFL.
> #EpicMojo
> #CampusWontBeTheSameWithoutHim
>
> ... Alpha BuzzFeed

RIMMEL

Weeks flew by.

I saw Romeo, but not nearly as much as I wanted to. Most of the time we spent together was during tutoring or stolen kisses between classes or other obligations. I longed to sneak off to his place for another night or an entire weekend.

We talked about it over texts and when we saw each other, but the past couple weeks, it had been really hard to find long stretches of time to be alone.

I was spending time with Valerie. Nothing too excessive; I was trying to take it slow. She didn't push me, and I wondered if Romeo told her about my hesitation to become close to her or if maybe she was just perceptive. We had lunch one weekend. She took me to some place I'd never been. It wasn't the type of place Romeo and I usually ate, with paper napkins and loud music.

This place was quiet and beautiful. The napkins on the table were cloth, and we had bread plates and special water goblets. It hadn't been stuffy, though, or awkward; it had just been elegant.

Mostly we talked about the shelter and the plans for the fundraiser. Valerie was a very organized woman. She had notebooks and a calendar for everything. She didn't much ask about my life. Occasionally, she would ask about Romeo, or I would mention my grandmother.

We also went around one afternoon looking at venues for the event. They were all very classy, and I worried how much they would cost. She merely brushed off my concerns and said the cost of the tickets would cover the room price.

I tried to be myself as much as possible, much to my own detriment. I was afraid if I was too much like myself, she'd be appalled and want nothing to do with me. So I always dressed nicely and had Ivy do my hair when I met with her. But I didn't change my personality. I didn't change my glasses.

There were some things about me she was going to have to accept. I did want her to like me—not some version I'd created, but the real me.

Michelle was beyond thrilled about the fundraising opportunity and went on and on about how lucky I was to be involved with Romeo, who had such a good standing in the community. But his status wasn't why I was with him.

I loved him.

His eyes.

His smile.

The way he loved me.

Even though football season was over, he seemed as busy with it as ever. The NFL scout we met at the championship game called.

The NFL was interested. They were talking contracts, teams, drafting him.

Romeo's dad was handling the negotiations. Apparently, he'd been studying up on the ins and outs of football contracts and deals since Romeo was in middle school. And since he was a lawyer and had Romeo's best interests at heart, he made the perfect manager.

So in addition to the contract negotiations and the meetings with his father, Romeo was training just as hard as ever. He wanted this so badly, and now that his dream was right there in front of him, he wasn't going to let it go.

I was proud of him.

When I first met him, I thought he was just another player jock. I thought he was a user, a slacker, and was lucky enough to have some talent he could exploit.

I couldn't have been more wrong.

He worked hard. Harder than most people I'd ever met. School might not be his strong suit, but he tried and he worked at it. He trained endlessly and perfected the talent he had. He didn't take any of it for granted either.

He deserved this.

Of course, I was a little sad too. If he got drafted, where would that leave us?

I never voiced that worry out loud, never even hinted at it. I wouldn't be anything but supportive of him, and I wouldn't do anything to take away from his dream.

I had one last class before I could break for lunch. I was meeting Ivy and Missy at the food court. The granola bar I'd eaten in a hurry this morning on my way to class just hadn't been enough and my stomach growled relentlessly.

I was excited for class, though.

Yes. I know. No one gets excited for class.

Except nerds.

I'd come to accept that title. I owned it.

I was getting my paper back today, the one I'd worked tirelessly on since the first week of classes. I'd researched a ton, spent hours putting together the topic and thesis. I wrote it, edited it, and then reworked it. My computer made it hard because lately it'd been running slow, and I made a mental note to take it somewhere to have it looked at.

This paper was important to me because it was for my animal science class. This class was an important part of my major, and I wanted to do a good job and prove this was certainly the correct career field for me.

Not only that, but high marks on a paper of this topic would help me stand out to veterinary schools when I graduated.

I just knew I'd get a good grade. It was well researched, thorough, and organized. I was proud of this particular assignment, and I was looking forward to seeing the high marks.

I took my seat in class and listened to a short lecture on what we were going over next week and also a recap of everything we'd gone over this semester. It was boring, and while I tried to listen, my thoughts kept turning to Romeo.

I decided when we got out of class, I was going to call him and see if we could see each other tonight.

The professor announced that the papers we'd turned in were graded and once he gave those out, we were free to leave for the day. I tucked my things in my bag and waited while he passed them out.

When he handed mine over, he didn't smile or even acknowledge me. It was like he was trying not to look at me.

Odd.

I didn't really think about it because I was too anxious for my grade and his remarks so I flipped up the professional cover page I'd designed and stared down at the red writing.

SEE ME!

I glanced around the room, wondering if anyone else got such an odd note on their paper. No one else looked the least bit concerned. In fact, most people were already up out of their seats and fleeing the room.

I glanced back down and flipped through the entire paper. There were no other comments or feedback. Many passages were underlined with red, but that was all.

What in world was going on?

I sat there in confusion until the last student left the room. The professor was at the front, sitting behind his desk. I flipped the pages closed and stood, clutching it in my hand.

"Professor Monahan? Was there a problem with my work?"

He looked up at me with an accusatory expression. I faltered and almost took a step back.

"I really am quite disappointed," he said.

"Excuse me?" My heart started pounding beneath my ribcage and something in my stomach turned sour. I didn't know what was going on here, but I knew it wasn't good.

"All this time I thought you were a conscientious student. I thought you were truly dedicated to your major."

Horror filled me. "I am!"

How could he think anything less?

He shook his head sadly and then looked at me like I was some sort of gunk on the bottom of his shoe.

"Do you know how serious plagiarism is?"

I looked up swiftly. "What?"

"It's a very serious offense, Miss Hudson."

"Yes, I can imagine it is," I said, wary. "Why are you asking me about plagiarism?"

"Oh, drop the wide-eyed, innocent act," he snapped and pushed away from his desk. "We both know you're guilty and the paper you attempted to pass off as your own is not yours at all."

"*What!*" I gasped. "Professor Monahan, I can assure you I wrote every single word of this paper and I did *not* plagiarize it."

"Do I look like a fool to you?" he asked, leaning over his desk and giving me a look probably meant to make me think he could see through me.

It only made me angry.

"Are you actually accusing me of plagiarism?"

"Oh, I'm not accusing. I have proof."

I snorted. "You couldn't possibly."

His laptop was open on his desk, and he hit a few keys and then turned the screen around so I could see. "The age of the internet has made plagiarizing papers rather simple. Students often assume we as professors are too stupid or old to realize such things exist."

I stared down at the screen, trying to figure out what I was looking at.

"This, Miss Hudson, is a website that I and several other professors here on campus use to crosscheck papers turned in against papers that are for sale on various sites around the web."

I glanced away from the computer and up at the man accusing me of being a cheater.

A cheater.

If I wasn't so freaked out right now, I'd laugh. "So you're saying you checked my paper on this site"—I gestured to the laptop—"and it came up as a match?"

"That's exactly what I'm saying."

"Maybe a few sentences were very similar by coincidence. I mean, it is a well-documented topic."

"Yes. I might be inclined to believe that if it had only been one or two sentences, but this was about ninety percent of the paper. Far too much content to be a coincidence."

Suddenly, I felt lightheaded. The disbelief echoing through my body was profound. How was this even possible? I didn't purchase this paper. I worked on it. For weeks.

"I think I need to sit down," I said, gripping the edge of his desk.

I thought I saw a flash of something that might be construed as pity or doubt in his eyes, but then they hardened once more. "Yes. Well, you can sit down in the dean's office."

"Excuse me?" My fingers tightened on the ledge of his desk.

"I've alerted the dean. This is a very serious matter. Your very future at this university is at risk."

"What?" I stumbled a bit but caught myself. My book bag fell over my shoulder and down my arm.

"Let's go," he said and picked up his briefcase and a set of keys. "I'm to escort you there."

In all my life, I'd never been treated like a criminal. I'd never felt the squirmy sickness of panic quite like this. My hands broke out in a clammy sweat as my heart continued to race. I followed him out of the room, down the stairs, and out of the building.

The entire time I walked, I stared down at the paper, now marked in all red. It was my paper. I recognized the words on each page. I'd worked so long on it I could probably recite most of it in my sleep.

"Professor Monahan," I pleaded as we walked. "You have to believe me. This is some kind of mistake."

He looked back over his shoulder as we walked. "I don't make mistakes. This was blatant plagiary."

I swallowed down the bile in my throat and tried to calm my shaking limbs. As we walked, the wind whipped about and snow started to fall more heavily and coat the grass and sidewalk. I wondered if Ivy would wonder where I was, if she would think something was wrong.

I thought about texting her and telling her not to worry. But I couldn't.

Something was wrong.

And I was worried.

When we walked into the staff building where the dean's office was located, we continued through halls that smelled like bleach and lemon. Phones rang constantly and the sound of high heels clicking on the floor felt like nails on a chalkboard.

I took a steadying breath when we walked into the small entryway that led to the dean's office. An older woman was sitting behind a desk, and when we walked in, she looked up and smiled.

I couldn't force myself to smile back.

It took everything I had to not vomit.

"Tell him Professor Monahan is here," the professor said.

The receptionist nodded and did as she was asked. When she hung up the phone, she nodded. "You can go in."

On my way past, she gave me an encouraging smile. Tears rushed to my eyes, and she frowned.

"Hurry up, girl," Professor Monahan said with his hand on the dean's doorknob. Startled, I rushed forward and my foot caught the edge of an area rug beneath the receptionist's workstation. I went flying forward. The paper I once thought of as my best work went soaring and skidded beneath a chair.

"Oh my!" The woman gasped and rushed around to help me. "Are you all right, honey?"

I sniffed. My knee stung and so did the palm of my hand. But I pulled myself up. "Oh yes, I'm fine."

"Trying to make yourself look pitiful will only make things worse on you in the end," the professor intoned.

The receptionist frowned and shot him a sour look. "Here, let me help you." She went to retrieve my paper as I stood and straightened my coat.

"Here you go," she said, and I reached out to take it.

"Thank you," I said sincerely. Her kindness was welcome at that moment as my entire world was falling apart.

The large door to the dean's office sprang open and a man with broad shoulders filled the door. "I thought my appointment was—" he said but then stopped when he almost ran into the professor.

"We were just coming in, Dean," he said. "She was stalling."

"She fell! She could be hurt," the receptionist scolded.

The dean stepped around Professor Monahan and met my eyes. He recognized me immediately. I saw it flicker in his eyes. "Miss Hudson," he said. Then he looked at the professor, who was suddenly very uncomfortable.

"This is the girl you are accusing of plagiarism?" the dean asked, raising an eyebrow.

Professor Monahan faltered and then straightened, his posture rigid. "Yes. And I have proof."

I blew out a shaky breath. The woman beside me patted my shoulder.

I gave the dean a pleading look, but he only sighed and gestured toward this inside of his office. "Inside."

Professor Monahan was the first to go in. The dean stood and waited for me to pass. As I was slipping by him, he leaned down and whispered, "You need to make a call. *Call him.*"

My eyes flew up to his face. He gave me an imperceptible nod. I moved farther into the room, and the man accusing me gave me a hard stare.

I turned away from him and toward the dean. "Sir, would it be okay if I made a phone call? I have a feeling I'm going to be here a while and I don't want those waiting for me to worry."

He moved around his desk and gave me a displeased stare. "Quickly."

It was obvious he didn't want Professor Monahan to know he told me to call backup. I clung to that little nugget of knowledge like it was the last crumb of food in a desolate world.

Quickly, I dialed Romeo and prayed he answered. As it rang, I paced across the room, putting my back to the men.

"Hey." Romeo's voice filled the line. It was so rich, warm, and welcoming that I whimpered. "Rimmel," he said immediately, all the warmth in his voice replaced with alarm.

"I think I might need you," I squeaked into the line.

"Who is that?" Professor Monahan said loudly from across the room. "Who are you calling?"

There was a heartbeat of silence on the line, and then with cold calmness Romeo said, "Who was that?"

"Son?" Romeo's dad came through the other end of the line.

"You're with your dad?" I asked, gripping the phone as tight as I could.

"Yes. At the house. What's going on, Rimmel?"

"I'm at the dean's office on campus. Can you come? And bring your dad. I think I might need a lawyer."

CHAPTER TWENTY-EIGHT

ROMEO

Something was wrong.

The second I heard her whimper, everything inside me went on high alert. And the man yelling in the background, who the hell was that?

I yanked the phone away from my ear and looked at my father.

"Something's wrong with Rimmel. We need to go. She said she might need a lawyer."

My father frowned and stood up immediately. As if sensing my urgency, he didn't ask me any questions. He just grabbed his briefcase and suit jacket and followed me outside.

The car roared to life as soon as I hit the door of the house, and I barely gave Dad time to close the passenger door before I went tearing down the driveway.

"Careful now," Dad said. "You won't be any help to her if you're wrecked on the side of the road."

I wasn't going to wreck. And if I did, I'd get out and run the rest of the way to campus.

"She's at the dean's office," I said, not taking my eyes off the road.

The little whimper she gave when she heard my voice pounded through my ears and haunted me.

"I hope this isn't about Zach." Dad sighed.

My knuckles went white. Was this his plan all along? Lay low for weeks, act like he was going to obey the restraining order, and not so much as speak a word about me or Rimmel to anyone.… and then *bam!* do something insane?

If this was him, I was going to kill him.

I was going to go to jail for the rest of my life for murder.

I slid around the corner of the parking lot and stopped the car at the curb, not bothering with a space.

"Son," Dad said when I was getting out of the car. "Don't go in there swinging. Be calm. Don't act until we know the situation. Being a hothead might just make whatever is going on worse for her."

I heard his words but didn't reply. I knew he was right, but the panic pumping through my bloodstream made it really hard to listen.

The woman behind the receptionist desk jumped to her feet when I strode in.

"I knew I recognized her," she said immediately.

"Excuse me?" I snapped.

"You're the football player, right? The one who jumped into the stands for his girlfriend."

"Yeah?" I said, impatient.

"She's in there," she answered, pointing at the office door.

"What's going on? Can you tell us anything?" Dad said as I paced to the door.

"I'm not really sure." The woman hedged. "But the professor was very mad. He yelled at her. Poor thing was so scared she fell on the floor."

And that was all I needed to hear.

I didn't even knock. I flung open the door so hard it hit against the wall. Rimmel was sitting in a chair opposite the dean's desk, looking frighteningly pale and worried. She jumped up when I stalked in, and her bag fell off her lap onto the floor.

"This is a private meeting!" A man to her right gasped. I assumed this was the asswipe who made her fall.

"Who the hell are you?" I growled and planted myself in front of Rimmel, facing the man.

To his credit, the dean sat calmly at his desk and just watched the unfolding scene.

The man I was itching to punch looked at the dean. "You're going to allow him to just burst in here?"

My father stepped into the room and calmly shut the door.

"Ryan," he said, calling the dean by his first name. "What's going on?"

The professor looked back and forth between the dean and my father.

"Ryan" stood from his chair and held out his hand to shake with my father. "So sorry to have to call you down here like this, Anthony."

"You called him!" the professor yelled.

I gave him a hard, dismissive look and he shut up.

"Professor Monahan," the dean said formally, "this is our school's quarterback, Roman Anderson, and this is his father, *lawyer* Anthony Anderson."

The professor swallowed. "I didn't recognize you Romeo," he said.

"Result's still the same," I growled.

"Miss Hudson is dating Roman. Has been for a while now. She also tutors him, helps him keep up his grades so he is eligible to play on the team."

"She's family," I said. I didn't like the way "dating" sounded. It just wasn't good enough. Not for Rimmel.

I felt her hand on the back of my shirt. I felt the way her fingers shook, and it pissed me off all over again.

"Facts are facts," Professor Monahan said.

The dean sighed. "Yes. I understand that."

He flashed my father a quick regretful look.

"What the hell is going on!" I burst out and shifted to wrap an arm around Rimmel. She sank into my side for a long moment but then pulled back and straightened.

"I've been accused of plagiarism," she announced.

My father and I both laughed.

She glanced at me with solemn eyes. "I'm serious. Apparently, ninety percent of the paper—*my* paper—that I turned in a few weeks ago is available for purchase on a website."

"Yes, and the other eight percent can be found on various other websites, the content word for word," the professor added like he'd somehow delivered the nail in her coffin.

"You have no idea how lucky you are that if I punched you right now it would only hurt her," I said low.

The professor paled.

My father stepped forward. "What kind of evidence do you have to back up these allegations?"

The dean handed him a stack of papers. He took several minutes to look them over and then glanced at me. His eyes didn't hold much good news.

"Are you charging her with something?"

I stepped forward toward the dean, my eyes narrowed. He glanced at me with the same kind of look he gave me the night the cops came and searched my car for his nameplate. His hands were tied.

"No." He hedged. "Not as of today."

The professor gasped. "This is ridiculous. You have everything you need to strip that girl of her scholarship and toss her out of this school."

Rimmel sank in her chair like she couldn't stand anymore. I was completely floored. This was that bad? They were going to kick her out of school?

"Are you serious?" I exclaimed. "Her grades are perfect. She's a model student. When she isn't studying or tutoring, she's volunteering at the damn animal shelter, for Christ sakes!"

"I have to agree, Ryan. Expulsion seems a little extreme at this time," my father said.

Ryan inclined his head. "Alpha University code of student conduct states that plagiarism of any kind will not be tolerated by this university and students will be asked to leave."

"Are you aware, Dean," my father said, snapping into lawyer mode, "that Miss Hudson here has been repeatedly harassed and stalked by one of your students here at Alpha U?"

He frowned. "Yes, of that I am acutely aware."

"And that a restraining order has been placed on that individual on behalf of Miss Hudson and for the safety of her person?"

"Yes, I am also aware of that, Anthony," the dean said.

"Then you must find it to be not improbable that this is some kind of elaborate payback for the loss of that student's status here on campus."

"You cannot deny the facts." The professor spoke up. "That paper is on the internet for sale. It has been for sale since before she turned it in."

I glanced at Rimmel and she nodded miserably.

"What reason would a student with a four-point average have to plagiarize?" my father asked.

Professor Monahan was ready for the question. "Maybe the pressure of maintaining that average became too much. As you already pointed out, she tutors and volunteers in addition to her heavy course load. Perhaps with all of that in addition to dating a very popular man on campus, she has become too overwhelmed to perform in class."

I fisted my hands at my sides. "That is bullshit."

"Roman," my father admonished.

"I think it best if we take a little time to process this. I'll go over the documentation, consult with a few colleagues, and then ascertain what the best recourse would be."

"Are you serious?" the professor intoned.

The dean gave him a withering look. "Careful, Harold, you're sounding like a teacher with an axe to grind. Is this personal?"

He flushed.

"Of course not."

"Then you will respect my decision." He turned toward my father. "Out of professional respect for your family and on behalf of the MVP player here at Alpha U, I also extend this as a courtesy to you. Anthony, I will provide my full cooperation in this matter, as I assume you will be representing Miss Hudson."

"Of course. Thank you, Ryan."

"I don't understand what's happening." Rimmel spoke up from her chair.

My heart lurched.

The dean looked at her. "Right now, Miss Hudson, you are on probation. You may remain here on campus, remain in the dorm, but you are not permitted to go to class. You need to remain on campus—"

"What!" I growled. I would not have her an inmate of the school. Hells no.

The dean ignored me and glanced over at my father. "However, you are permitted to go to the Anderson home as often as needed, as he is your legal counsel."

"What about my scholarship?" Rimmel worried. Her hands were clasped so tightly in her lap they were white.

"That is also on hold. The school provides the funding for you to attend this university under strict guidelines that you adhere to school policy. Plagiarism is a direct and serious violation. If after we have looked at all the evidence and I must conclude you are, in fact, guilty, then your scholarship will be stripped away and you will be expelled. Hence, you will be escorted off campus the day I make that call."

A tear slipped down her cheek and she lowered her head.

I wanted to scoop her up and protect her. This was all so ridiculous. Rimmel didn't have a cheating bone in her entire body.

"This is ridiculous," I swore.

"Roman, why don't you take Rimmel home? She's looking a little ill at the moment," my father said. "I have a few more things to discuss with Ryan. I'll call a cab when we're done."

I nodded and slid an arm around Rimmel and practically lifted her out of the chair. I picked up her backpack and the crumpled papers at her feet. When I turned, she was standing in front of my father with watery eyes. "Thank you for coming."

Dad's eyes softened and he cleared his throat. Even he was ruffled by her earnest and sorrowful eyes.

"Of course," he said and took her hand. "We'll talk later."

I pulled her into my side. On the way out of the room, I gave the professor accusing her of such bullshit another disdainful stare. My mind churned with ways I could punish him for hurting her like this.

Once we were out in the hall and the dean's door was closed behind us, she leaned back against the wood and let out a huge sigh.

"Hey," I said, turning so my body blocked her from the prying eyes of the receptionist.

She gave me a weak smile as another tear slipped over her cheek. "What the hell am I going to do?" she rasped.

"It's gonna be okay." I reached for her and, feeling the way her body trembled, I bent down and swept her up in my arms.

Her cheek fell against my chest and her hand curled up around my neck.

"Is she all right?" the woman asked from behind her desk.

I gave her a smile and winked. "She's just fine. She just likes it when I carry her."

The woman sighed. "Well, I can certainly see why."

Rimmel made a choking sound as I walked through the building. "My life is falling apart, and old women are hitting on you."

"I'm sorry, baby. I'll try to be less irresistible."

She snorted and wiped her nose on my shirt.

Outside, I shifted her weight into one arm and opened the passenger door with the other. I put her in the seat and tossed her book bag in the back.

"I don't want to go to the dorm. Not right now."

"My place," I said.

She nodded and laid her head against the seat.

"Hey," I said, taking her jaw and turning her head so she could look at me. "This is gonna be fine. We're gonna fix this."

Her eyes welled up with new tears, and I swore. After a quick kiss to her lips, I jogged around and got in the driver's seat.

We had to fix this.

If she lost her scholarship, she would likely go back to Florida.

Her whole life would be shattered.

And so would mine.

CHAPTER TWENTY-NINE

RIMMEL

Expelled.

Plagiarism.

Cheated.

Stripped of scholarship.

These were the words that went around and around inside my scattered mind. I was shell-shocked, confused, and embarrassed.

How could anyone think I would cheat?

How could almost my entire paper be found online?

What was I going to do if I got expelled from school?

The questions were relentless. The doubt that clouded everything nearly blinded me.

One moment, I was excited for class, sitting there in anticipation for a good grade that was well deserved. I was planning what I would have for lunch with my friends at the food court.

And the next moment, everything was blown apart.

"Rim," Romeo said from beside me. His voice sounded a thousand miles away. I blinked and realized we were at his house. I climbed out of the cold, ignoring the several inches of snow coating the ground.

I walked past the now covered pool and didn't bat an eye.

Inside the house, I took off my boots and hung my coat by the door. Romeo did the same, adding my backpack by the shoes.

I wandered into the living room aimlessly, not really knowing what to do with myself.

The familiar sound of loud purring and the feel of warm fur rubbing against my leg stole my attention, and I looked down to see Murphy weaving in and out of my legs. A sob broke free, one I hadn't even realized I'd been holding back, and I scooped up the cat and hugged him into my chest.

There were so many implications of what just happened I could barely sort through my thoughts.

"What the hell happened today?" Romeo gently asked from beside me.

I dropped onto the couch, still holding Murphy close. "I have no idea. He just accused me, right out of nowhere."

"My dad will figure this out," he said, sounding so sure.

I felt anything but sure.

"This could ruin my entire career," I said. "Before it even starts."

He started to shake his head, to say something to try and make me feel better. But I stopped him.

"Even if they prove it wasn't me, the cloud of dishonesty will follow me. I was supposed to start applying to vet schools this fall. Do you know how competitive it is to get into those? They look at everything, and everyone has a list of achievements. Now I'll be the girl who might have plagiarized."

"Rim—"

"No," I snapped. "This was my dream. It *is* my dream. And it's slipping through my fingers."

He ran a hand over his face and looked at me like he had no idea what to say.

"How am I supposed to sit here and wait for a room full of men to decide my future?"

"We aren't just going to sit here," he said, his face a mask of determination.

"Then what are we going to do?"

"We're gonna figure this out."

Murphy jumped down from my lap, and I turned my body so it faced Romeo. "You never even asked."

His head tilted to the side. "Asked what?"

"If I did it. You never even asked me if it was true."

"That's because I *know* you didn't. There's no way in hell."

Emotion so hard and swift squeezed my chest. He had faith in me, and it meant so much. "Thank you for coming when I called today."

"Baby, don't you know by now that whenever you need me, I'm gonna come?"

Suddenly, not everything seemed so incredibly terrible. Yes, it was still achingly bad and I still wanted to barf, but I no longer felt like my entire world was over.

I still had Romeo.

"He told me to call you, you know."

"Who?" Romeo asked, his eyes narrowing.

"The dean."

He nodded. "Makes sense. He must not think you did this either."

"But he suspended me. He's talking about expelling me."

"He has too, Rim. Just like when he had to search me and my car. He's bound by policy and rules." He threaded his fingers through mine and squeezed. "It's a good sign he wanted you to call. He knows if anyone can get you out of this, it's my Dad."

"I just wish I knew what happened," I said and laid my head against the couch.

"Hey now," Romeo said and reached for me. "What's this?"

"What?"

"I'm the only pillow you need." He spread out on the couch and tugged me between his legs so I was leaning against him. I turned on my side and laid my cheek on his chest, and he wrapped me in his arms.

I felt safe here with him. His arms were my safe zone. They were the most sure thing in my life.

"Romeo?" I whispered, not really wanting to put it out there, but unable to keep it in.

"Hmm?"

"Do you think it's possible Zach somehow had something to do with this?"

"Yeah. I do." His voice held a note of steel, and I shivered. Romeo was a laidback guy, but Zach was pushing him way too far.

"But how?"

"I don't know. But if your paper ended up on some site for people to buy *before* you turned it in, then someone had to have taken it and posted it up there." It made sense. It was the only way that could have happened.

"I never worked on my paper on any computer other than mine. Except that one night here with you."

"Has anyone had access to your computer lately? Borrowed it?"

"No, and it's been running so slow no one would want to use it anyway. I really thought it would last longer than a year and a half."

"You keep your computer in your dorm, right? Who all has access to the room besides Ivy?"

"No one," I replied. "Ivy didn't do this." I felt I had to point that out.

"Maybe someone snuck in to your room when you were both gone one night."

"Then it would have to be a girl. Someone who lives in my dorm. They're the only ones with access," I said without conviction because it just didn't seem right. Yes, there were girls that were jealous of my relationship with Romeo, but to go as far as to steal something and try and get me kicked out of school?

That was extreme.

"Not necessarily," Romeo said, his voice hard.

"What do you mean?" I lifted my head and looked up.

"Anyone can have access to the building if they're let in. They let me and B in all the time."

"But you're *you*." I pointed out.

He chuckled. "I'm not the only guy on campus, though." But then his voice hardened and his arm came back around me, tighter than before. "And clearly there's someone in that dorm with no standards or Zach wouldn't have been able to get in the building to stalk you in the shower."

And then I remembered.

I gasped and sprang up. I turned, sitting between his legs, and stared at him with wide eyes.

"He wasn't just in the bathroom that day," I rushed out. Memories of that morning came flooding back.

Ivy in bed. Ivy's clothes all over. Ivy hungover and then later her embarrassed confession.

"What do you mean?" Romeo said, flat.

"He was in my room. He spent the night there."

"What?"

"Ivy went to the pre-game party at the Omega house. She got really, really drunk."

"Are you saying she brought Zach back to your room and screwed him?"

"Well, I wasn't going to put it like that."

Romeo let out a string of cuss words and climbed off the couch to pace the room. "That guy has no fucking morals at all. He probably got her drunk just so he could take advantage."

"She was really embarrassed and didn't want to tell me."

"That girl," he muttered. "She seriously needs to keep her legs closed."

"Romeo!" I gasped.

He shrugged. "It's the truth. If she hadn't been so willing to screw him, he wouldn't have had access to your room. To the bathroom that morning. To your computer…"

"She's my friend," I said, firm. "You can't say things—"

"Forget Ivy." He cut me off. "Where's your laptop?"

I blinked. "At the dorm."

"We need to go get it."

"Why?"

"Because he might have left some kind of trail or timestamp behind on the hard drive."

I sighed. That seemed like such a long shot. "Even if he had snooped on my laptop that night, my paper wasn't done then. I had it started, but it wasn't completed."

"So?" He didn't seem to get what I was saying.

"So… over ninety percent of the paper was found on sites online. Whoever did this had to have taken it once I was almost finished writing it."

"We need to get your computer," he said again, just as anxious as before. "Maybe he somehow hacked into it and left behind some kind of open doorway that allowed him to access it from a different location."

"Is that even possible?" I wondered out loud.

"I'm sure as hell gonna find out." He stalked out of the room, and I heard the rustling of his coat and the jingling of his car keys.

I rushed after him, trying not to get my hopes up.

This *was* a long shot.

But it was the only shot I had.

CHAPTER THIRTY

ROMEO

My hands were tied.

By my father literally forbade me to go near Zach.

Frankly, I thought it was ridiculous for us to sit around and wait… and wait some more, when I could just go find him and beat the truth out of him in seconds.

Problem solved.

No one else seemed to agree with my logic.

Except Braeden.

But my father forbade him too.

And yeah, I could have gone and done it anyway. My hands pretty much shook with the desire every second of every day that passed. But I didn't.

I guess deep down underneath all my anger was a piece of me that agreed with my father.

Fuck. I was turning into an adult.

As much as I wanted to kill Zach, doing so would make this worse. It would give him and his father a reason to sue us. It would make Rimmel look guiltier than she already did, and it would fuck up my chances with the NFL.

The NFL whom I just signed with.

I was now a professional football player, a free agent who was being pursued by two major teams. It was only a matter of time before I was drafted, before I was given the chance to prove myself on the field.

My father was still in negotiations. There were meetings. There was training. There was a lot going on.

And I wasn't even excited anymore.

How could I be excited about my dream when Rimmel's life was being ripped apart?

We went and got her laptop and I looked around on it. I didn't see a thing, but that didn't mean something wasn't there. I wasn't a computer geek. But it was running slow, and I was taking that as a sign something was wrong.

I was going to give it to one of the guys I knew on campus to go through it, but my father didn't want it going to anyone associated with Alpha U. Instead, he called in a favor with a guy who did shit like this on high-profile cases around the country.

The laptop was overnighted to him, and we were sitting around waiting for him to get his thumb out of his ass and find something.

Okay, he wasn't sitting around with a thumb in his ass.

He was working on a high-profile murder case, but still. Rimmel was more important to me. And watching her wait was like pulling out my eyelashes one at a time with a pair of tweezers.

She was still on probation—basically campus arrest with permission to be at my place (under the assumption she was spending all her time working with my father, her lawyer). She couldn't go to classes, and the rumor mill was flying.

At this point, the BuzzBoss might as well just rename the Alpha app *Romeo & Rimmel's Reality Show*. I thought about hunting that guy down and punching him in the face too.

I found her with red eyes and blotchy skin too many times to ignore this was killing her.

On the third day of waiting, I stormed into the dean's office and demanded she be allowed to continue her volunteer work at the shelter. I couldn't stand seeing her so restless and lost. My mother even sent in a whole stack of paperwork and receipts to prove the work Rimmel was doing to put together a large fundraiser in the community to help.

He agreed, like I knew he would.

He seemed apologetic and even guilty that this was happening. But as he reminded me on my way out of the office, he had no choice.

And then he wished us luck on disproving the plagiarism allegations.

I thought being able to go back to the place she loved would help snap Rimmel out of her listlessness. It didn't.

If anything, she withdrew further away from me and hid at the shelter with her beloved animals.

A week after she was suspended from classes and basically shoved into limbo, I'd had enough. Going to classes, training (even harder than usual to work out frustration), fielding calls, and meetings with the NFL—basically living my life was getting to me.

I had everything I ever wanted, but it meant nothing.

Rimmel's misery overshadowed everything. I couldn't be happy unless she was.

My phone rang as I was walking in the door from a two-hour training session. "Dad?" I replied the second I saw it was him.

"I wanted to let you and Rimmel know that my contact is going to start combing through her laptop tonight. He should have some answers for us tomorrow or the next day."

"About friggin' time," I muttered.

"It's been a long week," Dad conceded. "He's going to find something, and when he does, I'll have all the allegations dropped and erased from her record so this can't follow her into next year."

"And what about Zach?" I asked, hard.

He sighed. "We'll deal with Zach."

I bristled and my father grunted. "Just keep your nose clean, son. You're a free agent with the NFL. You cannot afford any bad press, any arrests, nothing. You won't help Rimmel by ruining your life."

"Look, Dad, I have to go."

"You'll tell Rimmel?"

"Yeah, I'll go over there now."

"Maybe bring her by. Your mother is worried about her. It might make her feel better if she sees her."

"Yeah, okay." I agreed, then hung up.

My mother had taken a real liking to my girlfriend. She held back so as not to overwhelm her (per my request), but I knew it was only a matter of time before my mom would go full maternal on her and I wouldn't be able to rein her in.

Really, I thought it would be good for Rim. She didn't have a mother, and my mother always wanted more than one child. But I wasn't going to push that. Rimmel had to make her own choices about her relationship with Mom.

If she decided she couldn't be close to her, then that would be it. Either way, I was going to support her.

I glanced at the clock and knew Rimmel was still at the shelter, so I decided to take a quick shower and change before driving over to the dorm. On the way, I'd swing by the shelter and pick her up.

Only she wasn't at the shelter.

Michelle seemed confused when I walked in to pick her up.

"Rim in the back?" I asked.

"She left for the day. I thought you knew…" she said awkwardly.

"No. I'm here to pick her up."

"Well, she told me she texted you and then left a few minutes later." Michelle frowned.

I didn't want to make her feel bad. Clearly, she already felt somewhat guilty. "No worries." I smiled at her and she relaxed. "She probably walked back to campus." The thought gave me a rash. "She likes to walk." But I never let her. Because it was dangerous.

Irritation slammed into me. The distance between us was over. I was going to find her and fix this because I couldn't take it anymore.

"I'll just run by the dorm and see her. Thanks," I called and then left without waiting for a reply. I hurried to my car and drove to campus, looking for her as I drove.

She was nowhere to be seen, and I was partially glad. It was already dark out, and I hoped if she had walked, she'd done so before the sun went down.

One of the girls going into the dorm let me in, and I bounded up the steps and knocked on her door. I could hear music playing inside, and I pictured her sitting on her bed, singing off-key.

Ivy opened the door and her eyes widened. "Romeo."

"Hey," I said without my usual smile. I couldn't help it. I was still sort of pissed she'd let Zach in her pants.

"What are you doing here?" She seemed confused.

What the hell else would I be here for? "Uh, to see my girlfriend."

"But she went out with you." Then her mouth dropped open. "Well, at least that's what she said."

"Explain," I growled.

Ivy opened up the door all the way and waved me inside. She went across the room and pointed to a bouquet of red roses on the table beside Rimmel's bed.

"You sent her these…" she said like it was obvious. "You asked her to meet you." Ivy held up a small white envelope that had been propped up against the vase.

I was an asshole for two reasons:

1.) I did not send these flowers.

and

2.) I probably should have.

I slid the small white card out of the envelope to read the message that was "from me."

Meet me on the field at 8:00 -R

I glanced up at Ivy. "I didn't send this."

Her eyes got big. "Then who did?"

I let out a curse. "She went here?" I said, motioning to the card.

Ivy nodded. "She was surprised but happy. She thought she was meeting you."

Panic, sharp and pungent, filled me. I crumpled the card in my hand and rushed from the room.

Someone sent Rimmel a note, pretending to be me.

Someone who obviously wanted to get her alone.

And now she was.

CHAPTER THIRTY-ONE

RIMMEL

All the work was done. I'd spent so much time here the past few days that there was nothing left to scrub, organize, or feed.

The shelter never looked better, but me… I was a mess.

I missed Romeo, the closeness we usually shared. Even when we'd gone through stretches of time between us, I still felt close to him. But lately it'd been muffled. It'd been hard to grasp.

And I knew it was my fault.

I needed to stop hiding and stop pushing everyone away.

"Since everything is done, I thought I would leave early," I told Michelle.

"Of course!" she said. "This place is spotless."

"Great. Thanks!"

"Do you need a ride to campus?"

"Oh no, I texted Romeo." I lied.

The truth was I wanted to walk. I wanted to clear my head and organize my thoughts. I needed to compartmentalize some of my feelings and put them away so I could be there for Romeo. I barely knew what was going on in his life because I'd been so focused on the crash and burn of mine.

Michelle smiled and called out a good-bye before she went back to her office. I was relieved I didn't have to stand around and pretend to wait, so I hurried out into the cold and started in the direction of campus.

There was snow on the sidewalk and on the ground, so I walked carefully and tucked my head down against the wind.

The walk was good for me and I enjoyed being out in the fresh air. Even if it was freezing. When I got back to the dorm, I ignored the stares of some of the girls and went about my business. I took a shower and then spent more time than I liked blowing my hair completely dry.

I hadn't been trying at all with my appearance lately, and since I planned to call Romeo later, I decided to make an effort to look nice.

Once my hair was brushed out and falling around my shoulders, I dressed in a pair of light-colored skinny jeans, brown boots, and a white sweater with sparkly gold elbow patches.

Ivy walked in from class and gave me a onceover. "Wow, what's the occasion?"

I shrugged. "I'm just tired of being depressed."

She nodded with a frown. "I still feel terrible—" She started, but I held up my hand.

"Stop apologizing. You couldn't have known what Zach was after the night you brought him here."

She flopped down on her bed. "Is there any word at all from the computer guy? From Romeo's dad?"

"No," I said glumly. With a week already passed and no new proof in my favor, I was beginning to think there wasn't going to be any.

"Ugh!" Ivy shouted. "I can't believe he would do this to you!"

"Well, technically, we don't know it was him," I allowed.

Ivy made a rude noise. "Yes, we do."

There was a firm knock at the door. Ivy and I shared a look. "You expecting anyone?" I asked.

She shook her head. "You?"

I shrank back, suddenly worried it was more bad news. "No."

She jumped up from the bed and flicked her long hair over her shoulder. She pulled open the door only enough to poke out her head.

"Rimmel Hudson," a man said from the other side of the door, and I stiffened.

I heard her exclaim with excitement. "Thank you!" she called, then came back in the room, slamming it shut with her foot.

"Look!" she squealed.

I glanced over and gasped. She was carrying a huge bouquet of red roses. It was so large I couldn't even see her head behind the blossoms.

"It's gorgeous," I breathed, taking in the silky petals, the bright red, and the way they gracefully arched out of the large glass vase.

No one had ever sent me flowers before.

"Read the card!" Ivy exclaimed as she set them on the table near my bed. "Even though we already know who they're from."

I smiled and snatched the card off the little cardholder thingy in the middle of the bouquet. I giggled and pressed it to my chest. "He wants to meet me. Tonight."

Ivy pretended to swoon while I stood there with a goofy smile on my face. I guessed Romeo had enough of the distance between us too.

"What do you think he has planned?" Ivy asked.

"I don't know," I replied, gently setting the card with the vase. I leaned in to smell the blossoms. "I don't really even care," I mused.

Ivy sighed. "He's like the perfect guy."

I glanced at the clock. I had an hour before I was to meet him. I thought about texting him and saying how much I loved the flowers, but I decided to wait. I wanted to tell him in person.

Ivy started fussing with my hair and ended up flat-ironing it so it was sleek against my shoulders. She went on and on about romance, but I barely listened. I was too busy thinking about Romeo.

When it was close to eight, I pulled on my coat and tucked my phone in my pocket. "Don't wait up," I told Ivy.

She laughed and made me promise to give her all the details later.

I wasn't entirely sure what field to go to, but I decided the indoor field would probably be where he meant. He knew how much the cold bothered me, so it made sense he would have us meet inside.

It wasn't a short walk, but by the time I got there, my toes and fingers were numb. I didn't see his car anywhere outside, and I hoped that didn't mean I was at the wrong field. But I decided to go inside anyway. He might have parked on the other side where I couldn't see his car.

I walked inside, sort of at the underneath level (even though it was on the ground) because the stadium seats rose up above it, creating this hollowed-out space below where fans could buy their tickets to scrimmage games. There were also bathrooms down here and a concession stand, which was obviously closed.

As I walked, my footsteps echoed over the concrete, and the slightest inkling of fear slithered up my spine. I pushed away the shiver and continued on, wondering what kind of surprise Romeo had planned.

I walked up the stairs leading to the field and bleachers. "Romeo?" I called, thinking it seemed kind of still and dark in here for someone who had planned something.

He didn't answer, but I did hear a sound. The sound of scuffling feet above.

I paused but then continued the rest of the way up, thinking it must be Romeo.

"I got the flowers," I called. "They're so beautiful."

When I reached the top of the stairs, I walked across the floor toward the railing to overlook the field.

It was way too dark in here. There was only enough light for me to make out where I was going.

Clearly, I was at the wrong field.

Dreading the walk to the other field, I pulled out my cellphone to call Romeo. I would just ask him to come get me. I was too cold to walk.

A light kicked on and I jumped back and held up my arm to shield my eyes. It was so bright and intense that my eyes watered even as I shielded them.

"Hello?" I called out. "Romeo?"

Someone behind me laughed. Someone up higher in the stands.

Romeo didn't laugh like that.

The spotlight that had been blinding me swung around the large space, making me dizzy before it settled on its target.

"You're late," the voice said.

I gasped and looked up.

I knew that voice.

He was illuminated by the light, standing up on one of the bench seats, and staring down at me with cocky smile.

"Zach," I said, confused. "What are you doing here?"

"Waiting for you," he answered like it was obvious.

Fear slammed into me and I rushed forward to the steps. Two figures materialized out of the darkened stairwell and rushed me. The cellphone in my hand was ripped away, and I heard it break apart when it was thrown against the concrete wall.

I screamed.

A set of unrelenting arms wrapped around my waist, and even though I kicked and screamed, he held me captive.

"Bring her," Zach ordered.

I was dragged forward on the orders of a man who had truly lost his mind.

CHAPTER THIRTY-TWO

> #ItsSoCold
> I just saw a teenager with his pants pulled up.
> #ButtCracksGetColdToo #StayWarm
>
> ... Alpha BuzzFeed

ROMEO

Thirty minutes.

That's how long ago Rimmel was supposed to meet the person pretending to be me.

I was certain who that person was by now.

I called her phone for the millionth time as I tore across campus to the indoor football field and prayed to God I had the right place.

She isn't answering.

She's been alone with him for thirty minutes.

She isn't answering.

Fuck my future.

I was going to kill him.

I should have taken him out a long time ago. This was all my fault. If I had, then she wouldn't be in danger and I wouldn't be on the verge of panic.

The parking lot was empty, but I knew that didn't mean anything. I sped all the way to the entrance and slammed the brakes. I left the Hellcat sitting right there, pocketed the keys, and rushed in the door.

"Rimmel!" I roared and ran inside and up the stairs. "Rimmel!"

There was a bright light shining down on the field. It was pointed at the end, at one of the field goal poles. My eyes followed the light as the sound of muffled yells echoed through the stadium.

Holy.

Shit.

My entire body froze. It was as if for a heartbeat, everything in me stopped working. The horror of what I was looking at completely shut me down.

Rimmel was in the center of the spotlight. Her arms and legs were tied together and there was something binding her mouth so she couldn't speak.

But that wasn't the worst part.

The worst part was her location.

She was hanging from the goal post.

Thick rope wrapped around her middle and she was strung up like some kind of human piñata.

I'd never know this kind of rage before. I'd never known this kind of fear.

It was the kind that rendered me instantly numb, almost like my brain just couldn't comprehend the kind of shit it was seeing. Adrenaline surged through my system, making me feel jittery, and my stomach clenched so hard that I had to swallow back the gagging reflex forcing its way up my throat.

She was looking in my direction. I wasn't sure if she could see me, but she must have heard me call her name. Even from the distance between us, I could see her tearstained cheeks and the fear in her eyes.

Her glasses were gone.

She was yelling and screaming, but whatever was against her mouth made it so I couldn't hear anything.

"I'm here, baby," I screamed. "I'm gonna get you down."

I readied to leap over the railing to get down to the field, but movement below her stopped me.

"'Bout time you showed up," Zach said, stepping up close to where she hung. He was dragging something along behind him, and my eyes narrowed.

"Quit being such a fucking moron, Zach. If you got a problem with me, then be a man and come at me. Don't pick on a defenseless woman," I yelled.

"But watching you rush around to her defense is just so rewarding," he crooned.

What the fuck? This guy was seriously off his rocker. He needed a padded cell and meds. Like now.

"I wonder," Zach yelled as I leapt over the railing and landed on the field. "How long does it take hypothermia to set in?"

What the fuck? I started toward them.

"Or is it possible for someone to drown without being submerged in water?"

Rimmel started screaming, her muffled cries panicked, and her body began swinging back and forth.

Zach lifted what was in his hands.

Rimmel screamed more.

I was down at the other end of the field and I started to run. "Don't do it," I growled.

Zach laughed.

Then he held up the hose the maintenance team used and aimed it at Rimmel.

"No!" I roared and pushed my body as hard as it would go. I covered the field quickly, but I wasn't fast enough.

Water shot out of the nozzle and hit Rimmel. Her body jerked like it was shot as water drenched her entire body.

Zach laughed and laughed. He sounded like a maniac as he waved the hose all around, making sure to spray every last inch of her.

As I drew closer, I heard her struggling. I saw the water rushing into her face.

Pissed off didn't even begin to cover how I felt.

I crouched low and rammed into Zach from behind. He'd been so involved in torturing Rimmel that he hadn't even known I was coming.

I tackled him into the ground and he dropped the hose. I sat up, pinned him to the ground with my weight, and started punching him as hard as I could. I was so angry that I didn't even aim. I just punched and hit him anywhere. His moans and the sound of crunching bones were the most satisfying sounds I'd ever heard.

"Keep… hitt… ing." Zach laughed between hits. His teeth were outlined in blood. "She's… gonna… freeze.

I hit him again and his head rocked to the side, and he didn't move. I shoved away from him and looked up at Rimmel hanging from the pole, bound in rope, and dripping wet. She was already shivering.

"I'm gonna get you down, baby. Hang on," I said.

From the sidelines, two guys watched the unfolding scene like they were shocked. "What the fuck did you think was going to happen when you helped that pecker kidnap a woman?" I yelled. "Find something to cut her down!"

They snapped into action, and I gauged the distance that she was hanging above me. I wasn't going to be able to jump to reach her. How the hell had he even gotten her up there?

I felt Rimmel's stare as I moved around down below, looking around for anything I could use to get her down. Her eyes were glued to me like she was clinging to my image.

I stopped and looked up at her. "I'm not going anywhere. Everything's okay now."

More tears fell from her eyes, and for the first time, I noticed the bruise on the side of her face.

He hit her.

He. Fucking. Hit. Her.

Impatient and unwilling to venture too far away from her to look for a ladder, I took a running start and leapt up on the pole. I jumped as high as I could and wrapped myself around it. Because I was tall, I made it a good distance up.

The field goal was shaped like a giant U on a stick. Using my arms and legs, I shimmied my body up until I made it to the top of the stick part. Rimmel watched as I balanced myself on the bottom of the U-shaped part she was tied to. She was far enough out that I had to straddle the pole and work my way toward her.

The closer I got, the slicker the pole became. Everything was soaked. Her hair was in wet clumps hanging in her face, her skin was pale, and her lips were turning blue.

I took a steadying breath as I reached the place the rope was tied. The weight from her drenched body was pulling her down, and I knew the rope tied around her had to be cutting into her skin. It had to hurt.

"I'm gonna pull you up, okay?" I said.

She nodded. I locked my thighs around the pole and wrapped what I could of the hanging rope around one of my arms. Then I began pulling her up. She wasn't heavy, but I was balanced on a pole and her weight was below me, so it was awkward. But I refused to give up. I kept pulling, my bicep and shoulder shaking from the effort.

A small sound of pain floated up from below me, and it cut through me. Ignoring how badly my arm burned and the way the rope cut into my skin, I gave one last tug. I was able to wrap my other arm around her and tow her up between my legs.

I sagged forward from relief as she tried not to collapse against me. She was stiff and held as much of her weight as she could. I admired that because I knew she had to be in pain.

• • •

She had what looked like an old T-shirt shoved in her mouth and tied around the back of her head. I untied it and threw away the fabric.

She dragged in an agonizing breath and coughed. "Romeo," she said, her voice hoarse and weak.

"Shh," I said. "It's okay now."

One of the losers appeared at the bottom, and he was holding a pair of large gardening sheers.

"Toss 'em up," I yelled. I held out my arm away from Rimmel and opened my hand. "Right here."

The guy hesitated, and I made an impatient sound. He moved so he was standing under my arm and then used both hands to fling the things straight up. I snagged them out of the air on the first try.

"Balance, okay?" I said and pushed her forward away from me so I could cut her hands from behind her back.

The rope was thick and these sheers were pitiful, so it took me a few minutes, but when she was finally free, she sagged forward with a groan. I caught her around the waist and towed her up.

"I'm not sure if I can cut your ankles free up here and keep our balance," I said as I went to work on the rope that bound her to the pole. When I cut through it, the remaining piece was left draped over the post.

"I just want down," she rasped.

"Where's the ladder?" I yelled down.

But the asshole was gone.

Both of them were.

I glanced to where I left Zach lying.

He was gone too.

"It's just you and me," I whispered.

"Want me to jump?" she asked.

"No!" I replied quickly. "You can't jump from here. You're all tied up. You're weak. You'd break something."

"I don't think we have another choice."

I wasn't sure I could shimmy down the pole with her on my back. Her arms were probably too weak to hold on to me, and I would need my arms to climb down. Her feet were tied together so she couldn't wrap herself around the pole and slide down. Besides, she was shaking so bad her teeth were knocking together. She wasn't going to be able to do much of anything.

This was on me.

"Hold still," I said and balanced her on the pole. She gripped it like it was a lifeline as her body quivered and shook. She was so weak and cold she wasn't going to be able to hold on very long, if at all. I shifted so I was sitting beside her with my knees bent and my lower legs dangling off the side.

"What are you doing?" she asked.

"Getting you down."

I tucked the clippers beneath my arm and locked my legs around the pole. I lowered my upper half so I was hanging upside down by my legs.

"It's a good fucking thing I work out all the time," I muttered as I grabbed the clippers and dropped them on the ground.

Blood rushed to my head and I did a partial sit-up and reached for her. She looked at me like I was insane.

"Trust me," I murmured.

She nodded and came forward. I grabbed her around the middle and then lowered myself back down so I was hanging with my arms around her.

"Wrap your arms around my waist. Hold tight."

She did, and I basically slid her down my body until my hands were beneath her armpits. "I'm gonna lower you a little more. As far as I can reach. You're closer to the ground now. I'm going to drop you. Try to land softly. Once you there, get the clippers and free your ankles."

"I'm scared, Romeo."

"I got you," I said with a lot more bravado than I felt right then. Her safety was literally in my hands.

She took a shuddering breath. "I'm ready."

I released her arms and she fell, a little yelp of alarm ripping from her throat, but I caught her around the wrist before she even finished screaming.

"You ready?" I asked. The weight on my body was starting to make my muscles burn.

"Do it," she said.

I let go and she fell the rest of the way to the ground. She hit with a thump and her legs buckled under her.

"Rimmel," I called out.

She looked up at me. "I'm okay."

Relief flooded my body.

"What about you?" she called up.

I started to tell her I would slide down the pole, but the loud sound of a motor cut through the stadium.

• • •

What the—

My thought was cut off when one of the oversized zero-turn mowers the maintenance people used came lurching toward us as fast as it would go.

Zach was driving.

He looked even more sick and twisted with blood and bruises all over his face.

"Rimmel!" I yelled and stretched my arms out for her.

I couldn't reach her, but it was all I could do. "Run!"

But she couldn't run. Her feet were still tied together. She struggled with the clippers, sawing away at the rope.

Zach was coming fast.

But he lurched around her and our eyes locked.

He was coming for me.

I started to sit up, but it was too late. He stood and the mower jerked erratically as he snagged my hand and kept driving. The speed and pressure of the pull was too much for my muscles, and I felt myself slide right off the pole.

Zach let go of my hand and kept going, but the damage was already done.

I braced myself for the fall as the hard ground came rushing toward me.

CHAPTER THIRTY-THREE

#Spotted
The famous Hellcat stalling out
more than once on its way to the
local emergency room.
#FallenHero? #MoreUpdatesToCome
... Alpha BuzzFeed

RIMMEL

It all happened so fast.

One moment, Romeo was climbing up the goal post and shimming over to me, and the next, I was hitting the ground, finally free from the ropes that bound me.

When Zach and his friends grabbed me, I fought and kicked as hard as I could. Until one of them hit me hard enough to knock me out.

When I woke, I was hanging from the post.

The fear I felt when I first realized where I was couldn't be described. I imagined it would feel a lot like being dangled over a cliff.

I couldn't even beg to be released because my mouth was gagged and bound.

I couldn't even fathom that something like this would happen.

I got roses.

I expected a surprise.

I expected romance.

What I got was sheer horror.

Just when I thought the worst was over, I heard the revving of a small engine. Romeo was still hanging upside down from the pole, and I was lying there stunned. The next thing I knew, some crazy contraption driven by Zach came barreling toward us, and I watched helplessly as he stood on the thing and purposely grabbed Romeo and tugged him.

As Zach drove off, Romeo did a literal flip in the air and then landed with a hard slap on the field.

I screamed his name as I struggled with the clippers and finally freed my ankles from the rope. I surged up onto wobbly legs that tried to give out, but I wouldn't let them. I rushed over to where he landed, and he rolled over with a grunt.

"Oh my God," I cried and fell to my knees beside him.

"I'm okay," he said and struggled to sit up.

I noticed he wrapped a hand around his middle.

"Where are you hurt?" I rushed out.

He didn't get to answer because Zach had turned the mower around and was coming back at us.

Seriously. We were being attacked with a lawnmower.

If I wasn't so scared, I'd laugh.

Romeo rushed forward and picked up the hose. He turned it on full blast and sprayed Zach right in the face. As he drove closer, the pressure of the water grew more intense, and he lost control and the thing swerved and crashed into the nearby pole.

Romeo pulled his cell out of his pants and handed it to me. "Call the cops."

I called 9-1-1 as Romeo stalked forward to where Zach was slumped over in his seat. As soon as the operator answered, I launched into detail about where we were and what happened.

Well, as much as I could. I was pretty sure I was starting to babble as the shock of the night took full effect.

Zach was unconscious. His face was bruised and bloody and there was a gash on his head that was oozing blood. Romeo grabbed him by the back of the neck and pulled his limp body off the mower. Instead of dropping him, he held him up and plowed his fist into his face one last time.

"Motherfucker!" he spat and dropped him in a heap.

He glanced up at me. "Tell the operator we're not waiting for the cops. We're going to the hospital."

I relayed the information, and she tried to talk me out of it. But Romeo took the phone and pressed the end button.

"Come on. Let's go."

"I'm okay," I told him. "I don't think any of my injuries are an emergency. We should wait for the cops."

"You need to get looked at," he said, gruff. "And so do I." As he spoke, he wrapped his left arm across his body once more and rested his hand on his right arm.

"Romeo," I gasped. "Where are you hurt?"

He grimaced.

"Is it your ribs?" I said, forgetting about everything that had happened and focusing solely on him.

"No," he said and shifted. He looked up at me, his eyes grim and laced with pain. "My arm is broken."

I sucked in a breath and looked down at him. He wasn't holding his ribs. He was favoring his arm.

His right arm.

His throwing arm.

I blinked back the tears rushing into my eyes. He didn't need tears right now.

He needed me to be strong, just like he'd just been when he helped me.

"Give me your car keys," I said.

He looked at me like I had four heads.

"You can't drive with a broken arm. Shifting will only hurt it worse."

"Front pocket," he said.

I grabbed them and we started walking again. I glanced at him every few seconds because I was so worried.

When the Hellcat finally came in sight, I clicked the automatic start and rushed to climb in. When he was in, I glanced at him again.

"I'm okay. This is nothing."

I wondered if he really believed that.

I wondered if I did.

I nodded and looked down at the controls of the car. I wasn't very good at driving a stick. I'd only had the one lesson.

And I was missing the books I needed to help me see.

But I didn't say a word. Instead, I straightened up as tall as I could, adjusted the seat, and took a breath.

"Baby, please don't wreck on the way to the hospital," Romeo said.

I glanced at him and said with much more boldness than I felt, "I got this."

And then I drove.

CHAPTER THIRTY-FOUR

Cops rushing
to the indoor field. Students holding
vigil in the ER waiting room.
#SomeoneHasSomeExplainingToDo
#StillNoWordOnRomeo #WaitingSucks

... Alpha BuzzFeed

ROMEO

Pain radiated along my entire right side. My arm ached and the ice they placed on it only seemed to make it worse.

I'd just come back from X-ray.

We wouldn't know how bad the damage was until the radiologist looked at the images.

My arm was swollen, blotchy purple in some areas, and basically totally fucked up.

I'd just signed with the NFL.

Professional teams were making offers.

I was a quarterback.

I threw completed touchdown passes all day long. I had the best record in the state. My right arm was my ticket to the life I'd always dreamed of.

And now it was broken.

Everyone on staff here was solemn and morose around me, almost like I'd died. As soon as I walked in with Rimmel, they rushed me back. They tried to make her sit in the waiting room, but that only got people yelled at and me an elevated blood pressure.

She'd been fucking hanging from a pole. She was wet, cold, bruised, and battered. She was in worse shape than me, but they wanted to make her wait for treatment.

Hell to the no.

This was the first moment I'd been alone since I fell. Since I felt the bone in my arm snap, since I felt the stab of pain.

I knew immediately what it meant.

I understood my life as I knew it could be over.

What the fuck was I going to do?

My arm stung with the pressure of the ice, and I ripped it away and threw it across the room. It hit the wall with a loud slap as the door to my room opened.

Rimmel peeked inside.

She still wasn't wearing glasses because we didn't know what happened to them.

"Hey," she said quietly, hesitating in the doorway.

I held my arm out to her and she rushed inside. I folded her against me and she held her body stiffly so she didn't cause me any pain.

"Shouldn't you be with the doctor?" I asked.

"I snuck out of the room when they weren't looking."

I smiled. "Thanks for not tearing up my car on the way here," I said, tucking a strand of damp hair behind her ear.

She was dressed in nothing but a hospital gown.

I sweet-talked my way out of one and was just wearing a pair of scrub bottoms and no shirt. I have no idea where the nurse found these pants, and I didn't care. Gowns were for women.

"How bad is it?" she asked, her eyes filled with worry.

"Not sure yet."

She cupped her hand around my jaw. "It's gonna be okay. I know it."

"Yeah?" I asked, pain lancing through my chest. "How do you know?"

"Because you're number twenty-four. You have *epic mojo*."

"I signed with the NFL last week. There are offers on the table from two pro teams."

She gasped and excitement filled her eyes. I loved that look. It was so much better than the morose glances I'd been getting since I got here. "Romeo! That's amazing! Why didn't you tell me?"

"Because what's going on with you is more important."

She took my face and forced my head down so she could look into my eyes. "I am never more important than you are. *You're everything*."

"Kiss me," I demanded.

She did as she was told. When she was done, she sank back onto the balls of her feet. "Your dream is still right here. Your arm might be broken now, but it's gonna be fixed and you're going to play better than ever."

I finally said out loud what no one—not even me—wanted to hear. "What if it's not?"

"I don't believe that. Not for a second." She glanced at my battered arm and back up at me. "But if that's what happens, then something else just as amazing is going to happen for you. And I'll still love you. No matter what."

"I love you, Rim."

"I know you do. I just wish you hadn't gotten hurt like this because of me."

I started to reply, but the door opened once more. Two nurses came in with disgruntled looks on their faces. "There she is," the blond one said.

Rimmel grimaced.

"You can't be leaving your cubicle, miss." The dark-headed nurse scolded her.

"Ladies," I said and turned up the charm. "You'll have to forgive her. I was whining like a big baby and begged her to stay in here with me."

"That's the football player," the blonde whispered. Rimmel stiffened.

"Maybe she could just take that bed right there." I pointed to the one beside me. "That way we could all be in the same room, and I'll have more than one nurse to help me if I need it."

Rimmel sighed when they agreed immediately and rushed to get her chart and other supplies for the room. "Seriously? Do all women have to fall over themselves for you?"

"I wanted you in here," I said.

Her eyes softened.

The door opened again and my parents came rushing in.

"What the hell happened?" my father boomed. For once, his smooth feathers were ruffled.

Mom rushed to my side with tears in her eyes. "Oh, Roman."

"I'm fine," I said. "Just a broken bone. I'll live."

"Your arm," Dad said. I knew he was thinking about my career.

"We're still waiting for word on the break," I said. "Besides, Rim had it worse than me."

"Rimmel." My father came forward and put an arm around her. "The nurse told us about your ordeal. I'm so sorry. I thought the restraining order would keep him away."

"We all did," she replied and leaned into him a little. Her eyes slid to my mother, with a little bit of expectation in them.

Mom didn't even look her way.

In fact, it was like she was making an effort to *not* look at Rimmel.

What the hell is going on now?

"Shouldn't they be putting a cast on this by now?" Mom worried.

"I think they're waiting for the X-ray results," I said and glanced over at Rimmel. She had straightened away from my father and was looking a little lost standing there.

Clearly, my mother's rebuke had hurt her.

I really wasn't in the mood for this.

"Dad, would you mind going to see if the radiologist is done reading the results? I'm anxious to know—"

"Of course, son. I'll go see what I can find out."

On his way out, Rimmel's nurse came rushing in and demanded she get in bed. She bustled her off to her side of the room and pulled the curtain between us so she could check the rope burns Rimmel suffered around her midsection.

I almost demanded she leave the curtain open so I could see the damage, but I wanted this moment with Mom because I knew we wouldn't get this chance again anytime soon.

I pinned her with a hard look. She stared back.

"What the hell was that about?" I growled low.

"What?"

"Don't play games. I'm sitting in the hospital. My arm is busted, my girl is battered, and my career might be over. Why the hell did you snub her that way, especially after she's made such an effort to let you in?"

"I got a call from the PI I hired today."

"What the fuck, Mom? I thought you were done with that bullshit."

She didn't even scold me for my language. That's when I knew I wasn't going to like this.

"I was. But something came back and he thought I would want to know."

"What?"

"Her father is in debt up to his eyeballs. Apparently, he has a massive gambling problem."

I shook my head. "That's it?"

"That's not enough to prove she's after you for your money?" She lifted an eyebrow.

"No," I said, hard. "I'm only gonna say this once. Stop digging around in Rimmel's past and her family. You could find out that her entire family is full of murderers and I would still love her."

"Funny you should say that," Mom said. "Because it appears her father is the one who killed her mother."

An audible gasp filled the room. The curtain between the beds was shoved back and Rimmel stood there looking white as a ghost, her mouth wide open.

"How dare you?" she said. Her eyes were cold and hard as she stared at Mom.

"Rimmel…" I started, worried that after everything that happened, this would send her over the edge.

She stalked forward, intent on my mother. "How dare you come in here while your son is suffering like this to hurl unfounded and untrue accusations around?"

"They are not unfounded. Your father is a gambling addict. He was in debt years ago, so severely that his life was threatened. When he was unable to pay what he owed, the men he borrowed from took it back. In blood. Your mother's blood."

Rimmel swayed on her feet.

"Get out," I growled. "Get the hell out of this room and stay out!"

"Roman," Mom said, her voice shocked.

I turned away from her and held out my good arm to Rimmel. She rushed into it with a cry. I looked at my mother with hard, cold eyes over her head.

Seeing that she made a huge mistake, she backed away. I stared her down until she was gone.

Then I turned my eyes toward the nurse who was lurking behind the curtain by Rimmel's bed.

She jumped and rushed from the room.

My arm was screaming, and I wondered what my dad was learning.

"Rim," I said gently.

She lifted her head from my chest. "It's not true."

"I know," I murmured and hugged her close again. Yet... I couldn't believe my mother would say all of that if she didn't have the proof to back it up.

But that didn't excuse the way she delivered the news.

We had so many problems right now, so much hate shoveled our way, and now was not the time for more.

Rimmel's thoughts seemed to mirror my own. She pulled back to say, "What are we going to do, Romeo?"

Up until this point, I'd been sitting on the end of my bed, my feet on the floor. I let go of her now and moved up on the bed. Gingerly, I leaned back against the pillows and let out a sigh. Then I lifted my left arm and invited her beside me.

She climbed onto the bed, trying not to jostle me, and fitted herself against my side.

"We're gonna deal with it. All of it. One thing at a time. And we're going to do it together," I told her.

She rested her cheek against me and sighed.

After a while, her whisper floated through the room. "What if what your mom said is true?"

I whispered my answer. "What if my NFL career is over?"

Rimmel tilted back her head and gazed up at me. "We'll still have each other, right?"

"Always," I vowed.

I just prayed to God each other wasn't all we would have left when all the hate settled.

Find out what
happens with
Romeo & Rimmel
in their final book

#PLAYER

Coming
March 2015
Turn the page for a tease!

The Hashtag Series

The Hashtag Series #3

Players gotta play.

Hate is like a poison. It contaminates everything.
So does doubt.

Even though I deny what I overheard, even though I insist it isn't true, the seed of doubt has been planted. I can't help but be tormented with the endless what-ifs that have taken over our lives.

Romeo and I were happy in love. The future stretched before us brighter than any star in the darkest sky. Now everything is broken. Literally broken. Romeo's entire career is at stake. My entire future is threatened… And my past?

It's coming back to haunt me.
To haunt us.

* * *

Romeo says we're in this together, and right now the only sure thing is us. But how far can a love so new be pushed? The lengths we'll have to go to save each other puts everything at risk.

Romeo's a #player, but how much of the game can one person play?

AUTHOR'S NOTE

When I first started writing this book, I was scared. Scared it wouldn't live up to *#Nerd*, which has been so well loved, read, and accepted. It's a scary thing for an author, following up a book that has been widely well received with another that people are asking for.

As I was writing, I smiled a lot and I fell in love with Romeo a little bit more, so I hope that is a sign that you readers will enjoy this one just as much as *#Nerd*, and I hope it's been worth the wait.

#Hater is actually the longest book I've written in over a year. It kept going. And going. LOL. I'm pretty much a #Zombie right now. I've been typing and writing constantly. I honestly don't even know what to say (maybe because this book #BrokeMyBrain), because looking back on the past couple weeks that I've been writing like a fiend, I can't really remember much.

You ever drive home from somewhere and pull in your driveway and think, "Wow. I don't even remember driving home?" Well, that's what the last couple weeks have been like for me. I spent so much time deep in the world of Alpha U that everything else kind of fell away.

The only thing I really remember feeling as I was writing (besides the feels that Romeo gives me, haha) is surprise. Surprise that Zach was being so vile. I also worried that he was taking things too far, but I wrote what the characters were telling me. Poor Rimmel really got the short end of the stick in this book, ya think?

But through it all, I loved how her and Romeo stuck together, how they never let the #Hate tear them apart. It will be interesting to see how everything works out in *#Player*.

And yes, for so many of you that have asked, Braeden is getting a book. It will be *#Selfie,* and I plan to write that after *#Player*.

I'd like to thank my editor, Cassie McCown, who was patient and waited for me to finish this book even after I blew my deadline. My cover designer, Regina of Mae I Design, for not killing me over all the designs and photos we went through to find the cover that "spoke" to me for this book. I mean, seriously though, is this cover not #Epic? Like it just screams the awesomeness that is Romeo.

Also, to all the readers. To YOU. I seriously didn't know how *#Nerd* would be received. The enthusiasm for Romeo and Rimmel totally touched my heart. I feel so blessed to be given another opportunity to share more of the characters you loved so much. I sincerely hope this latest installment did them justice!

#HappyReading,

XOXO —**CAMBRIA**

Cambria Hebert is a bestselling novelist of more than twenty books. She went to college for a bachelor's degree, couldn't pick a major, and ended up with a degree in cosmetology. So rest assured her characters will always have good hair. She currently resides in North Carolina with her children (human and furry) and her husband.

Besides writing, Cambria loves a caramel latte, staying up late, sleeping in, and watching movies. She considers math human torture and has an irrational fear of chickens (yes, chickens). You can often find her running on the treadmill (she'd rather be eating a donut), painting her toenails (because she bites her fingernails), or walking her chorkie (the real boss of the house).

Cambria has written within the young adult and new adult genres, penning many paranormal and contemporary titles. Her favorite genre to read and write is romantic suspense. A few of her most recognized titles are: Text, Torch, Tryst, Masquerade, and Recalled.

Cambria Hebert owns and operates Cambria Hebert Books, LLC.

You can find out more about Cambria and her titles by visiting her website: http://www.cambriahebert.com.

And don't forget to sign up Cambria's newsletter!
http://eepurl.com/UsdBj

www.ingramcontent.com/pod-product-compliance
Lightning Source LLC
Chambersburg PA
CBHW050948210726
48287CB00004B/1179